To my sister Amelia,
whose first visitor to her new house
in Alaska was a moose.
Love you!
Can't wait to follow
your next artistic adventure.

One Fine Duke

LENORA BELL

piatkus

PIATKUS

First published in the US in 2019 by Avon Books,
An imprint of HarperCollins Publishers, New York
First published in Great Britain in 2019 by Piatkus
by arrangement with Avon Books

3 5 7 9 10 8 6 4 2

A CIP catalogue record for this book
is available from the British Library.

ISBN 978-0-349-41768-4

Printed and bound in Great Britain by
Clays Ltd, Elcograf S.p.A.

Papers used by Piatkus are from well-managed forests
and other responsible sources.

MIX
Paper from
responsible sources
FSC® C104740

Piatkus
An imprint of
Little, Brown Book Group
Carmelite House
50 Victoria Embankment
London EC4Y 0DZ

An Hachette UK Company
www.hachette.co.uk

www.littlebrown.co.uk

Chapter 1

London, 1830

"STOP THE CARRIAGE!" roared Andrew, Duke of Thorndon, pounding on the ceiling with his fist.

The carriage slowed and swerved to the side of the avenue. He unlatched the window and stuck out his head. Unfortunately, his eyes hadn't been playing tricks on him.

His younger brother Rafe was sprinting down the Strand holding up the front of his breeches with one hand, arse shining behind for all of London to see.

Drew briefly closed his eyes. *Dear Lord, why me?*

This time Rafe had gone too far. Running through the streets of London with his trousers undone wasn't the worst of it. Not even close.

Drew unclenched his fingers from the crumpled scrap of paper and read the chilling words one more time:

> *I know what your brother is doing. You must PAY. Await further instructions and TELL NO ONE or Lady Beatrice will be KIDNAPPED.*

He'd left his estate in Cornwall within hours of receiving the letter. He wasn't going to sit around waiting for another threatening letter to arrive. Anger infiltrated his mind like weeds choking a wheat field.

He would never allow his innocent younger sister, Beatrice, to be kidnapped and held for ransom. Whatever trouble Rafe was in, Drew would fix it swiftly and be back in Cornwall well before the July barley harvest.

His manservant, Corbyn, opened the carriage door. "Is anything the matter, Your Grace?"

Drew pointed back the way they'd come. "*That* is the matter."

Corbyn's mouth gaped open. "Is that . . . Lord Rafe?"

"Indeed."

"And is he . . . ?"

"Bare-arsed naked? Yes, yes he is. Probably being chased. Possibly by an angry mob brandishing pitchforks."

"Good heavens!"

"Heaven had nothing to do with it."

Rafe stumbled and nearly collided with a gaggle of shop girls who turned to giggle and stare at his retreating posterior.

"He appears to be rather intoxicated, Your Grace," Corbyn observed.

"Hasn't been sober since our father's death."

In the five years since the old duke had died of a ruptured spleen, Rafe, always their father's favorite, had spiraled downward into a debauched life of gambling, mistresses, and misdeeds.

Drew had traveled in the opposite direction, retiring from the maelstrom of London society to the quiet seclusion of Thornhill House in Cornwall, where he led an orderly, predictable, and useful life. He'd discovered a talent for agricultural innovations. If successful, his new system of crop rotation would mean better yields for his tenants—more crops to feed more hungry mouths on his lands, and hopefully, on the lands of other noblemen.

Rafe caught sight of Drew and waved frantically, nearly losing his trousers. "Thorny," he shouted. "Thorny, it's me. Give us a lift?"

Heads swiveled. Inquisitive gazes drilled into Drew like beetles boring through rotting wood. He retreated into the gloom of the carriage. "Hoist him in, Corbyn, and try to be discreet about it."

"Very good, Your Grace."

Drew closed the blinds. The last thing he wanted was more notoriety.

London brought the past careening back, threatening to smash the hard-won equilibrium he'd finally achieved.

He'd been kidnapped as a boy of fifteen and held for ransom by a desperate tenant farmer seeking revenge on Drew's father, the duke, because the farmer lost his leasehold when he couldn't pay his rent, taxes, and the Church's tithes after several years of poor crops.

His kidnapper had kept Drew chained in the small, dark hull of a ship in the London harbor for ten endless days, feeding him only thin gruel.

Drew's kidnapping had gripped London, whipping the newspapermen and the public into a feeding frenzy. *Duke's Heir Held for King's Ransom. Will the Duke Pay?*

The duke hadn't paid.

Drew had negotiated for his own freedom. Clawed his own way back from Hell.

Long-buried memories hooked his mind, trying to drag him down.

Smell of filth and bilge water. Straw pallet crawling with vermin. Gray metallic taste of thin gruel coating his mouth, leaving a film on his mind.

He clenched and unclenched his fists, fighting for control. He took a deep breath in through his nostrils and exhaled slowly.

I am not my thoughts. I am not my memories.

I'm carved from ice. Impervious. I feel nothing.

He would never allow the same fate to happen to Beatrice.

Never.

The door opened and his brother landed in a heap on the opposite seat. The carriage shuddered back to life. Rafe buttoned his breeches and tucked in his shirt. He wasn't wearing a coat, or a hat, and his blond hair was a tangled mess.

"Is someone chasing you, Rafe?" Drew asked.

"Fitzbart. With a pistol. Not loaded . . . least I don't think so. Can't be sure."

"Because . . . ?"

"Caught me tupping his mistress."

"Of course he did."

"Don't look at me like that." Rafe gestured defensively. "He'll forget all about it tomorrow. Sod it, I need a drink. Don't suppose you keep any tipple in this hearse?"

Drew steadied his breathing. He wasn't the same man who'd left London five years ago. He was in complete control of his life and his emotions now.

"You don't look well, Rafe." His brother's face was bloated from too much drink and unhealthful living, his blue eyes bloodshot.

"And you look disgustingly fit," replied Rafe. "Still dressing like a country parson, I see. What brings you to London after all these years?"

Drew winced. "I've been meaning to visit, it just never seemed like the right time." The letter had forced his hand.

"Why are you here now?" Rafe asked. "Must be something dire. Finally decided to cut me off?" Spoken with a laugh, though Drew caught the underlying panic.

Drew smoothed the creases out of the letter. "I received this and departed for London immediately." He handed the letter to Rafe. "Been searching for you all afternoon."

Rafe read the brief words. "Christ." He wiped a trembling hand across his brow. "I honestly have no idea what this means. I . . . Christ. It's bloody hot in this carriage." He plucked at the collar of his shirt, which was stuck to his chest with sweat. "A fellow can't breathe."

Drew leaned forward, bracing his forearms on his knees. "What the devil are you up to?"

"It's just a jest. Someone trying to scare you."

"Then why did you shudder when you read it, as if someone had walked over your grave?"

Rafe shrugged. "Too much drink last night."

Drew caught his gaze and held it. "You'd better

tell me what this is all about. Don't forget that I've been financing your gambling sprees, buying your mistresses diamonds, paying off all of those jealous lovers. Who sent this?"

"None of your concern." Rafe handed him back the note. "This is my problem, not yours. Beatrice is quite safe. Go back to Cornwall, we don't want you here." Rafe didn't meet his eyes. He was hiding something.

"How do you know that Beatrice is safe?" Drew asked. "Do you know who sent this?"

"I don't," his brother replied quickly—too quickly. "But I'll find out and I'll take care of everything."

"Can you promise me that?"

"Absolutely."

"There's something you're not telling me."

Rafe glowered at him. "Not your problem. I'll see that it ends here. Go and visit Beatrice. You'll have enough problems once Mother catches wind of your arrival. The prodigal son returns, and all that. She'll have every debutante in London nipping at your heels within hours."

Which was another item on the long list of duties Drew had been delaying for far too long: taking a wife. It was high time he produced an heir. "Have to marry someday, don't I?"

"Can't have a wastrel like me inherit," said Rafe.

"Precisely." Rafe would undo all of the hard-earned progress that Drew had made on improving the living conditions and livelihood of the tenants who worked his holdings.

Drew wished he knew the right words to say to make his brother see that the path he was on would lead to an early grave. "Have you forgotten that I used to be you? I know the low places you frequent. I know the emptiness, the self-loathing. The evil waiting to swallow you whole."

"Spare me your sermons, parson."

"I have a duty to this family. There must be a stouthearted lady so desperate to become a duchess that she's willing to wed an uncivilized duke and live in the wilds of Cornwall in a crumbling old house."

"Crumbling old *haunted* house," amended Rafe. You know as well as I do that Thornhill House is just a house, not some gathering ground for ghosts and devil worship."

"There was a double murder there."

"In fifteen seventy."

"England has a long memory."

"Especially when you keep feeding it fresh details. I know you've been spreading rumors about me and Thornhill House. A malevolent headless horseman . . . a young mother with a dead baby inhabiting a mirror . . . really? Does it all have to be so very gothic?"

"Well, you're not here to counter the rumors. I'll tell whatever stories I please."

"I'm here now. And I'm not amused."

"I don't know how you can stand living like that. Only sheep and fields as far as the eye can see. I'd go mad."

"That's what they say about me, I hear."

"Mother will be overcome with joy to see you.

She's gone marriage-mad. Won't stop hounding me. And poor Beatrice, Mother's hosting a ball in her honor tonight. Not that she'll receive any proposals."

Drew couldn't believe that Beatrice was old enough to marry. When he'd left London she'd been a scrawny, bookish young girl with her hair in plaits. He'd been gone too long.

Guilt pricked his heart like stinging nettles.

"I'm sure she's grown into a lovely girl. She's always been fiercely clever. If the bachelors of London can't see her charms, then they're blind fools."

Rafe gave him an incredulous look. "Not exactly a beauty, now is she? My friends call her Beastly Beatrice." He caught sight of the look on Drew's face. "'Course I always defend her."

"Case in point. Your friends are idiots. One of them could have written this letter. *Someone* wrote it." Drew prayed that it was only a prank.

He would never allow history to repeat itself.

"A MATTER OF WEEKS?" Mina's voice cracked. "But you said I could stay in London for the rest of the Season."

"I changed my mind," said her guardian, Sir Malcolm Penny, in a flat tone that brooked no argument.

"Uncle, you can't just change your mind. This is my life. I've been waiting for this chance for years. I have plans."

So many plans.

This was her very first taste of freedom and she

meant to make the most of it. She'd been hidden away in the countryside so long—she had so much to learn, so much to experience.

"That's what I'm afraid of," her uncle said drily. He stroked his graying black beard. "Someone must keep a close watch on you."

Guard her. Restrict her movements. Curtail her opportunities.

He'd kept her under lock and key at Sutton Hall, his country estate, for ten long years. Ever since that bitterly cold February day when she'd learned that her beautiful, glamorous parents had perished while abroad.

Sir Malcolm's own wife and daughter had died in a poison attack meant for him. So many deaths, so close together, had made him overprotective of Mina, to say the least.

"I have to leave England unexpectedly," he said. "It's not safe for you to remain in London alone."

It's not safe. It's for your own good. You'll thank me someday.

If Mina heard those words one more time her mind would crack. Her uncle was cold, dispassionate, and unyielding. If she flew into a temper it would only make things worse. She must be logical and state her case clearly.

"I have Great-Aunt Griselda to watch over me." She spoke calmly and kept her expression neutral. "She'll strike fear into the hearts of any gentlemen with nefarious intentions."

She'd certainly plagued Mina during her brief time in London with her strict lessons in etiquette and decorum.

Docile and decorous didn't come naturally to Mina.

"I may be away from England for some time. The contents of an Egyptian tomb have been donated to the Louvre Museum and I'm off to help identify and catalogue the items," said Sir Malcolm.

His face betrayed nothing as he lied.

To the world, he was an expert on antiquities and president of the Society of Antiquaries. In secret, he was a spymaster who trained and handled an elite British force of secret agents.

I know why you're going to France, and it's not because of some dusty old relics, she nearly blurted out. *You're going to hunt Le Triton—the evil genius of the Paris criminal underworld. The man who was responsible for the death of my parents. Take me with you!*

She came from a long and illustrious line of spies. Her father, her uncle, and generations of the Penny family before that. All she'd ever wanted was to follow in her parents' footsteps, claim her heritage—for the family honor—and avenge the death of her parents.

Chin up. Shoulders back. Make direct eye contact. "If I find a match in the next few weeks, you can't force me to return to Sutton Hall." Marriage was her means of escape and her pathway to freedom. But marriage to a man of her choosing, one who would further her goals, not hinder them.

She'd already determined the perfect candidate: Lord Rafe Bentley. The wickedest rake in

London . . . and one of her uncle's spies. Theirs would be a mutually beneficial union culminating in hitherto uncharted heights of espionage.

Sir Malcolm sighed heavily, staring at the bizarre groupings of stuffed hedgehogs and other woodland creatures dressed in tiny formal clothing that occupied most of her Great-Aunt Griselda's chimneypiece. "Mind you, there are only four suitors I will approve of in all of England." He handed her a small leather binder.

"What's this?"

"A Duke Dossier."

"A *what*?"

"A detailed analysis of London's eligible dukes, in order of preference. If you marry, you will become no less than a duchess, with all of the privileges and protections the rank affords."

Marry a duke? *Never*. Controlling, arrogant men had dictated her life long enough.

Dukes, by sheer virtue of their exalted status in life, were proud, vain creatures who thought of nothing but themselves, and they certainly wouldn't allow her to pursue an exciting life of international espionage.

She knew of only one exception—the Duke of Ravenwood, one of her uncle's spies, but he'd given up espionage to hunt antiquities with his archaeologist wife in far-flung corners of the globe.

Mina unwrapped the silk cord and opened the binder.

"Study these dukes closely, Wilhelmina," her

uncle instructed. "You'll become a duchess, or you won't marry at all." He shifted his weight on the lumpy purple velvet settee.

Mina could have told him that there was no comfort to be found in Great-Aunt Griselda's mausoleum of a house that smelled of dried rose petals, camphor, and the oil of turpentine she used to paint the fur of her stuffed and mounted animals.

Every rap on Mina's knuckles as she attempted to wrest something resembling a melody from the pianoforte, every book piled on top of her head to correct her posture, every sip of watery tea felt like a penance for some crime she'd never committed.

It wasn't her fault that she'd been raised in the countryside without the benefit of a governess or the society of other girls.

The Duke Dossier was further punishment. *You've been a bad, headstrong hoyden. Now you must study the lives of dukes.*

"Did I hear someone mention dukes?" Great-Aunt Griselda, or Grizzy, as Mina thought of her, glided into the parlor on the invisible gladiator's chariot Mina always pictured her riding upon. "My favorite subject."

Sir Malcolm rose and kissed her withered cheek. "I was saying that if Wilhelmina is to marry, she must become a duchess."

"Are you certain that she can aspire to a duke?" asked Grizzy. "I haven't had much luck with her etiquette lessons, and she's sadly lacking in accomplishments."

If one considers proper forms of address to be an accomplishment. Mina preferred modifying and inventing weaponry for use in service to the Crown. A timepiece she'd modified had been instrumental in helping the Duke of Ravenwood defeat an enemy in Paris.

"There are only four eligible dukes this Season," said Grizzy. She was an expert on eligible dukes. "I don't count Thorndon—since he never comes to London, and I won't mention Borthwick, since he's seventy-five and Wilhelmina's just turned twenty."

Mina shuddered. "Thanks ever so much."

Grizzy perched on the edge of her chair. "There's Granwall, but they say he murdered his first wife. And Westbury, but he hasn't a farthing to his name—lost it all in the gaming hells. Marmont might do, though he's quite peculiar. He invents a new illness every day of the week."

"Thorndon," said Sir Malcolm. "He's the only clear choice."

Mina stifled a snort of disbelieving laughter. Thorndon happened to be Lord Rafe Bentley's elder brother, but the two of them were like night and day. "Uncle," she said, "Thorndon is a recluse who shuns society. I heard that he wanders the moors at night, howling at the moon. They say village maidens have gone missing."

"Oh no, Sir Malcolm, Thorndon will never do," said Grizzy. "Everyone knows he's gone quite mad living in that cursed house in Cornwall."

The very name Thornhill House conjured images of vine-twisted walls. Wind howling across moors. An ancient, haunted house. Craggy cliffs and crashing seas.

A prison.

"Utter rubbish," said Sir Malcolm. "Those ridiculous rumors are complete fabrications. I have incontrovertible proof that the sixth duke of Thorndon is as sane and hale as I am. It's all detailed in the dossier."

"Yes, but Thorndon never visits London, and therefore I'm not likely to meet him, much less elicit an offer of marriage," said Mina firmly.

Sir Malcolm's impassive expression took on a hint of smugness. "He arrived in Town today. He's staying at his club. And he's in want of a wife."

Blast. Mina should have known her uncle had a card up his sleeve. "He may be in want of a wife, but I'm not in want of a duke."

"Nonsense." Grizzy patted the black lace cap perched atop her towering mound of iron-gray curls. "Every young lady desires a duke."

"Not this one," Mina said.

"His mother's ball tonight is your best chance," said her uncle. "A preemptive strike will be best. The other young ladies will be frightened of his reputation but you will be armed with the truth."

Blast all dukes to eternity! Tonight was when she'd been planning to approach Lord Rafe. This duke dossier business could ruin everything.

"And just how am I supposed to launch this preemptive strike?" Mina cocked an imaginary firearm. "Waylay Thorndon and hold him at pistol point in the gardens?"

Sir Malcolm's upper lip twitched. "You are quite fearsome with a pistol. Steadier hand than most gentlemen I know."

"Pray don't encourage her, Malcolm," said Grizzy. "She's unconventional enough already."

"Do you still have that flintlock pocket pistol?" asked her uncle.

Mina patted the silk reticule sitting on a side table. "Right here."

"Do you mean to tell me you have a firearm in your reticule? What if it should discharge accidentally and harm a footman?" asked Grizzy.

"Mina's an expert markswoman," replied Sir Malcolm with a touch of pride. "She must be ready to defend herself should a gentleman make unwelcome advances. A pistol tends to cool the ardor."

"No gentleman will dare take liberties under my piercing gaze," promised Grizzy.

First order of business: evade Grizzy's piercing gaze.

"I expect you'll find that Thorndon is already predisposed to court Wilhelmina," said Sir Malcolm. "I wrote him a letter describing her excellent managerial skills, her facility with a ledger, and her suitableness for a solitary life in the countryside. I told him that she was delicate in stature, yet strong as a horse."

"I'll be sure to neigh loudly and nuzzle his palm for apple slices while we dance," said Mina tartly.

"Really, Wilhelmina," said Grizzy. "What's wrong with you? You should be grateful to your uncle. He's trying to make you a duchess."

He was trying to protect her, lock her away someplace safe, silent, and hidden away.

She was so tired of hiding. She longed to be more than her uncle's secretary. She was going to make her own mark on the world, instead of making entries in his ledgers. The world had no idea what she was capable of.

"Thorndon is the very pinnacle of English manhood," said Sir Malcolm. "Dignified, statesmanlike, admirable, and, above all else, honorable. He'll keep you out of trouble and out of harm's way."

Trouble was her reason for being here. Trouble, adventure, revenge . . . *freedom*.

Everything she'd been denied her whole life.

"He's a remarkably fine figure of a man," said Sir Malcolm, continuing the plaguing topic of the Duke of Thorndon. "He towers over me and I'm not small. His features are noble and his eyes are an unusual shade of amber—rather like honey."

"Sounds like *you* want to marry him," said Mina.

"Don't be impertinent, Wilhelmina," Grizzy scolded.

"Study the dossier carefully," Sir Malcolm instructed. "Memorize portions of Thorndon's excellent treatise on the rotation of turnips and clover to produce hospitable soils and quote them back to him while you dance."

Turnip rotation. *Good Lord*. Mina would rather poke out her eyes with a pitchfork than memorize agricultural treatises. She was here for *adventure*.

"Marry Thorndon and your future will be assured," said Grizzy. "You'll be a duchess."

"In a crumbling haunted house on the moors," said Mina.

"A small price to pay," replied Grizzy. "I'm sure that Thorndon would allow you to travel to Town after you give him an heir and a spare."

Frustration sizzled through Mina's mind like a fuse ignited by a spark.

No man was going to *allow* her to do anything, ever again.

She was going to seize control of her life. Shape her own destiny.

A destiny that most certainly did not involve being imprisoned on the moorlands as a brooding duke's broodmare.

Chapter 2

❧

"THERE HE IS, Wilhelmina," Grizzy whispered, staring reverently across the crowded ballroom. "The Duke of Thorndon."

Holy Hell, he's handsome, thought Mina.

Jaw-dropping-on-the-floor handsome. Drool-on-your-lace-fichu handsome.

Distract-her-from-her-plan-with-his-brother handsome.

Her uncle had been right. Thorndon was a fine figure of a man. Objectively speaking, the finest she'd ever beheld.

Tall as a door frame, with a face hewn from the same granite as the rugged Cornish coastline.

A face rendered seductive by contrasts: sharp cheekbones and curved, sensuous lips. Gleaming ebony hair brushed his collar. His eyes were a light, gold-tinged brown—the only warm thing about him.

He owned this ballroom. Literally. And he owned everyone in it by dint of his oversized presence and the cold, unsmiling arrogance scrawled across his face.

He didn't even follow the dictates of fashion, preferring plain black attire to the white pantaloons and gaily-colored waistcoats of the other gentlemen.

Why should he follow the dictates of fashion? Everyone should follow him.

"When you're introduced to Thorndon, pray speak as seldom as possible," Grizzy whispered. "Attempt to appear biddable and do try to recall my decorum lessons. Remember, no one in London knows anything about you, thank the Lord."

Mina had seen several polished, elegant young ladies staring at her, nudging one another and whispering. She was an outsider, a usurper, her proper place in the social hierarchy not yet established.

They needn't worry. She had no designs on their prize duke. And she was about as unpolished as a debutante could be—as rough as an unsanded plank. If anyone touched her they might get splinters.

She longed to shed her country skin swiftly and emerge as the sophisticated social butterfly her mother had been. But she knew that it would take time, observation, and experimentation.

Her first flirtatious conversation, first kiss, first taste of brandy, first adventure . . . it was all ahead of her.

She couldn't wait to taste it all.

"There are many lovely young ladies here but we have the advantage," Grizzy continued, "because Sir Malcolm has already written to Thorndon about you. The duke will regard your secluded country upbringing favorably as he's seeking a bride able to thrive in the wilds of Cornwall."

He wanted a biddable lady that he could control—a secretary he didn't have to pay. An investment expected to produce a return in nine months' time.

"Are you listening to me, Wilhelmina?" asked Grizzy. "You only have one chance to make a favorable first impression. Pray do not squander this precious opportunity."

"I'm planning to be absolutely memorable." Memorable for her utter lack of desirability.

Grizzy sniffed. "Not *too* memorable. Practice restraint, delicacy—your speech must be measured, your laughter modulated. Not one flash of temper."

"I'll do my best," Mina said sweetly. She'd do her best to be everything the duke disdained.

Thorndon was everything she was escaping—duty, restrictions, and boundaries. He was the jailer her uncle wished her to wed—could legally force her to wed.

A huge, unyielding obstruction of a duke, standing between her and her true target.

She was merely biding her time until Lord Rafe arrived. She'd done her research. He never appeared anywhere before midnight, preferring to make a fashionably late entrance. Once he arrived, she could set her plan in motion.

She would evade Grizzy's sharp gaze long enough to secure a private audience with Lord Rafe in the moonlit gardens. During which, Mina would propose an espionage partnership in such a compelling way that Lord Rafe would accept her offer immediately.

Her life of freedom and adventure began to-night.

But first she must repel the duke.

As soon as one dewy-eyed debutante left Drew's arms, his mother introduced another one.

There seemed to be an endless supply of them. All encased in frothy layers of white or yellow or pale pink. All with impossibly slender waists and delicate arms emerging from enormous ruffled sleeves that reminded him of abandoned wasps' nests.

Hair adorned with bows and feathers.

Eyes adorned with fear.

They touched him gingerly, as though he were made of eggshells and might crack in front of them. Which made him irritable. So he growled and glowered but it only made them smile with more determination, bat their eyelashes harder, and pile on the flattery.

He shouldn't have agreed to attend the ball. He was exhausted from days of hard travel and frustrated by his conversation with Rafe—which had gone nowhere, damn him. His brother had stubbornly refused to admit anything and had escaped at the first opportunity, literally leaping from the carriage and racing away.

Drew would be out searching for him if he didn't have to be here, to warn his sister.

Lady Beatrice will be kidnapped.

Not on his watch.

He shouldn't have agreed to the ball, but it had made his mother so happy that he hadn't had the heart to say no. Especially when he'd seen the hurt in her eyes when she spoke of how long he'd been absent.

The same hurt in Beatrice's hazel eyes.

The violins were out of tune, couldn't anyone else hear it? The shrill scraping sound of strings about to snap.

The gossips clustered in knots, waiting for him to slip up and display some sign of madness, their sharp gazes dissecting him like a fresh cadaver in the lecture hall of a medical college.

He knew what London thought of him.

Such a dreadful shame, a duke gone so far astray. Hiding in that cursed house. Wild and uncivilized as the Cornish coastline. Gone half mad because of his ordeal, sympathizing with his kidnapper and ranting about tenant rights. Sweating in the fields like a common laborer.

He must be as mad as they said he was. He couldn't bring any of these London hothouse flowers to Thornhill House. They would wither after one winter.

He wanted a marriage of convenience with a stouthearted and sturdy lady who wouldn't suffer an attack of vapors at the sight of cobwebs, leaky roofs, or mold creeping along a wall.

A lady who had experience with living in the countryside beyond the occasional summer retreat to a well-tended, luxurious family seat.

He loved Thornhill House in all its time-eaten, rickety-boned glory. It had been long deserted when he arrived, cared for by only a skeleton staff of elderly retainers nearly as decrepit and tottering as the desolate mansion they tended.

He'd renovated one wing of the house, and would start on the next section soon, but it was in no state to receive a pampered young lady with expectations of luxury and modern amenities.

Beatrice twirled past him in the arms of a bored-looking dandy with ridiculously forward-swept hair. How did the dandies make their hair stay that way? It looked like tree branches trained by sea winds to grow all in one direction.

His sister had a martyred expression on her face. She wasn't enjoying the dance any more than the dandy was. Mother had forced her to remove her spectacles. She stumbled and her partner sneered.

Drew's heart clenched into a fist. If any man in the room so much as cracked a joke at his sister's expense he would pummel him to within an inch of his life.

The dance ended and Beatrice chose an opportune moment to slip behind the wall of potted ferns in front of the glass doors that led to the gardens, one of her favorite hiding places as a young girl.

He began making his way toward her hiding place, hoping to finally be able to seize a moment alone with her, when his mother pounced.

"There you are, Thorndon." Her round face wreathed into a hopeful smile as she slipped her hand into the crook of his arm. "I have a lady to introduce—Miss Wilhelmina Penny, Sir Malcolm Penny's niece."

"I'm afraid that I'm rather exhausted from my—" he began, but his mother blithely ignored him.

"Miss Penny is a lovely young thing, raised *entirely* in the countryside. She has such a charming, rustic air. She's very good with bookkeeping and estate management, and her great-aunt tells me that she has a fascination with agricultural pursuits."

Of course she did.

His mother rose to her tiptoes to whisper in his ear. *"I think she could be the one."*

Drew cleared his throat. "I truly am tired from—"

"No refusals." His mother tugged him toward Miss Penny and her black-garbed pirate ship of an elderly chaperone. "She would be devastated. Just look at that angelic face."

Yet another fair-haired wisp of a lady encased in frothy white. Miss Penny looked as though a stiff breeze could carry her away. A duke's refusal to dance with her might crush her entirely. Her name rang a bell, though he couldn't recall why.

"One more, Mother, and then I'm finished for the evening."

Moments later he clasped a tiny-boned wrist. "Miss Penny, may I have the pleasure?"

A panicked expression crossed her pretty face but then she smiled one of those sugar-spun smiles that would melt so quickly outside the comforts of London. "Your Grace, the pleasure would be mine."

He led her out for the waltz.

She was so dainty that he had to stoop slightly

to reach her waist. One of her hands drifted onto his shoulder like a petal falling from a flower onto a brick wall. He clasped her other hand gently, cognizant of how huge his hands were in relation to hers.

The music started and his feet followed the order to dance.

She smelled good, like the honey of clover buds when you crush one between your fingers.

They all smelled good.

Artificial blooms raised in the confines of London, raised to be ornamental.

She floated in his arms like a wraith, her gaze fixed at some remote point in the distance.

Were her eyes blue or gray? Some color in between, he decided. More gray than blue. Like a tide line in an ocean. Or the sky before it rained.

She had an oval face with a pointed chin and lush, full lips.

Kissable lips.

Sir Malcolm Penny's niece. Ah, that was it. He'd received a letter from the eminent antiquarian right before he left for London. He had it in his traveling trunk, unopened.

"I believe your uncle wrote to me recently, Miss Penny."

Her gaze snapped to his face. The panic returned to her eyes. "All lies."

"Pardon?"

"Lies. He lied to you. I hate the countryside. I'm hopeless with account books and estate management. I'm not useful in the slightest. My health is delicate. I catch a cold at the slightest provocation."

"Uh . . . you hate the countryside?"

"I hate open fields. Sheep are such insipid creatures. I detest sunshine. I'm only happy in lamplight. And I can't abide nature walks. I only consent to walk when there is a trinket or a new pair of gloves for purchase at the end of my exertions."

She told him all of these details in a rush, as though she'd been rehearsing the speech and hadn't quite perfected her delivery.

Drew stared at her, taken aback. While he couldn't agree with the sentiments she was expressing, this was at the very least a far cry from the other conversations he'd had this evening.

The last lady he'd danced with had professed a hyperbolic adoration for all things Cornwall, from grazing sheep to legendary ghosts, to a profound ambition to stand on the cliffs at Land's End and "absorb the transcendent power of Nature."

"You hate taking nature walks," he echoed.

"Especially along the moors. Or on cliffs overlooking the ocean," she confirmed, with a decisive little nod of her determined wedge of a chin.

A brunette with bright brown eyes waltzed past and gave him a brilliant smile.

That's what debutantes were supposed to do when they encountered a single duke in possession of a vast fortune.

Smile. Flatter. Flirt.

Miss Penny must be confused.

"I haven't read your uncle's letter yet," he admitted. "But I certainly will now, if only to spot the untruths."

"Oh." A pink flush spread across her cheeks. "I thought you had read it already."

"Why do you hate the countryside?"

"Let me count the ways. The loneliness. The lack of excitement. Every second of every day you know precisely what will happen. The exact same thing that happened yesterday. Nothing."

"That's not even one bit true. There's always something happening—a calf being birthed, a field to plow, seeds to sow, or a fence to repair."

"My point precisely. Nothing. No opera house, no museums, no Vauxhall Pleasure Gardens, no London Tavern where the intellectuals and radicals debate weighty matters. Only turnip fields and sheep as far as the eye can see."

"You sound like my brother," he muttered.

"Lord Rafe?"

"That's the one. Are you acquainted with him, Miss Penny?"

A smile played at the corners of her lips. "I met him on several occasions when he visited my uncle's estate."

"He shares your distaste for sheep. And what do you have against turnips?"

For that matter, what did she have against dukes?

She certainly wasn't hoping to become a duchess. It was almost as if she'd planned what to say to make herself least appealing to him. For some perverse reason that made her more intriguing.

"I sneeze when I walk across country fields. I break out in red welts all over my face. It's dreadfully unattractive."

Drew paused for a second and she tugged on his shoulder to keep him in step with the music.

"Of course I know the rotation of crops is one of your passions," she continued blithely. "I've read your treatises on the subject and they are so utterly scintillating and fascinating." Her tone spoke the opposite, her laughter tinkled, brittle as spun glass.

"Do you know, Miss Penny, my mother told me that you had a charming, rustic air."

"I do not," she said indignantly. "I'm worldly and sophisticated. There's no air of the country about me. I'm no obscure, provincial female with piffling concerns or countrified manners."

"And yet your complexion has a healthful glow."

"From staring at London sunsets. Coal smoke creates such pretty shades of violet, don't you agree, Your Grace? Although you wouldn't know, since you spend all your time in Cornwall."

Ah, here it came at last. Perhaps now she would finally say that she'd always wanted to visit the southland in all its craggy glory, or some such nonsense.

"I suppose you've always wanted to visit Cornwall?" he prompted.

She wrinkled her pert nose as if he'd suggested she might want to visit the privy at a sporting tavern.

"Certainly not. I hear there are more sheep than people. Not a circumstance to recommend a place, to my way of thinking."

Perhaps she was only being contrary to differentiate herself from the other ladies. A tactic which was working beautifully. He'd forgotten all about the gossips, how stifling the air in the ballroom was, and how he couldn't breathe deeply with such a crush of people around him.

Her rudeness was somehow refreshing. He was beginning to enjoy Miss Penny. He liked stroking the ridge of her spine. Delicate, yet sturdy.

He liked that she was challenging him. That she was brave enough to insult him.

Some would say foolhardy enough.

She'd dared to antagonize a dangerous, half-mad duke. He wanted to know why. And he wanted to throw her off balance. Fluster the bold, brave Miss Penny.

Show her just how bad and mad he was.

"Miss Penny, you put me in mind of a Cornish bog. You're pretty to look upon, but one false step and a man could be sucked to a muddy death."

She appeared to be genuinely delighted by this. She grinned. "I'm so glad you think so, Your Grace."

"Yes, Miss Penny, you put me in mind of bogs . . ." he stared into her eyes and lowered his voice to a husky whisper ". . . and beds."

Her smile wobbled. "Did you say *beds*, Your Grace?"

"Beds are much nicer than bogs, wouldn't you agree, Miss Penny?"

"Ah . . . I suppose so."

"So many wonderful things happen in beds."

She blinked. "I'm quite fond of sleeping. I never rise before noon. I never help with household chores, I prefer to laze abed."

"Mmm. Yes. Lazing about in bed can be so very diverting."

"About your treatise on the rotation of turnips and clover, Your Grace—"

"I'd rather talk about beds than turnips, wouldn't you? I have a nice bed. It's big. Comfortable. Has crimson velvet bed hangings. Beeswax candles to light my way in the dark."

"Quite as I pictured a ducal bed to be," she said gamely.

"Do you picture ducal beds often?"

"Er, almost never," she mumbled. "That is never. I never, ever picture beds. Or dukes in beds." She clamped her mouth shut.

"Are you quite sure about that?"

No, she wasn't sure about that.

She was picturing his bed right now. With him in it, wearing the bedclothes and nothing more. Soft linens sliding down a heavily muscled expanse of chest to reveal . . .

When he gazed at her and spoke of beds in that low, husky voice that sent shivers between her shoulder blades, well, any red-blooded young lady would experience at least a little bit of thrill.

Except that this was a full-blown quake, as if her body wanted to split along the seams.

He had the most disconcertingly gentle grip, as though he thought her hand the most precious gift he'd ever received.

There was an indefinable quality about him, a majestic ownership of his body that Mina felt on her own skin, within her own body.

He was the heated, menacing atmosphere right before a thunderstorm. The zing of attraction zipped from where their hands touched, up her arms, and spread throughout her body.

Her hair might be singed when the waltz ended.

She wished Thorndon would stop talking about beds. And she wished she could stop picturing him in bed.

Gather yourself together, Mina.

Stairs and doors.

That's where her attention should be. Lord Rafe would either come through a door or descend the central stairs.

"You keep glancing at the entrances," said Thorndon. "Are you waiting for someone?"

Your brother. Who is my pathway out of the prison of rusticating spinsterhood and into a thrilling life of international intrigue and espionage.

So stop distracting me with your molten gold eyes and molded jaw.

She had to regain the upper hand here. All of that talk of beds . . . he'd been trying to fluster her, but what if he truly was taken with her? It would ruin everything if he decided to want her.

She had to antagonize him further.

"Of course not. Why would I be waiting for someone? I'm dancing with the very pinnacle of English manhood. The very essence of a country nobleman. You're ever so rustic and *quaint*."

"Quaint?" he growled.

She widened her eyes. "Don't you enjoy striding across the moors with a hunting rifle swinging at your side and a pack of foxhounds baying at your heels?"

"Of course I do."

"And if your carriage becomes stuck in the mud, you drag it out yourself instead of waiting for your servants to unstick you?"

"With one hand tied behind my back."

"Rustic," she said. "Quaint."

"I was told you were the rustic one. My mother said that you were raised in the countryside and had a talent for estate management. I pictured you churning butter with one hand while balancing account books with the other."

"Ridiculous!" As a matter of fact, she had learned to churn butter, but she certainly wouldn't admit that to him. "What do you think I am, a combination milkmaid and secretary? You'll have to seek elsewhere if that's what you're looking for. This ballroom is filled with ladies who are finished and polished to a highly reflective sheen."

He glanced around the room. "You're right. But you're not one of them."

Blast. She should have made more of an effort with Grizzy's decorum lessons. He saw right through to her rough and splintered heart.

She stared up at him as if he were a squashed insect on the ceiling, and not a virile, devilishly good-looking, and highly infuriating duke. "If you're insinuating that I'm not a proper dance partner for a duke, then have no fear, Your Grace, there are dozens of ladies dying to take my place. I would be more than happy to relinquish you to one of them."

He took a leisurely perusal of the room, stopping to gaze at several beautiful, elegant, and poised young ladies. "You're right, Miss Penny." He caught her gaze and held it. "You're infinitely replaceable."

The music ended. She retrieved her hand from his grasp.

His bow was perfunctory. Her curtsy nearly insulting.

He stalked away. She whirled around and marched in the opposite direction.

Goal achieved. He wasn't the least bit interested. She wasn't memorable. She was infinitely replaceable.

He'd find some graceful, meek, biddable lady, sweep her off her feet, and install her in his desolate mansion on the moors.

And why that idea rankled so much, she had absolutely no idea.

...

Chapter 3

🦎

Now that Mina had driven away the duke, her
one purpose for being here was to speak with
Lord Rafe. She had a proposition to make. She and
Lord Rafe would forge an equal partnership—one
based on mutual skills and ambitions.

Lord Rafe was affable, charismatic, and infinitely more manipulatable than his brother. Perhaps he wasn't the most brilliant of men, but he
was perfect for her purposes.

With his charm and access to society, and her
pedigree in espionage, they would bring the
criminal underworld to its knees, starting with Le
Triton, the notorious French antiquities thief and
spy who had murdered her parents. She burned
to have revenge on the cruel man who had cut her
parents' lives short and left her so alone.

She planned to corner Lord Rafe and explain
her proposal for building his career as a secret
agent and establishing their partnership.

After which he would agree to marry her.

After which he would spirit her away to the
gardens for her very first kiss. He was a wicked
rake, after all, and would be woefully unimpres-
sive if he didn't steal a kiss.

She wouldn't close her eyes while he was kissing her because she'd want to soak it all in, to remember it for later, remember what freedom looked like. Tasted like.

His kiss, their partnership, would mean her escape from her uncle's control, her legitimate entrée into the world of espionage, and her freedom.

He wouldn't close his eyes, either. He would feel the connection between them, the inevitability of their partnership. His eyes would glow hot and gold.

Wait. No. His eyes were cool and blue as the ocean.

What was wrong with her? She'd actually pictured Thorndon kissing her. *Thorndon*. The man her uncle had decided would make an excellent substitute jailer. Her uncle wanted to hand Thorndon the keys and have Mina locked away in Cornwall.

Blast her guardian. And blast all arrogant dukes.

Grizzy appeared at Mina's side. How did she move so swiftly through a crowded room at her advanced age?

"I didn't think you had it in you, Wilhelmina," she said, steering Mina toward the back of the ballroom. "But you did it."

"Did what?"

"Dazzled the duke."

"No I didn't."

Grizzy stopped walking. "Take a look. Not too obvious, now. A small backward glance will suffice."

What was she on about? Mina glanced over her shoulder.

Good lord. Thorndon was staring at her. Glaring might be a better word. Their gazes locked and time stopped. The crackling energy that surrounded him arced across the room, setting her cheeks ablaze and her heart pounding.

Why did he have to be so overbearingly good-looking?

"Thrust out your bosom," instructed Grizzy. "Laugh a little. Toss your hair. Like this." She made flipping motions against the precise gray curls hanging down from her towering coiffure.

When Mina just stood there, Grizzy glowered at her. "Flirt, girl, *flirt*. The Duke of Thorndon is staring at you."

"I thought I was supposed to maintain an air of detached decorum."

"There's a time and a place for everything, and now is the time for thrusting out your bosom and flirting. He's entranced."

"You've had too much rum punch."

Grizzy shook her head. "I know an entranced duke when I see one. He couldn't take his eyes from you the entire time you danced. What were you speaking about?"

Grizzy must be wrong. Mina had thoroughly antagonized the duke. "He's not entranced, he's incensed. I insulted him."

Another darting glance told her he was *still* staring. She swiped a lock of hair out of her eyes impatiently. What did she have to do to be rid of his attention?

"That was perfect," said Grizzy.

"I wasn't flirting. My hair was in my eyes."

"Now walk slowly away. Don't look back again."

"I think I'll go to the retiring room and splash some water on my face."

Grizzy gave her a knowing look. "Feeling a little faint? I don't blame you. He's handsome as sin."

"It's not that, it's only the room is unbearably close and hot."

"Take a moment to compose yourself, but then you must return and dance with another gentleman, to make the duke jealous."

Mina promised to return even though she had no intention of dancing with anyone else until Lord Rafe arrived. She would have promised anything to make her escape.

Dancing with Thorndon had thrown her mind into a spin, like a child's top set in motion. He was everything she'd thought he would be—rude, arrogant, controlling. He'd all but propositioned her on the dance floor and he'd done it just to make her blush, to assert his mastery over her emotions.

She should be angry, and she was, but she was also . . . spinning.

Splash her face with water. Attempt to restore equilibrium to her thoughts.

She might require a whole bucket of ice water to find her footing again.

She'd nearly made it to the retiring room when she saw the dreaded Duke of Marmont, another of the marriage prospects highlighted in the Duke Dossier, and his mother heading her way.

She dove for the first cover she saw, a large grouping of potted ferns.

"Pardon me, but this is my hiding place, I'll thank you to move along," whispered a female voice from inside the cover of the plants.

"Just let me stay for a few moments. Please. It's a matter of great urgency." She squished in beside the other girl, holding her breath and praying that the duke hadn't seen her.

"Miss Penny," called Marmont. "Where has that girl gone off to? I swear I saw her come this way."

She could only see pieces of him through the fern fronds. A knobby knee. A blade-thin nose.

"Never mind, Eugene," said his mother. "We'll find her. If she's the one you want, she's the one you'll have."

"Marmont. Ugh," whispered the girl. "You can stay here as long as necessary."

"Bless you," Mina whispered. Her companion had pale red-gold hair and a thin face with purplish shadows under hazel eyes behind wire-rimmed spectacles. The yellow gown she wore did her complexion no favors.

The duke and his mother finally took their search elsewhere.

"He's a proper nincompoop," said the girl when it was safe to talk. "Which is a corruption of the Latin non compos, you know. He's a fool."

"I'm well aware. I had the terrible misfortune of dancing with him earlier. He has a horror of communal punchbowls. He also advised me on the most efficacious methods of avoiding phlegmatic ailments."

"He's a hypochondriac."

"A what?"

"Borrowed from the Greek *hypochondria*, meaning the organs of the upper abdomen, behind the ribs, thought to be the seat of melancholy." At Mina's blank look, the girl added, "he suffers from a depression of the mind that centers on imaginary physical ailments."

"Oh."

"Just learned that one." The girl held up a book. "*Whyter's Etymologicon Magnum*. Have you read it?"

"Can't say that I have," said Mina politely. "Is it very good?"

"It's wonderful, though I'm going to become a lexicographer and compile a much better one. Mine will be much thicker. Words are my passion." She pushed her spectacles up her nose. "I'll be a confirmed old maid after this interminable Season is finally finished and I'll devote myself fully to my etymological studies. I've been invited to join a secret society of professional-minded ladies—oh dear, I'm not supposed to tell anyone that."

"Your secret's safe with me. I'm Wilhelmina Penny, by the way."

"Lady Beatrice Bentley."

Rafe and Thorndon's sister—a stroke of luck. "I was hoping to meet you tonight, Lady Beatrice."

"You were? I suppose it's to do with my brother the duke. Everyone's being so nice to me now, even Lady Millicent Granger told me she liked my ribbons, when she's never said two words to me before and always calls me Beastly Beatrice behind my back."

"Why would she call you that?"

Lady Beatrice turned her head fully toward Mina for the first time. The right corner of her mouth and her right eyelid sagged slightly downward. "Facial palsy. Slight partial paralysis."

She pronounced the medical diagnosis with such naked emotion that Mina's heart ached for her.

"Paralysis: Latin, from the Greek *paralyein*, to loosen," said Lady Beatrice.

"Honestly, I didn't even notice," Mina said.

"Thank you for saying that. I know it's not true but I appreciate the sentiment. And I appreciate that you're not staring. Most people stare."

"You'll have to point out Lady Millicent so that I may find some appropriate torture for her. She'll never see me coming. Stealth is one of my talents."

"She's there, dancing with the Earl of Mayhew. And the best torture for her would be to steal her coveted prize, ergo my brother, the duke. I saw you dancing with him. He appeared to be entranced."

"He was *not* entranced. It was loathing at first sight, I'm afraid. For both of us."

"Oh dear, I'm very sorry to hear that. I know we just met but I quite like you, Miss Penny. I don't want him to marry Lady Millicent, though she is this Season's reigning beauty."

"Don't you have another brother?" Mina asked casually.

"No respectable girl speaks about Rafe these days if she doesn't want to be tarnished by association."

That's precisely what Mina wanted. Bring on the tarnishing! Bring on the adventures.

"Will he be attending this evening?" she asked, keeping her tones admirably modulated.

"He usually arrives around midnight with his inebriated friends. They dance with a few ladies, say scandalous things, and then leave again for the night's real entertainment in the demimonde. That goes on until he stumbles home to his nearby town house in the early hours of the morning. Repeat *ad nauseam*."

"You don't think very highly of your brother."

"You obviously haven't met him."

"I have met him. That is, he visited my uncle's estate from time to time."

Lady Beatrice gave her an alarmed look. "I do hope you're not thinking of reforming him."

"Of course not."

"You can't, you know. Many have tried. All have failed."

"I've no interest in reforming your brother." At least not in the sense Lady Beatrice meant.

"Do reconsider my brother Andrew—Thorndon—won't you? He may be brusque and he may appear to be unfeeling, but he improves upon acquaintance, I promise. I know he has a good heart, be it buried ever so deep. His life has been . . . troubled."

Mina hadn't read the Duke Dossier closely enough to uncover any troubles.

Peering through the fronds, Mina searched the room for Lord Rafe. He wasn't there, and neither was Thorndon, not that she was looking for him.

Now was her chance to escape. "If I go back out there, Marmont will claim me for another dance," she said.

"You can hide here with me, I don't mind," Lady Beatrice offered.

"That's very kind but I think some air would do me good. Is there a way for me to access the gardens from here without being seen by everyone?"

Lady Beatrice nodded. "There's an entrance to the gardens directly behind us. You can hide there until Marmont loses interest."

"Thank you, Lady Beatrice. It was very nice to meet you."

"Likewise. I do hope we'll see each other again soon."

"I would like that."

It was nice chatting with Lady Beatrice but Mina had urgent plans.

She was still wearing the demure gown Grizzy had chosen for her, but not for long. She had a transformation to complete. She must be ready to make a truly memorable impression when Lord Rafe arrived.

She'd made her plan carefully, considering all of the variables. She'd followed the path of logic, written everything out, every possible outcome, and then burned the paper.

If she stayed at Sutton Hall she would die slowly inside and go dull, and eventually flicker out. Lord Rafe was her escape route.

He would be the handsome face of the operation, and Mina would do what she excelled at:

keeping thorough records, cracking ciphers and codes, piecing together small tidbits of information into a greater whole, and modifying and inventing weaponry.

With Mina at his side, they couldn't lose. They would become even more celebrated than her parents had been. Together they would defeat Le Triton and Mina would finally have her revenge.

He'd thought he could do this. He'd thought he'd banished the memories.

Drew pressed his forehead against the rough wood walls of the gardening shed at the back of his mother's rose gardens, where he used to retreat as a child. Normally he didn't like small, enclosed spaces but this one was familiar. Comforting.

A small thing had happened—inconsequential to everyone else in the ballroom. The candles had sputtered overhead and one small drop of wax had hit his cheek.

Smell of beeswax filling his nostrils.

Only it wasn't beeswax, but tallow. The cheapest, foulest tallow, which smelled of burned animal hair. Tallow mixed with the odor of bilgewater. Floor beginning to sway.

Irrational fear intruding on his mind.

It was London that dragged this out of him, this lingering edge of madness.

London, gossips, large gatherings of people, unfamiliar carriages, unfamiliar small spaces.

A drop of wax on his cheek.

Many things triggered his attacks, or had triggered them until he left London and built a new life. He thought he'd mastered his emotions, that nothing could take him back over the side and plunge him into the storm waters again.

He ran his hands over the walls. He hadn't brought a lantern. There had been enough moonlight to walk along the garden path. Cold metal. A three-pronged gardening fork hanging on the wall. A good, sturdy shape for his palm to enclose.

He pressed harder with his fingertips on the sharp tines of the fork. If the gossips could see him now they would have their proof that he wasn't right in the head, that he'd gone mad.

When he'd left London for Thornhill House, he'd only been dimly aware of the army of servants it took to keep his life humming along smoothly.

As far as he'd known, food had arrived on the table in seven courses prepared by a French cook. He'd certainly known nothing about growing and harvesting plants.

The tool in his palm reminded him of the work he had to do at Thornhill. When he had first arrived there he hadn't known the sharp end of a spade from the handle.

Old Caleb, the gardener here when Drew was a child, was buried and gone, but his roses lived on, unfurling every year in brilliant crimson, waxy white, and a heated fuchsia color that seemed to pulse when you looked at it.

Most of the bushes were naked right now, snipped to the bone so that the ballroom could be festooned for the night.

The new gardener wasn't so careful with his tools as Caleb had been. Things were scattered about. Seeds in muslin bags not put away in their proper wooden boxes.

He sifted through the seeds, as if sorting them into piles would do something similar in his mind, every thought in its place, orderly and neat.

Nothing mixed up or out of place.

Just a little longer in the velvet caress of utter solitude.

A few more breaths and he would go back inside.

Think about the life of a seed, how if it rains and then the sun shines, it can seem like a fresh green seedling appears overnight, so eager and hopeful, stretching thin fibers to the sun.

For some unaccountable reason, instead of a green seedling his mind's eye pictured Miss Penny. She'd been the most interesting thing to happen to him tonight. While he'd been talking to her he'd forgotten to be wary, forgotten all of the people watching them.

He pressed his cheek against the rough wall and thought about the smooth line of her profile, that plump lower lip, and the mystery in her blue-gray eyes.

Why had she been so intent on making him dislike her? Had he lost his charm, along with his sanity?

The door of the shed scraped open. For a moment he wondered if he'd imagined it, but then a slight figure dressed in shimmering white appeared.

He flattened against the back wall, hidden by the wooden shelves.

The woman carried a small lantern, which she placed on the hook near the door. When she turned toward him he nearly betrayed his presence with a surprised sound.

Miss Penny.

He could almost believe her to be a ghost . . . except that she glowed with life. She was so very alive. She was muttering to herself. She made these little impatient gestures. He couldn't make out all the words but she was angry about something.

"Phlegmatic ailments," she muttered. "Really? You think that's a scintillating topic of conversation? Pah." She removed her shawl and folded it carefully, setting it on the low bench that flanked the wall closest to the door. "And beds. Let's talk about beds, shall we? Do you often picture ducal beds?"

Her mimicry of his voice nearly made him laugh aloud. He'd managed to get under her skin in the same way she had lodged under his. It was good to know that the feeling was mutual.

"Why did he have to be so handsome?" Miss Penny peeled off her gloves and set them atop the shawl. "And that delicious almond-y scent of his. I can still smell it in the air. I have to stop thinking of him." She removed the garland of white and pink silk flowers from her hair and flung it to the floor. "Damn all dukes to a specially created duke hell."

She grabbed a spade from the wall and used it to open the bench seat. She reached inside. What the dickens was she doing?

"*Replaceable.* I'll show him who's irreplaceable."

She knelt down on the wooden floor of the shed in front of the bench, in her pristine white gown, and reached inside, bringing up a linen-wrapped parcel.

She stood up and unwrapped the parcel. Lantern light caught shimmering scarlet silk.

A gown by the looks of the bows and frills.

She hugged the gown to her breast. "There you are, my beauty. You're not replaceable in the least."

Mystified, all Drew could do was watch as she danced a few steps of a waltz with the dress as her limp partner.

She set the gown on top of the bench. And then she did something truly unexpected.

She began unfastening the white dress she wore.

"Demure," she said as she unhooked the back of her gown, twisting and contorting to reach the buttons. "Charming and countrified." Another button. "Biddable and decorous." The gown slipped down her shoulders.

He should turn away. Stare at the wall. Stare at anything other than the smooth expanse of flesh she'd just revealed.

"I am. None. Of. Those. Things." Each word meant another button undone.

He couldn't look away now. The sight of her captivated him. Her hair escaping her coiffure and falling around her face. She bit her lip, twisting her torso to reach the final buttons.

Every loosened button made her gown slip lower.

He really should leave. If only there was a back

exit out of the shed. If he revealed himself now, she would be mortified.

She wriggled and danced. "Devil take it," she swore. The last button was giving her trouble.

Do you require a hand with that? he nearly asked.

Finally the gown came loose. She tugged it over her head and tossed it aside.

She reached inside her bodice and plumped one breast higher over her corset and chemise. Then did the same on the other side.

Blood raced away from his brain and made a rush on his cock.

She had beautiful breasts. Lush and full for her slight frame.

He shouldn't be looking at her breasts, but damn it, he'd come to this shed first and he'd come here to escape from all the scrutiny.

A terrible thought struck him—what if she was preparing for a tryst? He could be stuck here while Miss Penny and her lover, the lucky bastard, made use of the garden shed.

Then he would feel like a complete lecher. He had to say something. He had to stop her from disrobing any further. There was only one honorable course of action.

Spying on a young lady changing clothing was not good form.

Though this was his garden shed. On *his* London estate. At *his* ball.

Who was the trespasser here?

How was he supposed to know that his childhood haven would be invaded by a debutante changing from her virginal gown to what could only be described as a Covent Garden confection?

The bodice barely covered her corset.

"Blast," she cursed, wiggling with her hands behind her back, attempting to fasten the gown.

It was the most erotic show he'd ever seen. He had to leave. Now. Or she had to leave. He backed away and his heel must have hit a rake, because the handle flew up and smacked him in the back of the head.

I suppose I deserved that, he had time to think, before he realized there was a pistol pressed against his chest.

"Don't shoot." Drew raised his hands, palms outward. "I'm a duke."

Chapter 4
❦

$\mathcal{P}$RECISELY THE STATEMENT most likely to make Mina fire.

Especially when she realized which duke she held at pistol point.

Thorndon towered over her, huge and solid, so near she could smell his cologne—a faint trace of almonds and spicy musk.

Eyes glowing gold in the lamplight. Eyes which had seen her disrobe.

She dug her pistol into his chest, over his heart.

He'd seen her disrobe. Had he heard her mutterings? And, most importantly, had she said anything incriminating about his brother, Lord Rafe? She quickly tried to remember everything she'd said from the moment she'd entered the shed.

She wished she could swallow the last few minutes like the torn-up shreds of a secret message no one but she would ever read.

Talking to oneself was a dangerous habit. She'd spent so much time alone at Sutton Hall that it was ingrained behavior.

Lord Rafe didn't like innocent debutantes, so Mina had planned to transform herself into a sophisticated woman of mystery by wearing her mother's scarlet silk dress, which she'd paid to have altered according to today's fashions.

Only now Thorndon was ruining everything.

Great big barrier of a duke.

"What are you doing, lurking out here in the shadows, Your Grace?" She got the sense that he'd been hiding. But why would a duke hide from his own ballroom?

"I could ask the same of you, Miss Penny. It's my shed, after all."

He didn't seem terribly concerned about the firearm targeting his heart. She was embarrassed and it made her want to throw him off balance.

"I assure you I know how to use this weapon."

"I didn't suggest otherwise. I'm sure you're skilled with a gun, having been raised in the countryside, and being so fond of the hunt."

"I was raised in the countryside but I'm no simple country miss."

"Not in that gown. No one would mistake you for anything simple. That's a complicated gown."

"This is a stunning gown," she huffed.

Wearing her mother's gown was the closest Mina could come to touching her mother. She'd even purchased the same rose scent her mother had worn.

She wanted to become just as glamorous and sophisticated as her celebrated mother had been.

"Has too many ruffles," said the duke. "It looks like a rose mated with a bawdy-house sofa. I liked the other one better."

Now he was insulting her mother's dress. He was the most irritating man in the world, and she had to be stuck in a garden shed with him. "You would, wouldn't you?" She nudged his chest with her pistol. "You want young ladies to be demure, biddable, and silent."

"I didn't say that. I only thought the other gown suited you better. You looked sunny and pretty, like a daisy."

"A daisy?" she sputtered. "I'm nothing so ordinary or conventional as a daisy. Take that back."

"As you say, Miss Penny. You have the pistol. You're not a daisy. There's no air of the country about you. You're not sunny or fresh or pretty."

Not pretty. Why did that upset her?

Everything about him was infuriating, especially that smirk, as if he knew the effect his proximity had on her. The way the backs of her knees wobbled and her belly tightened.

He had to be in control, didn't he? Well. Who was the one with the pistol?

"Despite the firearm, I'm at a decided disadvantage here, Your Grace, wouldn't you say? You've seen me in my chemise, and you're still fully clothed. I think we should even the playing field, don't you agree?"

Some demon was shaping her words. It's just that he was so very in control, even when she had a pistol pressed against his chest.

She wanted him at a disadvantage. She wanted to dictate the tenor of this encounter.

"Remove your coat, Your Grace."

"Are you sure that's a good idea, Miss Penny?"

"I demand retribution. A . . . chest for a chest. You saw mine."

"This is my garden shed. I was here first. You're the trespasser. Why did you hide a change of clothing in my gardener's work bench?"

"No questions until we're on even footing."

"Very well, I agree that I had you at a disadvantage. Shall I remove my coat?"

His words spoken with a mocking inflection that clearly insinuated he thought that she'd back down easily.

She wasn't going to back down, be silent, hide away. Not anymore.

"If you please," she said boldly, if a bit breathlessly.

"You'll have to move your pistol, Miss Penny."

"Oh, of course." She took one small step away from him. Not too far. She wasn't born yesterday.

He removed his tailcoat and hung it on a peg. His waistcoat was plain black silk but there was a thin band of gold around the edges that matched his eyes. She hadn't noticed that before, because she'd been too busy staring into those eyes while they waltzed.

"There, are you happy?" he asked.

"The cravat, if you please."

He loosened the knot of his cravat and undid the elaborate bow until the ends dangled down his chest.

She swallowed. Perhaps she hadn't thought this all the way through. Watching Thorndon disrobe was disconcerting and rather . . . addictive. She wanted to see more of him. The well-defined arm muscles she'd felt beneath his shirt as they danced.

Perhaps a flat, muscular abdomen.

She glanced down.

Fatal error.

In one ruthless move he knocked the pistol from her hand, grabbed her by the waist, and lifted her against the wall, reversing their positions.

"Oof," she exhaled, more from surprise than pain.

He lifted both of her wrists with one of his hands and held her trapped against the rough wood wall. She tried to squirm free but he was too strong.

Waltzing with the man had been a breathless moment of anticipatory awareness . . . this was the storm.

Her emotions rioted, and her body betrayed her mind, reacting to the feel of his hard, long body covering hers.

Desire shot an arrow through her belly.

A dark shed. A mad, half-clothed duke.

"Let me go," she said, panting, her breasts rising and falling against his unyielding chest.

Hold me closer. Give me my first kiss. Up against a wall in the dark.

Eyes glittering as you claim my lips.

"It's not every evening that I'm held at pistol point by a debutante and forced to undress," he said. "If I let you go, how do I know you won't lunge for your weapon?"

"You'll just have to trust me, Your Grace."

"Ha." His thumb caressed the inside of her wrist and the longing in her belly, her mind, intensified.

Kiss me now. I want to know what it's like. I want you to be the one.

What was wrong with her?

"I don't trust you, Miss Penny. I hardly know you. Whom are you planning to meet?"

"That's none of your concern."

"Why did you work so hard to make me dislike you while we were dancing?"

"Has it ever occurred to you that not every unmarried lady in the world wants to wed you?"

"Actually, no it hasn't. Becoming a duchess is a powerful prize. And I am a handsome, virile specimen, despite my bleak reputation."

"Ha." Conceited, controlling dukes.

His lip quirked. "You don't think I'm handsome, Miss Penny?"

"Certainly not. Too brooding to be handsome. You prowl around with your own private thundercloud above your head."

His lips tilted higher in a predatory half smile. "But I heard you muttering about how handsome I was. And how I smell delicious."

"I must have been speaking of some other duke," she replied flippantly.

He did smell delectable. A heated blend of spiced musk and sweet almonds that made her want to nuzzle his neck with her nose.

"You're really not frightened of me at all, are you?" he asked.

"You're hardly going to murder a debutante at your mother's ball. Bad for the family name."

"What's left of it," he said, with a wide streak of bitterness in his voice.

"I'm not scared of anything." That wasn't true. She was scared of lots of things.

She was frightened of herself, right now, not of him.

Her mind felt foggy and her body wanted to do scandalous things. Being trapped and held at his mercy should have made her furious but apparently made her wanton instead.

"Is that so?" His fingers tightened around her wrists. It was a good thing that the lighting was so dim because the position stretched her breasts over her corset until her nipples were nearly visible. Nipples which were embarrassingly hard, as if it was snowing out and not a mild summer evening.

He glanced at her breasts, his gaze like hot candle wax searing her skin. If he touched her skin it would be hot, like the barrel of a pistol after being discharged.

"I'm fearless and worldly and sophisticated," Mina insisted. "I don't even care that you saw me in my shift."

"Yes you do. You were blushing."

"It's too dark for you to tell."

"You're only pretending to be a sophisticated London lady, Miss Penny." He touched the edge of her bodice with his free hand. "This gown doesn't suit you, and I think you know it. Why change into it?"

Maybe she was still an awkward, country-bred hoyden. Maybe she wasn't worldly yet, but she had to pretend to be—for Lord Rafe.

Blast. She'd forgotten about him again. How much time had passed?

"This may be my very first ball, but I'm a woman of the world. I have a proposition for someone and this is the right costume," she said.

"A proposition. Am I to understand that you are planning your ruin?" he asked, his voice husky, as though he might volunteer for the job.

She shivered. Her eyes closed.

She might want to hire him.

Focus, Mina.

"Not a carnal proposition, a business one," she said tartly. "Now, if you'll excuse me." She made another attempt at freeing herself.

"I'll let you go now, Miss Penny." He released her wrists and stepped away. "Since you have an assignation to keep."

She lowered her arms.

He stooped down and when he rose her pistol lay in the palm of his hand. "I believe this is yours."

"Aren't you afraid to give it back to me?"

"You wouldn't shoot a duke at his own ball. Bad for a lady's reputation."

She accepted the pistol and stuffed it into her reticule.

"And now I'll make myself presentable and leave the garden shed to you, Miss Penny." He began fumbling with his cravat.

It must be late. Nearly time for Lord Rafe and his friends to make their entrance. She'd be watching from the gardens and when he entered, she'd meet him halfway.

Grizzy would be livid, but there wouldn't be anything she could do about it.

They'd have to elope to Gretna Green to be married, since her uncle would never consent to the union. He'd never allow her to marry one of his spies, especially one who'd disgraced himself and was currently out of Sir Malcolm's favor.

The duke was still attempting to retie his cravat into something resembling a fashionable knot. The sight was somehow endearing.

"You've no idea how to tie that, do you?" she observed.

"Not a clue." He tied the ends into a large bow directly under his chin. "How does this look?"

"Dreadful." She squelched a giggle. "Your valet will murder you."

The duke undid the bow and started over again. "Cursed cloth."

"You're doing it all wrong."

"Thank you very much. The problem is that my fingers are too large."

All of him was too large. He had dwarfed every other man in the ballroom.

He would tower over Lord Rafe, taking up all the space in the ballroom, drawing Mina's eyes to him instead. She must stop having these thoughts.

"Here. Let me help you," she said brusquely. The sooner he had his cravat tied, the sooner he would leave. Then she would have time to tidy her coiffure and restore her composure before doing what she had come to do.

She stood on her tiptoes and untied his cravat. She hadn't considered how intimate such a simple gesture might be. Unknotting a cravat, unloosening his clothing.

"I met your sister, Your Grace. A lovely girl."

He glanced down at her. "That's what I think, but she's not popular because of the shortsightedness of London dandies."

"That's just silly—all because of a slight affliction of her facial nerves."

"She's marked as other. She's an easy target."

"I thought she was remarkably clever and well-spoken."

He smiled at her for the very first time and she had the sensation that he was seeing her—truly seeing her—and that he liked what he saw. "You're right. She's sharp as a knife. She should have dozens of suitors."

"Perhaps she doesn't wish to wed."

"Why, did she tell you that?"

"Not in so many words . . . but she did say that she was looking forward to being an old maid."

Her fingers shook slightly. Her whole body was vibrating, as if she were stretched over a crossbow and had been plucked by strong fingers.

He had to lean down so that she could reach his cravat.

He would lean in much the same way to kiss her.

And there her mind went again, wishing he would kiss her. It was beyond irritating.

He sank to his knees. "Is this better when I'm down here?"

She made a mistake in the tying and had to start over again. "I could use more light."

Instead of moving the lantern closer, he placed

his palms on her hips and moved her closer to the lantern.

"It will have to be undone," she said breathlessly. "I'll get it right eventually."

DREW WAS UNDONE. Mixed up and tangled.

The intimacy rolled over him in a wave. Her small fingers at his neck.

Kneeling before her. He wanted to wrap his arms around her and bury his face in her breasts. Tease her nipples to peaks with his tongue.

It had been too long. And she was very, very pretty. And he was only a man.

Her beauty was straightforward. It hit him in the solar plexus. Her hair smelled fresh and sunshiny, like a field of wildflowers.

He'd like to loosen those tightly coiled ringlets on either side of her cheeks with his fingers, muss her hair . . . unfasten that scarlet seduction of a gown.

It had been a long time since he'd felt this buzz in his stomach. Attraction. Awareness.

Whom was she wearing this dress for? While they were dancing, she'd been glancing at the door. She's made a comment about Rafe. What had she said? That she'd met him on several occasions when he visited her uncle.

Dear Lord.

Not Rafe.

He grabbed hold of her hands. "Please tell me you didn't change into this gown to impress my brother."

"Don't be ridiculous, Your Grace." She extricated her hands from his grasp and gave one final tug to the ends of his cravat. "There. You're presentable."

He wasn't presentable. He was a raging beast. The thought of Miss Penny throwing herself away on Rafe made him see red.

He took a deep breath. He could be wrong. "My brother isn't coming to the ball tonight."

"Not coming—why?" Dismay in her eyes, quickly followed by nonchalance. "That is, why should I care?"

Damn it. He'd been right. She'd changed into this seductive red silk gown for Rafe.

It was written all over her face, though she strove to hide it.

"You shouldn't care, Miss Penny." *Please don't care. Not for Rafe.*

"I don't." She tossed her head and one ringlet fell into her eyes. She blew it away with an exasperated breath.

He rose to his feet. "Rafe's not attending the ball. I don't know where he is. We had an argument today and there's no way he wants to be in the same room with me."

"Oh." The one syllable saying so much. She'd been waiting for Rafe, watching for him, she was . . .

"You're in love with my brother," he said.

"Absolutely not," she huffed. "I told you, he visited my uncle sometimes. And I've read about him in the papers. That is all."

"He took an interest in you?"

"He may have taken a passing interest."

Drew nodded. "He takes an interest in every pretty girl he meets. I'll wager he plucked a rose from his lapel and promised to marry you someday."

Her eyes clouded over. "Something like that."

"And you took his words literally." Now he was beginning to understand. Vulnerable young girl meets handsome rake. An obsession blooms.

"He was kind to me at a time in my life when I felt very much alone," she said.

He saw it very clearly. She was infatuated with his brother because of some episode in her past that had meant less than nothing to Rafe, and everything to her.

It was a tale as old as time.

It made Drew want to slam his fist into the shed wall.

"Please listen to me very carefully, Miss Penny."

By the mutinous tilt of her chin, he could tell that she wouldn't listen, but he had to say the words anyway. "The Rafe you think you know only exists in your mind and your heart. You've fabricated him from lonely girlish longings. He would chew you up and spit you out. He would crush you and leave you ruined. He's done it before."

"None of this is any concern to me," she said breezily. "I've no idea why you're speaking of it."

"Admit that you changed into this red gown for Rafe."

"I'll admit nothing of the sort."

He closed his eyes for a heartbeat. He had to fight this surge of protectiveness, the need to warn her. She wasn't his problem. She could throw away her virtue if she wanted to and it was no concern of his.

But he didn't want to see the light extinguished from her eyes. Or the smile fall from her lips. She had such nice lips, and her eyebrows were particularly appealing. They were always flying up when she spoke in such an expressive way.

"You probably think that you can reform him," Drew said. "Well it's just not possible. He's no half-hearted dissolute. He's leapt fully into the hellfire. Find someone else to want, someone who will love and respect you in return."

"I'll tell you what I want, Your Grace. I want adventure." Her eyes glittered in the gloom. "I'm longing for it. I'm so tired of the humdrum, the predictable. I want my heart to beat faster, and my blood to rush through my veins. I want to take risks."

And I'm the exact opposite. I need routine, predictability. My blood is too icy to rush.

He knew from personal experience that young ladies sometimes thought that wicked rakes were the answer to all of their midnight longings.

"Miss Penny," he said gently, touching her shoulder. "Let me make one thing very clear. Stay away from my brother. Do you understand me? He's in some kind of trouble right now. He won't tell me what it is, but that's why I'm here—to drag it out of him and set about fixing whatever mess he's made."

She raised her eyebrows. "I'm still not sure why you're speaking to me of your brother."

Smooth voice, not a hint of a telltale tremor. So that's how she wanted to play this.

He dropped his hand. "My apologies. I didn't mean to cause offense."

"None taken. Now, if you'll excuse me." Her gaze traveled to the door.

"You should change back into your other gown, Miss Penny, because my brother will not be making an appearance."

"Good evening, Your Grace." She wasn't a woman to heed warnings—he saw that as clear as day in the determined set of her jaw.

If she wanted Rafe, she was damned well going to have him.

She wasn't his to save. All he could do was warn Rafe away from her, make it very clear that if he took advantage of her in any way, Drew would make his life miserable.

"Good evening, Miss Penny," he said coldly.

He cloaked his fingers in white gloves and set off down the garden path back to the ballroom.

He wasn't here to save adventurous debutantes from their own worst impulses.

He was here to protect his sister, rescue Rafe from his difficulties, and return to Thornhill with a sensible bride who agreed to a convenient, loveless arrangement.

Or the bride business could wait another year and he could return alone.

He just wanted everything to go back to the way it had been before he left Thornhill. He hadn't had one of these attacks in years. He followed a schedule, knew precisely what would happen every second of every day.

The right bride would only make a small ripple in his life. No waves. Nothing to engulf or destroy the tenuous peace he'd finally forged out of the darkness and the painful memories.

Miss Wilhelmina Penny was treacherous ground. She wanted to fling herself headfirst into life and damn the consequences. He should stay as far away from her as possible.

I'm so tired of the humdrum, the predictable. I want my heart to beat faster, and my blood to rush through my veins. I want to take risks.

She wasn't only longing for adventure—she wanted love. That's what ladies meant when they said they wanted their heart to beat faster. They wanted to be swept away by love.

He hoped she found everything she desired and never had to learn the hard lessons—the harsh lessons.

Love was a false sense of security. Fathers refused to pay ransoms. Love offered no protection from the darkness.

No one came to your aid.

He had no one to rely on but himself.

He was alone with his memories. Alone with his pain.

He could trust no one.

Chapter 5

It seemed far away now, his loss of control. Green-striped silk lined the walls of the family sitting room. The walls weren't closing in on him. The floor wasn't swaying.

The room smelled of lamp oil and their house-keeper's lemon biscuits.

His mother had gone to bed after the last guest departed, giving Drew the opportunity to speak to Beatrice about the letter.

His sister sat across from him, her spectacles flickering with the reflection from the fire. She was so tall and so slender, her hair a pale shade of copper.

He didn't know how to talk to her. She was a stranger to him.

"When did you grow up?" he asked her.

"While you were gone for five long years." She sipped her tea.

Drew winced. He was drinking whisky. It dulled the scythe edge of rage that sliced through his mind every time he thought about Miss Penny going to all the effort of changing into a seductive gown for Rafe.

"Why did you stay away so long?" Beatrice asked calmly.

"Thornhill is the best place for me. I'm never at ease in London. Too many bad memories here. Too many gossips passing judgment."

"Memories of the kidnapping."

"Of many things."

"Why don't you ever talk about it? It might do you some good to share the bad memories with someone who cares about you."

"I don't want to talk about it." *And don't care about me. I'll only wound you again by leaving.*

"I was so young when it happened," said Beatrice. "I didn't understand what was happening. As I grew up, you were never home, always out with your friends, just like Rafe is now. And then you left. I have so many questions, which everyone refuses to answer. Why wouldn't Father pay your ransom? How did you free yourself?"

"I said I don't want to speak of it," he said shortly. There was no use talking about the past. After he'd freed himself, no one had wanted to talk about his ordeal——his mother had tried to pretend it had never happened, his father had told him that it was best forgotten, that he must be strong and silent and bear the nightmares in secret. "I don't want to talk about me," he continued, "I'm here to talk about you. There's been a warning given——one I take very seriously."

She lowered her teacup. "What kind of warning?"

Society kept sheltered young ladies in the dark about so many things. His fear for his sister's safety forced him to ignore convention and share everything with her. It was better for her to be on alert. "I don't want to alarm you, but I feel strongly that you should know so that you will be cautious and careful."

"Now you are alarming me. What has happened?"

"I received this letter." He handed the letter to Beatrice and watched her read it.

She whistled, low in her throat. "How very strange."

"Now do you understand?" he asked. "When I read the words I dropped everything and rushed to London." He caught her gaze. "I would never let anything happen to you, Beatrice. I would never allow you to suffer in the way that I did. I would give my life to keep you safe."

She smiled, her lips wobbling slightly. "Let's hope it doesn't come to that. What do you suppose Rafe is up to now?"

"That's what I want to know. I couldn't extract anything from him earlier today. He ran away at the first chance and hasn't been seen since."

"He's been a regular terror lately, even worse than usual. His town house is a veritable den of iniquity. Mama doesn't allow me to visit him there even though it's only a few steps away. She turns a blind eye, of course. He's her golden boy who can do no wrong."

"Until the mystery is solved, my manservant, Corbyn, and I will take turns guarding your bedchamber door. I'll hire additional footmen and post a guard outside the house. I'll stay in Rafe's town house instead of going to my club. Once word is out that I'm in London I expect to receive another letter, this one asking for money."

"Or the extortionist may retreat now that you're here? Maybe they wanted to conduct things from a safe distance."

"That could be, but for now I'm not taking any chances with your safety."

"How can I help?"

"Be wary. Don't trust anyone. Talk to the servants in a general way. Ask them if they know anything about Lord Rafe's troubles, or if anything out of the ordinary has happened recently."

She nodded.

"I'll protect you, Beatrice. I won't let anyone hurt you."

As they'd hurt him. Wet rag stuffed into his mouth. Gagging, unable to breathe. Chained to the wall, the iron around his wrists chafing.

Two bowls of gruel per day. No privy. No sunlight.

"The memories plague you still," she said softly.

He nodded, unable to speak, the phantom rag still choking him.

"Why don't you take me back to Thornhill House with you?" she asked, mercifully changing the subject. "I'm so tired of society. I'll never be a success. I have designs on your library—I hear you have one of the largest collections of books in the entire kingdom. I hope you're protecting the library from mildew?"

"The collection is intact, but I don't think Mama would be very happy if you abandoned her before the end of the Season."

"She'll live. I'm sure there's a wing at Thornhill you could dedicate to your eccentric spinster sister, isn't there? I want to live surrounded by books. And perhaps a few cats. And I'll write the best etymological dictionary the world has ever seen. And don't say that it sounds lonely because that would be the very height of hypocrisy."

This was no passing whim. Drew could tell that she had it all planned. "Finish this Season and then I'll speak with Mother. Thornhill is still being renovated and it's quite rustic. It's not for everyone."

"I'm not cowed by leaky roofs or resident ghosts. Thornhill House needs another monster."

"You're not a monster."

"I'm Beastly Beatrice."

"I wish you wouldn't say that."

"Why not? Everyone calls me that behind my back."

"If you hide yourself away, you won't be living your life."

"That's what you did, isn't it? Hide yourself away. Withdraw from life."

What a wonderful example he'd set for his sister. "I've created a new life with a new sense of purpose. My agricultural experiments. The simple, straightforward sense of satisfaction that comes from helping feed people."

"I want to have a useful life. I don't want to marry a man who doesn't love me and who marries me for my fortune or, worse still, out of pity."

"Before I left London, you told me that you didn't want to be pitied. I see the sentiment is stronger than ever."

"*Pity: to feel compassion for the wretchedness of another.* If someone pities me, I must be wretched, but really I'm not. I find happiness and acceptance in books. They never judge me or pity me."

"Have I told you that you looked lovely tonight?"

"I didn't. That shade of yellow is death to my complexion."

"Then why agree to wear it?"

"I don't care what I wear. Do you know who looked lovely tonight?" she asked with a glint in her eyes. "A lady I met for the first time."

Don't say it. Don't—

"Miss Wilhelmina Penny." She watched him closely. "I saw you dancing with her."

A memory of their dance rose in his mind like the dawn.

Miss Penny's laughter making the candles flicker, the line of her rose-colored slippers contrasting with his black shoes, milky gauze swirling around slender ankles . . .

In the shed, he'd caught a tantalizing glimpse of pink stockings and pink garters tied with rosettes, and a slender waist, curvaceous breasts . . .

Whisky. And lots of it.

"What did you think of Miss Penny?" Beatrice asked, glancing at Drew over the top of her teacup.

"I thought she was trouble." Pretty, perplexing, arousing peril. Best avoided. Best forgotten.

Beatrice laughed and propped her feet up on the fender, turning her skirts up at the hem so they wouldn't catch on fire. "I liked her. She didn't stare at my face at all, and she offered to mete out punishment to Lady Millicent for making fun of me. She was quite ferocious about it. Reminded me of you, actually. You have the same warlike expression on your face right now."

"You know I won't countenance anyone who makes fun of you."

"It's part of my life," said Beatrice, staring at the flickering flames. "The Almighty placed this mark on me for a reason. I'm a wallflower. A complete and utter failure in society."

"You'll never be a wallflower to me."

"You have to say that. You're my brother. Besides, I've made my peace with it. I intend to find a new and different way to become a triumph."

"*I* CALL THAT A complete triumph," said Grizzy as they returned home after the ball. "Sir Malcolm will be very pleased with the progress you made tonight, Wilhelmina."

More like a total disaster, thought Mina as she climbed the stairs to her room.

Lord Rafe had never arrived because of some feud with his brother, the duke.

Thorndon.

Had she gone temporarily insane in that garden shed? Holding him at pistol point. Demanding that he undress. And then the commanding way he'd disarmed her . . .

"You achieved success where all the other ladies failed, Wilhelmina." Grizzy followed her into her room. "He was quite taken with you—everyone was whispering about it. The scrutiny of your deportment will be more intense than ever. We must resume our decorum lessons immediately."

"I'm tired."

"No rest for you, my girl. Not until I'm satisfied that you will be able to converse knowledgably on the arts when the duke invites you to visit the opera with his sister and mother, as I'm quite certain that he will."

"I met Lady Beatrice tonight. She's wonderfully engaging and clever. I hope that we'll become friends." She'd always wanted a friend growing up. She'd been so very lonely with no one to play with.

"Perfect. Now then, I'll name the opera, and you name the composer . . ."

Mina's mind wandered back to the shed as Grizzy tested her.

She couldn't shake the suspicion that Thorndon had been hiding from something when she'd surprised him in the shed. She needed to read the Duke Dossier more closely.

The surprising thing was that Thorndon had warned her about Lord Rafe. Which either meant that he was jealous of his brother or that he was capable of empathy and of caring for something beyond himself, not a very dukelike emotion, to be sure.

"I can see that you're too fatigued to concentrate on your lessons," said Grizzy. "We'll resume in the morning. I'll send Addison to help you undress." Mina hadn't brought her own lady's maid to London, because she'd never had one.

Her life had been entirely unconventional. She'd grown up as a hoyden, allowed to roam as she pleased around the grounds of Sutton Hall but never allowed to venture past the woods.

"I'll have to start a new naturalist tableau." Grizzy cocked her head. "I think I'll call it the Wedding of the Hedgehog and the Vole."

"Oh, please don't." Mina had seen the chamber of horrors that Grizzy called her workshop.

The iron pincers, the spools of metal wire, the cotton batting she used for stuffing. Grizzy had lent her a stomach-churning book entitled *Taxidermy: the Art of Collection, Preparing, and Mounting Objects of Natural History*, by her idol, one Miss Sarah Lee. "That is, don't start planning a wedding just yet," she said. "I only had one waltz with the duke."

"Nonsense. You dazzled him. I have every hope that an invitation from the duke will arrive for you tomorrow. A whirlwind courtship and then . . . Duchess of Thorndon. I never would have thought it possible."

Was that an approving glint in Grizzy's flinty eyes? Mina never would have thought it possible.

"Good night, Great-Aunt."

"Sleep well, Wilhelmina."

The duke had said that Lord Rafe was in some kind of trouble. If she knew what kind of trouble it was, she could be the one to fix it for him, and he'd be so grateful that he'd agree to her plan.

The problem was that in order to set her plan in motion, she needed to actually speak with Lord Rafe. She couldn't write him a letter—what she had to say must be spoken in person.

Her uncle had said Thorndon was staying at his club. Obviously Lord Rafe would know that as well, and so it would be clear for him to return home after the ball was over.

It was high time she stopped dreaming about becoming a secret agent and tested her capabilities in the real world.

She'd pretend to go to bed, wait until Grizzy was asleep, and embark on her very first clandestine mission: sneaking into Lord Rafe's chambers.

If he were there, she could make her proposition. If he weren't, she'd search the apartments for clues about the trouble the duke had alluded to.

Mina had kept a satchel packed and ready for a swift escape ever since her parents had perished. She'd even attempted to run away from Sutton Hall, but Uncle Malcolm had swiftly found her and brought her back home.

He had a network of informants spread throughout England and the Continent.

Tonight she'd take the first steps toward true freedom.

If only she'd been able to bring the red silk dress with her. After she'd changed back into her ball gown, she'd reluctantly left the red silk in the garden shed, bundled up and hidden in the workbench.

This mission called for invisibility and stealth.

Let's see, she would need a dark cloak. A stout rope. Sensible boots.

And her trusty pocket pistol.

THREE HOURS LATER, Mina crouched in the shrubbery outside of Lord Rafe's bedchamber window at his nearby Mayfair town house, which was adjacent to his mother's town house where the ball had been held.

She'd scaled his iron gate and made her way, silent as a mouse, around the back of the town house to the courtyard, stopping at the mews to examine the carriages.

Lord Rafe's dashing cabriolet had been missing. He wasn't here, which meant that instead of convincing him to become her partner, she'd be searching his apartments for information about his whereabouts, debts, current mistress, and other salient details of his life that she might use as leverage.

A few more minutes and then she'd climb the low wall and enter through a window left helpfully ajar. It was either a sitting room or a study. The bedchambers were on the floor above.

She crouched low, hidden by rosebushes from the house, but able to observe everything.

The house was dark and silent.

Thorndon was probably snoring in his bed at his club. No doubt he was dreaming of finding a demure, biddable country lass to milk his Cornish cows and churn his . . . butter.

Not that she should be thinking about Thorndon.

Only . . . there was the garden shed, halfway between the two houses. Inside that shed she'd entertained all manner of wild fantasies.

He'd held her wrists trapped over her head and flattened her against the wall with his overwhelming strength and muscular body.

She'd longed for him to kiss her. Touch her.

Wrong desires. *Wrong brother.*

Chapter 6

WALKING WITH MISS PENNY in a field of daisies, petals open to the sunshine, bees buzzing around their heads.

All the time in the world. No reason to rush.

No one to see them but the sheep. They could make love in the summer breeze.

He laid her down on the sun-warmed flowers. She watched him through half-lidded eyes. She lifted her arms and he came to her, resting his head against the swell of her breasts.

Her heart beat beneath his ear. Life danced and hummed around them.

He slid his hands up her skirts, over her smooth thighs. She wasn't wearing any drawers. How delightful. He squeezed her buttocks, angling her hips, spreading her thighs for his tongue, like a marauding bee sucking molten sunlight from a . . .

Drew woke with a gasp and a stiff cock. *No, just a few more minutes, please. Or maybe an hour?*

Christ. What was he, sixteen? Erotic dreams about a girl he just met. And why had his dream been so damned *flowery*? His sleep was usually invaded by nightmares, or else he was too exhausted from his labors to dream at all.

This dream had been filled with sunshine, flowers, and Miss Penny.

The sun on his back, breeze cooling the sweat from their brows, tucking daisies into her hair . . .

There he went again.

What the devil was wrong with him? He blamed it on the whisky.

It must be bothering him more than he cared to admit that a lady possessed of such spirit and intellect, not to mention such a sharp wit, would choose a wastrel like Rafe.

Corbyn stood sentry at Beatrice's door even now because of Rafe.

Drew was sleeping here in the hope that Rafe might return, and then Drew could continue the interrogation.

The bastard who had sent the letter would send another one soon.

It was his move.

Come on, you miscreant, come and find me.

He thrust off the tangled covers and left the bed, walking to the window. He opened the casement and leaned into the night air, taking great gulping breaths.

He couldn't stop thinking about Miss Penny. The zing of attraction between them. The unevenness of her breathing as she'd tied his cravat.

Or had it all been one-sided? Perhaps she hadn't felt a thing. She'd been humoring him, or worse, trying to be rid of him so that she could hold her tryst with Rafe.

Why in the name of everything unholy would

she want Rafe? It made no kind of sense. His brother wasn't the marrying type—even a girl who'd been raised by her uncle in the countryside would know that.

So what did she want with him? Did she think she could reform him?

Good luck with that. Drew had been trying for years now and Rafe wasn't ready to change. He might never be. If he'd truly done something so heinous that the family could be extorted because of it . . . well then, Miss Penny was putting herself in danger.

Changing her gown for Rafe. He didn't deserve to have a young lady go to so much trouble to please him.

More important, Miss Penny didn't need to change. She was absolutely perfect just the way she was.

Stop thinking things like that.

It was late. He was tired. He'd just had an erotic dream that had been cut short in a very unsatisfactory manner. His cock was still semi-hard.

There was something deliberate about the way she'd hidden the dress in the shed. She had specific plans. She had secrets.

She was the last lady he should be thinking about. She'd never be happy in Cornwall.

You're only thinking about her because she chose Rafe over you.

Just because he'd abandoned his rakish ways and found some purpose for his life didn't make him stuffy and boring. Just because he didn't gamble, consort with courtesans, or have a cravat style named after him didn't make him unappealing to adventurous ladies.

It had never occurred to him that a young lady might not find him attractive. He'd never had any trouble finding female companionship. Women used to flock to him, they couldn't get enough. His prowess in the sheets had been legendary. He'd been the wickedest rake of them all.

Past tense. All of it past tense.

All of the ladies at the ball—they'd only wanted him for the title and the fortune.

Had he lost his devilish charm? He used to be irresistible. He was still attractive, wasn't he?

The standing glass in the corner of the room said he was still handsome.

Moonlight was a nice, flattering light, not that he required flattering.

He examined his face in the glass. Chin still firm. Not a hint of wattle.

Jawline strong. All of his own hair. His father had been balding much earlier. Drew was only nine and twenty.

He lifted his nightshirt over his head and threw it on his bed.

He flexed both of his arms until his fists framed his head and his biceps popped into impressive relief.

Not bad.

It wasn't fashionable to be so muscled. His valet had said it frightened delicate young ladies and had advised Drew to go on a reducing diet.

In Drew's experience, once you got a woman

into bed, she was inclined to appreciate strength if employed for her pleasure.

He could lift most women with one arm. Wrap their legs around his waist and carry them to bed.

He could lift two women with one arm. Not that he'd tried anything so sporting lately.

As a youth, he'd tried all of the dark and secret ways to forget the trauma of his kidnapping— loveless couplings, brandy, whisky, living midnight to midnight.

He hadn't found anything that helped until he moved to Thornhill House and the enormous scale of the problems with the estate had dwarfed his own suffering. He'd thrown himself into improving the estate and he'd found a kind of tranquility of mind.

Good, honest hard work not only honed the body, but it also quieted the mind.

He tensed the muscles of his abdomen and slapped his belly with one hand. Taut and firm. No hint of a paunch.

He angled his hips forward and spread his legs wide. He had a damn fine cock, if he did say so himself. Never had any complaints there. Though it hadn't seen much action in the last few years. He'd been so focused on his work.

Remove your coat, Your Grace.

What kind of young lady forced a duke to strip at gunpoint? It had been outrageous and . . . arousing. Extremely arousing.

He gripped his prick with his fist, wondering what Miss Penny might say if she could see him now. He had no clothing to remove.

He was entirely naked. Hard and ready for her.

Remove your gown, Miss Penny.

That's what he'd say to her if she were brave enough to be in this room with him.

Lie back on that bed. Spread your legs. Touch yourself for me.

His breathing caught in his chest as he pictured her obeying his instructions, spreading for him like a flower opening to the sun.

Chapter 7

WHAT THE . . . ? WHAT was happening right now?

Mina ducked further into the shrubbery and averted her eyes. Despite her bonnet's protection a sharp thorn scratched her cheek.

When she'd first seen the lamp flare to life in the upstairs room, she'd thought it was Lord Rafe, until Thorndon had come to the window and started parading about as though he wanted her to buy his wares.

Heart thumping, palms sweating, she tilted her head back and risked another glance up at his window.

He was still there. Still standing directly in front of the window, completely naked. Illumined from behind by lamplight, and from the front by the full moon.

And he still had his hand on his . . . on that part of him which young ladies were not supposed to see until their wedding nights.

A part fashioned upon the same majestic proportions as the rest of him.

Thick and long and jutting right out in front of him at a nearly perpendicular angle. The observer in her took note of all the details she could make out from this awkward and distant vantage point.

At first she'd assumed he was doing some sort of exercises, with all the flexing of arms and the turning this way and that, and then she'd realized that there must be a mirror near the windows and he was preening in front of his reflection.

As an arrogant duke would do.

But when he'd begun to . . . when his hand started stroking up and down, she'd realized what was happening.

Her first glimpse of an unclothed gentleman was much more than a small taste.

It was an entire meal. A veritable ten-course feast.

It wasn't like she didn't know about the pleasure to be found by touching oneself. Her fingers had . . . strayed. Under the covers. Thinking about wicked rakes.

But she'd never imagined how a man might produce the same sensations.

It was a much more forceful and frenzied operation, apparently. Head thrown back. Muscles in his neck clenching. Fist pumping faster and faster.

Her breath coming faster, her heart beating. Little fireworks going off in her belly, in her chest, tiny explosions that left her lightheaded.

The hot-and-cold shivery feeling between her thighs increased to an almost unbearable pitch, but she was buried in too many layers of sturdy woolen clothing to seek any kind of relief.

Wool cloak, cotton dress, petticoats, drawers.

Far too much clothing.

If she were naked, and if she were in the room with him, and if they moved over to the bed (because she wouldn't want the neighbors to see, which apparently he had no such concerns about) then he would know how to give her relief.

She knew that deep down in her bones. The way he'd held her as they danced. This was a man who knew his way around a woman's body. So why was he pleasuring himself and not seeking the company of some willing female?

He backed away from the window, still holding himself. Maybe going toward the bed? Falling on the bed and finishing the work. Depriving her of seeing what occurred when the . . . finishing . . . happened.

You've seen quite enough. You'll never be able to unsee it.

If she saw him in public she would picture him stroking himself, eyes closed. His ridged abdomen rippling with effort. Sheen of sweat on his broad chest. Powerful arms bunched with muscles.

You're not here to ogle a duke. You're here to search for clues.

At least the duke would sleep like the dead now, or at least she always slept well after similar exertions. And if he were sleeping in the house, it meant that Lord Rafe wasn't here, unless they'd had a miraculous reunion in the last few hours.

The lamp died. The house was dark again.

She waited for what seemed like an eternity while her heartbeat slowed and her pulse stopped racing.

Carefully, watching for any movement, she crept from her hiding place. She loosened the bow under her chin and eased her bonnet down her back. Then she tied her skirts between her legs and found a handhold.

She made her way up the jagged wall step-by-step and handhold by handhold. The trellis of climbing vines made it easier and reassured her that if she lost her balance on the way up she'd have something to grab hold of. On the way down she'd use the long coil of rope she'd brought.

She'd been climbing trees and walls since she was a young girl allowed to roam within the confines of the estate grounds. No one had ever told her that her running and climbing were unladylike pursuits.

No one had cared enough to scold her.

She'd been bored and lonely, so she'd learned how to pick locks, to access the places on the estate where she wasn't allowed to roam.

And that's when she'd found the secret room behind a bookshelf in her uncle's library. Inside the room, she'd found her mother's diary—it had been coded but eventually she'd been able to crack it. And that's how she'd discovered her family's secret lives as spies for the Crown.

Sir Malcolm had denied everything and forbidden her to speak of spying, but it had only made her resolve stronger.

She'd begun to piece together the true nature of his work. He wasn't only an antiquarian. All of the men coming and going from the estate were not just fellow antiquities enthusiasts.

They were spies.

She kept her ears and eyes open, spying on the spymaster. She'd found books about code breaking in her uncle's library and studied them. She'd discovered a talent for solving puzzles, for finding patterns. She started taking apart clocks, pistols, anything mechanical, and finding new and better ways to put the pieces back together.

Spy craft was in her blood. It was her legacy and her destiny. The only method remaining for her to feel close to her parents.

Her future began now.

She wedged the window open first and then slowly inched upward, balancing on the ledge.

When it was open far enough, she shimmied inside and dropped to the floor. She held her breath, hoping that the carpet had muffled her landing.

This was a study by the looks of it. One wall was covered by floor-to-ceiling bookshelves and there was a large desk crouching against a wall.

Nothing moved in the household. No sounds of approaching footfalls. The duke was sound asleep in his bed upstairs, exhausted by his exertions.

Huge fist clasping huge . . . *ouch*! She stubbed her toe on the claw foot of the desk.

Had she made a noise? She held her breath.

Nothing stirred.

She needed more light to read by. She lit the lamp on the desk, keeping the wick low and the light dim. Jumble of receipts in a box on the desk.

Good Lord. That was an extravagant amount of money to pay for waistcoats.

She opened the drawers and found more receipts. Nothing about travel plans—no coaching timetables or names of ships.

She found a pamphlet of bawdy verses underneath a bottle of . . . she opened it and sniffed . . . brandy.

She could use some brandy after what she'd seen tonight. She took a long drink from the bottle, sputtering as the strong spirits burned down her throat.

Why did men like drinking this stuff so much? It wasn't very pleasant. But if she was going to be a real spy, she'd have to develop a taste for brandy, in the event that she had to drink with someone in order to wheedle information out of them.

The brandy wasn't so bad the second time around. Didn't burn so much and produced a lovely warm sensation in her belly, much like the feeling she'd had when she watched the duke's self-ministration. Was that what one called it? Self-stimulation, perhaps?

She'd have to ask him the next time they spoke.

Oh good Lord. Perhaps brandy was a bad choice. She untied her bonnet strings and set her bonnet on the desk.

The verses could be a clue, or even a code. She had an aptitude for deciphering codes.

> *Her nimble tongue, love's lesser lightning, played*
> *Within my mouth, and to my thoughts conveyed*
> *Swift orders that I should prepare to throw*
> *The all-dissolving thunderbolt below.*

Um. No hidden meaning there. Quite clear, that.

She perused the rest of the topmost verse, which had been written by John Wilmot, Earl of Rochester, apparently a man after Lord Rafe's predilections. Oh dear. It got worse.

Much worse. She thrust the poem aside. She wasn't here for bawdy verse—she needed cold, hard answers to such questions as where was Lord Rafe? And what new trouble had he found?

In a small drawer tucked into the side of the desk, she found a stack of letters written in a feminine hand and scented with jasmine perfume. Finally a clue. Jasmine perfume could spell trouble.

Why haven't you come to see me lately? Your turtledove is cooing with impatience.

Ugh. Turtledove?

The letters were all signed with a flourishing letter *F*. She pocketed one of them.

Nothing else of interest on the desk or in the drawers. She patted the bottom of the desk, listening for the hollow sound that would indicate a false bottom. *Voila.*

It only took a few seconds to pick the lock and access the hidden drawer. She reached inside and found a crumpled sheet of paper.

She smoothed the creases from the letter against the surface of the desk and pushed the lamp closer. Bending over the paper, she whispered the words aloud:

I know what your brother is doing. You must PAY. Await further instructions and TELL NO ONE or Lady Beatrice will be KIDNAPPED.

Her mind was a little fuzzy from the brandy but she guessed the significance of the note instantly. Thorndon had come to London because of this letter.

Lord Rafe was doing something reckless—unless the letter was an outright lie, a daring ploy to extort money from the duke.

She traced the words with her fingers, intent on deciphering the possible identity of the scribe. So intent that she didn't notice the approaching footfalls until a gruff, incredulous voice sounded, nearly in her ear.

"What the devil? Is that you, Miss Penny?"

Thorndon.

Acting on instinct, she hastily rolled the note and stuffed it down her bodice before straightening.

She turned to face the duke.

It must be the brandy, because she suddenly felt like she was standing on the deck of a ship in the eye of a storm.

Now that she'd seen him completely naked, albeit from a distance, he was even more attractive. His huge, sculpted body was mostly covered by a blue silk dressing gown, knotted at the waist. Her gaze darted downward.

His legs were covered by undergarments, but his feet were bare. That must be why she hadn't heard him padding toward her, creeping up and surprising her. She should have been more alert, more cautious.

What explanation could she possibly give

for her presence here? One of her uncle's agents would have a convincing cover for any occasion.

"Yes, it's me. Miss Penny," she said.

Oh brilliant. Truly innovative.

Think, you foolish girl. You want to be a spy, right?

His brow furrowed, eyes dark in the gloomy room. "What the deuce are you doing here?"

"I saw you," Mina whispered. "In your bed-chamber window. I was crouching below in the shrubbery." Her heart hammered. He was so much more formidable from this close-at-hand vantage point.

"My window," Thorndon echoed. "You saw me."

Understanding dawned across his face like the sun rising over a rugged sea cliff. She would have called it a blush, if a duke could be said to blush.

"I hope you didn't see *all* of me," he said darkly.

"I saw everything. From the crown of your head to the . . ." her gaze swept bravely downward, " . . . area below."

"Bloody Hell," he muttered. "I didn't know anyone was watching."

"Clearly."

"What were you doing lurking in my shrubbery, Miss Penny?"

She swallowed. There was only one thing to be done, one explanation for her presence that wouldn't betray her true intent. "What I saw gave me . . . ideas."

"Ideas." Alarm flashed in his eyes. "Now see here, Miss Penny, you're a young lady of good family and you should be home safe in your bed, not spying on—"

"Ideas about *kissing*."

"Kissing." He crossed his arms over his powerful chest. "Absolutely not."

"If you don't mind, Your Grace, I think I'll kiss you now."

And she did.

Chapter 8

She kissed him. *Really* kissed him.

It was so surprising that Drew didn't respond. He just stood there like an oak tree as she twined her arms around him, tugging his head down to her level.

Clinging lips. Scent sweet and clean. Soft breasts against his chest.

Just like his dream, only sans daisies and sheep.

Like a dream, only so achingly real. Solid, warm woman kissing him, trying to coax a reaction from him. She made a disapproving sound in the back of her throat and redoubled her efforts.

You've still got it, you handsome devil.

Their interlude in the garden shed hadn't been enough for her. She'd been gazing at his window and she'd been overwhelmed by the sight of him pleasuring himself. Which was somewhat embarrassing and . . . damn it, she was still kissing him.

He should do something about that.

Clearly the girl had a taste for danger. She couldn't just go around kissing anyone she fancied.

Her tongue slipped inside his mouth in a tentative yet brave exploratory expedition. She tasted of brandy.

He pulled back. The brandy bottle on Rafe's

desk was suspiciously uncorked. "Have you been drinking my brandy, Miss Penny?"

Her lips curved into a smile. "Maybe?"

"You taste like caramelized sin." He should end this now but he wanted more.

Just one more taste of her lips.

He should tell her to leave. Or he could take control. Kiss her again, but slower this time. More deliberate. Set a new tempo.

When he deepened the kiss, she followed his lead, opening wider, taking more of him and giving more of herself.

All the time in the world. No reason to rush.

She moaned and he swallowed the sound and asked for more. He'd been starving, he realized. Starving for this . . . for her. He'd thought of little else since he'd seen her undressing, like some mirage summoned from his most secret desires.

Her hands tangled in his hair, her head tilted back, throat exposed. He kissed the base of her throat, the delicate hollow of her shoulder.

Skin like driftwood worn to silk by the pounding of the ocean.

He wanted to push her clothing aside to find more smoothness to devour, but he couldn't allow himself to touch her. That would be going too far.

"You're so sweet," he said roughly. He kissed her cheek. "So soft."

In answer, she slid her hand inside his robe and traced the muscles of his abdomen.

"You're . . ." She tugged on the knot of his robe but it held fast.

Thank the Lord for small favors.

When she couldn't gain access, she slid both her hands inside, around his waist, down his lower back.

"You're . . . hard. Everywhere," she said. "There's not an ounce of softness, or give."

She had no idea. The things he wanted to do to her. Show her where his hardness was meant to slide. Give her so much pleasure.

But this was just a kiss.

He touched her cheek. "You have a scratch."

"From the rosebushes when I was watching you."

"Your punishment."

"And this is my reward."

One more kiss and he'd send her on her way.

MINA HAD PLANNED a swift, distracting kiss on his lips and then a swift escape.

That was at least a quarter hour past.

They were still kissing and she never wanted it to end. She was discovering so many things about herself. Kissing was her new favorite thing in the world. Better than decoding a secret message.

Or, rather, very similar to deciphering a code, only better. If she moved her hands *here*, he moaned. If she opened her mouth wider, he took more.

When her hands roamed, exploring the solid contours of his body, he grew even more solid.

A thick ridge of *solid* against her belly.

My, what an intoxicating feeling.

She felt beautiful, and powerful. She sensed that he was holding himself in check, refraining from touching her with his hands. He was an honorable gentleman.

She was safe.

Except there was nothing safe about this kiss. This was skirting the edge of something that might swallow her whole. Desire. Distraction.

She'd forgotten why she kissed him. Oh yes. The brandy. She'd kissed him because she drank the brandy. Also to distract him. Oh, and something to do with his brother.

Did there have to be a reason? Because right now all she wanted to do was enjoy her very first kiss, memorize it, own it.

He was so tall that she had to stand on tiptoe to reach his lips, brace her hands on his wide shoulders to stay upright.

She wanted to melt. Make him melt with her. Until they were lying on the storm-tossed floor.

Their lips met. Really met, had a conversation, got to know each other.

If she were connecting the fragments of this encounter to form a lasting memory, she would focus on small details—the faint stubble along his jawline that pricked at her cheek, how his hands remained tight against his sides, moving slightly sometimes, as though he wanted to touch her but had forbidden himself to do so.

She felt no such qualms. His body was firm and solid and warm beneath her questing hands.

So warm.

She wanted to find a bed and curl up against him like a kitten. A bed would be nice. A nice bed with soft sheets.

A feeling of warmth inside her body, centered between her thighs. Heat and wanting. A melting sensation in her belly. She couldn't quite catch her breath.

She should have ended this kiss long ago, but his hands still remained at his sides and her new goal in life was to feel his hands on her bare flesh.

She was softening and he remained so stiff. He didn't wrap his arms around her or whisper sweet things in her ear. He kissed her almost punishingly. She wanted passion from him, she would coax it out of him.

At least she could tell that his body responded. She could feel him hard and thick, pressing against her through all the layers of clothing separating them.

"Miss Penny," he moaned. "Wilhelmina."

She liked the sound of her name on his lips.

"How did you feel when you were watching me in the window, Wilhelmina Penny?" he asked.

She licked her lips because they'd gone dry as dust. "Hungry."

"And how did you feel when you saw me stroking my . . ." he stared into her eyes, "cock?"

"Your . . . ?" She was in over her head. She should make a run for it.

"Cock," he said again, the consonants like little explosions. "Do you call it something else? A bold lady such as yourself who holds dukes at pistol point and spies on them during private moments must have a word for everything she sees."

"Erm . . . manroot?"

The ghost of a smile, nothing more. What would

it take to make this man laugh? She really wanted to know. She was discovering so many new goals tonight.

"Charmer?" she suggested.

"Absolutely not," he growled. "Charmer makes it sound like he's a dandy dressed in green-striped trousers and a yellow waistcoat who twirls his moustache and uses a quizzing glass."

"So it's a he?" she asked.

He tilted his hips forward, bringing her into more intimate contact with the body part in question. "Most definitely. And he likes bold ladies who spy on him."

"He appears to be fashioned on a grand scale. Not that I have much to compare him with. Some classical etchings. Some disappointing statuary."

"I have a big cock. Is that what you're trying to say?"

He kept repeating the word. *Ah.* He was trying to frighten her into running away.

"You should know that I'm not easily frightened, Your Grace," she said bravely.

"Please, by all means, call me Drew. We're intimates now, since you've seen my—"

"Cock." There, she'd said it.

"Very good, Miss Penny."

She held her breath as his fingers skimmed across the edge of her bodice. He dipped his fingers lower and she shivered.

Bodice. Letter. Hidden between her breasts.

"I have to go now," she blurted.

A crashing thud interrupted his exploration. They both turned.

A man had entered through the same window Mina had used and was sprawled on the carpet.

"Bollocks," the intruder groaned. "Meant to stick that landing better."

"Rafe?" the duke asked incredulously.

"Don't mind me," slurred Lord Rafe, sitting up. "I can see you're entertaining. Carry on, carry on." He waved an unsteady hand. "Just gathering a few things. I'll be gone in a trice."

Chapter 9

"OH NO YOU won't," Drew said, rushing to his brother, who reeked of gin. "Where have you been? What trouble are you in?" He reached for his hand and hauled him off the floor. "What nefarious plans do you have?"

Rafe gripped the sides of his head. "Too many questions."

"I'll give you more than a headache if you don't cooperate," Drew threatened.

"Don't think you can best me easily anymore, Thorny. I've become something of an expert with knives." Rafe felt around his pockets. "If I were carrying a knife, I'd show you."

"I'm sick and tired of your evasions. This ends now. Tell me what's happening or I'll force you to tell me."

Miss Penny strode toward them. "Allow me to try, Your Grace."

Rafe looked her up and down with an appreciative grin. "Your strumpet might have better luck, Thorny."

"I'm not his strumpet. I'm Miss Mina Penny and I must speak with you, Lord Rafe."

"You don't want anything to do with me, Pretty Penny," slurred Rafe.

"*Miss* Penny," she replied.

"Righto, Miss Plummy." Rafe stumbled to the desk. "Just a few things and I'll be off." He stuffed some bank notes into his greatcoat pockets.

"Who sent the letter, Rafe?" Drew asked. He was running out of patience.

"I've no idea," Rafe replied. "I have more important things to think about."

"More important than our sister's safety?"

"I told you that was an empty threat."

"But you can't be sure because you don't know who sent it."

Miss Penny looked on with growing irritation, judging by the set of her jaw. She crossed her arms. "Lord Rafe, I was going to speak with you in private but this will have to do. I know that you have fallen out of favor with Sir Malcolm because of what happened at the gambling house."

"What's that you say, love?" Rafe glanced at her. "Dashed pretty doxy, Thorny. Well done, you."

"Kindly refrain from impugning Miss Penny's character," said Drew. "She's not a lady of easy virtue."

"Made you work for it, did she? Good on you, Peggy."

Miss Penny stamped her foot. "For the last time, I'm no doxy. I'm Sir Malcolm Penny's niece. You obviously don't remember but I've met you on several occasions when you visited Sutton Hall." She grabbed Rafe by the shoulders. "If you'll tell me what's happening, I'll help restore you to my uncle's good graces. In exchange for your promise to marry me."

Drew's jaw dropped. What in the blazes had just happened? How much brandy had Miss Penny consumed? "Now wait one second—"

"Your trollop just proposed marriage to me, Thorny," crowed Rafe. "That's got to hurt."

Drew's vision blurred. It did hurt. Like a serrated blade to the belly.

"For the love of God. I'm not a trollop!" insisted Miss Penny.

"Should be. You're devilish pretty." Rafe plucked the red rose from his lapel. "I'll tell you what, turtledove, if I arrive back in London in one piece after this mission, I might just marry you." He tucked the rose behind her ear.

Drew's vision went as red as the rose.

"What mission?" asked Miss Penny, flinging the rose to the floor. "Where are you going?"

Drew grabbed Rafe by the collar and shook him until his teeth rattled together. "You're not going anywhere, do you hear me? I'll hold your head under the pump and sober you up and then you'll finally answer my questions. And you'll stop insulting Miss Penny."

"I have something that works wonderfully to sober a man." Miss Penny searched her cloak pockets and came up with a small vial. "This should be effective. It's my own blend of smelling salts."

She uncorked the vial. Drew forced Rafe's head close to the vial.

"Damn." Rafe shook his head. "That burns the nostrils."

"Tell me, is someone after you? The Manor Boys? The Newgate Six?" asked Miss Penny.

Rafe peered at her groggily. "How do you know about those organizations? And no one's after me. I'm after someone. A much bigger prize."

"I know these things because I'm Sir Malcolm Penny's niece. I'm also his secretary. And I'm an excellent shot. There's a pistol in my reticule. Wherever you're going, you'd best bring me with you."

"'Fraid not, poppet. I never mix business and pleasure," said Rafe.

"I'm going to punch you soon," Drew warned his brother. He'd lost the thread of the conversation a while back and felt dreadfully unbalanced.

All he knew was that Miss Penny had proposed to Rafe.

He was having trouble moving past that hideously awful occurrence.

"Which target are you after?" Miss Penny asked. "Tell me."

"I'm setting a trap to catch the biggest prize of all. This is my chance to redeem myself, so kindly allow a man to gather a few things and then I'll be off to vanquish a bloodthirsty foe."

"Rafe, you can't leave, this is idiocy—we'll pursue this, whatever it is, together," said Drew. "Let me help you."

"Brothers side by side, is that it? I don't think so. We're past that possibility. And the target isn't in London. He's in . . ." He closed his mouth.

"France?" asked Miss Penny. "Is it a certain

antiquities thief?" She was thinking of Le Triton. If Rafe had a plan to capture him, she must find a way to join him for the mission.

Rafe's face turned a paler shade of green and he peered at Miss Penny. "What did you say your name was?"

"Miss Wilhelmina Penny."

"What do you know about antiquities thieves, Miss Penny?"

"Even more than you do, I'll wager."

Drew had had just about enough of this enigmatic, nonsensical conversation. There was obviously something that he was missing. Miss Penny and his brother appeared to share a common language and it was irritating him to no end. "Rafe, tell me right now, is Beatrice in danger of being kidnapped?"

"Who wrote the letter, Lord Rafe?" Miss Penny asked. "I didn't recognize the handwriting." She dipped her fingers into her bodice. Drew couldn't help watching as she wriggled until her bodice loosened, giving her access to the shadow between the luscious mounds of her breasts.

The last thing Drew saw was Miss Penny drawing a small scroll of paper from between her breasts.

And then everything went dark.

IT HAPPENED SO quickly that Mina didn't have time to stop Lord Rafe. He seized a candlestick from the desk and hit the duke on the back of the head. The duke staggered, and then crashed to the floor with a thunderous thud.

"I'm sorry. Sod it, I have to go." Lord Rafe raced for the window and lowered himself out, leaving Mina with an agonizing choice: follow him and demand he take her wherever he was going, so that they could vanquish the foe together . . .

Or stay and make sure the duke wasn't dead.

Chapter 10

❦

MINA CHOSE THE DUKE.

Well she couldn't just leave him sprawled on the leaf-patterned carpet like a mighty oak tree felled by lightning. What if the blow from the candlestick had drawn blood? It was her fault, after all.

She'd reached down her bodice to retrieve the threatening letter in an effort to make both brothers pay attention to her—and only one of them had taken the bait.

Thorndon had been so distracted by her bosom-baring tactics that he hadn't even noticed his brother approaching with the candlestick, and neither had she.

She'd been too distracted by Thorndon's heated gaze.

A fine pair of fools.

Now she'd lost her chance to find out where Lord Rafe was going and which target he was after.

She sank to her knees beside the duke. He was breathing, so there was that. She used both her hands to lift his head—no blood in his hair. No blood on the carpet. She lowered his head carefully. He would be badly bruised, no doubt.

She loosened his dressing robe and set her ear to his chest. His heartbeat was strong, his skin warm beneath her cheek. She inhaled the delicious, masculine scent that made her want to lick his throat.

Where were her smelling salts? Apparently she might require them more than the duke.

What had they said about loss of consciousness in the training class she'd eavesdropped upon at her uncle's estate?

Elevate the knees.

The duke's knees were so heavy she had to take them one at a time. And they wouldn't stay propped up once she'd placed them where she wanted. She grabbed a cushion from a chair and pushed it under his legs.

One of his knees kicked up, tumbling her off balance. She landed face-first in a heap on top of his chest.

"Oof." The breath left her lungs. Before she had a chance to right herself, an enormous hand clamped over her right bum cheek.

"Your Grace," she squeaked. "Your hand."

An involuntary spasm? Or was he faking unconsciousness? If he was faking . . .

"If you're only pretending, Your Grace . . . I swear." She struggled out of his grasp and was nearly free . . . until his other hand clamped on her other bum cheek, gluing her hips to his unyielding frame.

The door opened. "I heard a crash." A tall, hook-nosed man wearing a tasseled, red-striped nightcap stopped just inside the door. "Pardon me, Your Grace. I do apologize. I wasn't aware that you had company."

The servant backed toward the door.

"No," cried Mina. "Don't go. I require your assistance."

"My . . . assistance?" asked the servant.

"His Grace had a mishap," said Mina, finally managing to pry the duke's fingers off of her nether regions. She staggered to her feet, prepared to run after the servant if he attempted to flee. "You must help me revive him and convey him to bed."

"Ah." The servant nodded his head and the tassel on his nightcap swayed decisively. "I understand completely. Say no more, madam. During a feat of impressive athleticism, perhaps involving the desk, His Grace's limbs gave out from under him."

What was the man on about? "It wasn't his limbs, he had a blow to the back of the head."

"You accosted the duke, madam?" asked the servant sternly.

"Certainly not. It was—"

"A cowardly thief!" The servant pointed a bony finger at the open window. "A sneaking pilferer crept through the window. His Grace arrived to investigate and the burglar accosted him and fled back out the window. Did the craven larcenist abscond with anything of value?"

My hopes. My dreams. My freedom.

"It was Lord Rafe," she said.

"The thief absconded with Lord Rafe?"

"No, Lord Rafe hit His Grace on the back of the head with a candlestick."

"Ah." The servant nodded sagely. "That's happened a time or two. They've always fought tooth and nail, ever since they were lads. There was the time the young marquess (that would be His Grace now) caught his brother reading his private journal and, after locking the journal away, upended a chamber pot over Lord Rafe's head." The servant sighed happily. "Oh it is so wonderful that he's back. I do hope he'll take a bride. We're all longing for a little heir to coddle. A child would mean he wouldn't stay in Cornwall the whole year round. Now, if you ask me—"

"Er," Mina broke in. "I don't suppose you might help me revive the duke before you marry him off and make a father of him?"

"Of course, of course." The servant moved closer. "My name is Crankshaw, madam. I'm at your service."

"Thank you, Crankshaw."

"I've no idea who you are, madam, and I don't want to know. You speak with the tones of a lady of Quality but I have no desire to know if you are truly a lady. I'm famous for my discretion. No one shall ever hear a word about what I've seen tonight."

"Thank you, now if you might raise the duke's—"

"Have you tried smelling salts?"

"I was about to when I was . . . capsized. The salts are there on the floor."

Crankshaw retrieved the vial.

Bending over the duke, she slapped his cheeks lightly. He groaned.

Crankshaw passed the vial under the duke's nose.

His eyelids fluttered open. He had long, dark eyelashes. She hadn't noticed that before. Dark eyelashes and glowing amber eyes. Very confused eyes. "Where am I?" he croaked.

"In the study, Your Grace," said Crankshaw, enunciating very loudly and clearly. "You've suffered a blow to the head."

"No I haven't," said the duke. "I'm dreaming in my bed."

"Afraid not," said Mina. "You're lying on the floor of the study."

"No I'm not," said the duke. "Do you know how I know that? Because you're here. I'm obviously dreaming. The dreamiest dream. Daisies. Cows. Sunshine on my bare skin." He smiled warmly and gave her a sensual wink. "And on your skin. Why are you still wearing so much clothing? I specifically dreamed that your dress was already slipping off your shoulders."

Now she knew the knock on his head had caused damage. This was the first time she'd seen him smile and the sight was disconcerting.

When he smiled, it touched a fuse in her mind that sparked and burned dangerously close to her heart. And winking? He was *not* a winker.

"His Grace is disoriented," she whispered to Crankshaw.

The servant nodded. "He'll come 'round eventually."

"Help me carry him to bed," Mina whispered.

"Bed sounds nice." The duke gave her another wicked wink.

The blow to his head had scrambled his brains like eggs. He needed rest, and possibly a physician.

Crankshaw slid his arms under the duke's armpits from behind and hoisted him to a seated position.

"Are you able to stand, Your Grace?" Mina asked.

The duke rose to his knees but when he tried to stand he swayed and nearly fell back down. Crankshaw caught him around the waist.

"Perhaps if you . . . pull his arms . . . from the front," huffed Crankshaw.

Mina grabbed hold of the duke's large hands and pulled with all her strength.

Finally upright, he gave her another lopsided smile. "Seem to be having a bit of difficulty staying on my feet. Must have had too much brandy. Don't worry. Won't affect my performance."

Whatever that meant.

Crankshaw draped one of the duke's huge arms over his shoulders and caught him around the waist. The duke reached out and snagged Mina by her waist, pulling her tight to his other side.

He lowered his lips to her ear. "Ready for bed?" he asked in a husky whisper that sent a shiver between her shoulder blades.

"Take his other arm over your shoulders, madam," Crankshaw instructed. "It'll go easier that way."

Mina lifted the duke's arm from her waist and wrapped it over her shoulders, reeling under the sudden transfer of weight. His hand infiltrated her cloak and settled over her right breast.

She immediately moved his hand back to her shoulder.

"We're going to have fun tonight." His hand moved back to her breast and he squeezed softly.

"All right-y," she squeaked. "One, two, three and away we go."

Transfer the duke to his bed and make a hasty retreat. That was the goal.

If she was very, very lucky, Thorndon wouldn't remember any of this in the morning. She would be a shadowy dream memory, overridden by a devil of a headache. She could even replace the note in the drawer before she left, and none would be the wiser.

She must leave quickly, before anyone else saw her here. She'd go back to her bedchamber, take out a sheet of paper, and begin piecing together everything she knew thus far.

Lord Rafe had said he was going to set a trap for the biggest prize of all and that it was his chance to redeem himself. He'd called it a mission, and said he was going after a target, so there was every probability that it had something to do with espionage, and he most likely thought of it as a way to restore himself to the ranks of Uncle Malcolm's agents.

Tomorrow she would go about solving the mystery, finding Lord Rafe, and rendering herself indispensable to his mission.

If she met the duke again in Society she would simply ignore his existence. Though truly, he was difficult to ignore. The man was as heavy as an ox.

They half dragged, half pushed him out of the study.

His palm still covered her breast, as if he'd found the anchorage he craved.

In his addled mental state, a woman taking him to bed meant that she had designs upon him and he was free to fondle her at will.

He didn't even know who she was—just a female with soft breasts. Only a dream to direct to his satisfaction.

Every lurching step brought his palm against her nipple. The friction sensitized her breast. Despite the presence of the servant on the duke's other side, arousal spiked from the tip of her breast down her belly.

Did she enjoy being handled this way? Or did she enjoy being touched by *him*?

By Thorndon.

He'd told her to call him Drew, which of course would be the very height of impropriety.

Impropriety. Ha! They were well past that point. Just look where his hand was resting.

"Drew" must be a shortened form of his Christian name, Andrew. The name fit him. His kiss had drawn her into a new world of sensation.

Drawn vivid colors—hot reds, bursts of gold—where her imagination had drawn only lines in charcoal.

Her very first kiss.

Something to savor, a secret only they shared. A mistake, surely, but a glorious one, a memory to relive slowly in her bed at night.

"That was quite a kiss," he whispered, his lips nuzzling at her ear.

Blast. He remembered the kiss. Did that mean he remembered who she was?

"Were you dreaming about a kiss, Your Grace?" she asked innocently.

"Yes. And so were you."

"Your Grace," she said firmly, "kindly refrain from talking. It's taxing your strength. You need a b—to rest." Better not to mention beds again.

"Good idea. I'll conserve my strength for later. In bed." His head lolled to the side and he stopped talking.

Conducting the prodigiously heavy and woozy-headed duke up a narrow flight of stairs was a tricky task. If she and the servant weren't careful, their charge would fall backward and drag them down with him.

"I've escorted many a drunken lord to his bed in this very manner," said Crankshaw, breathing heavily as they made slow progress up the stairs. "Oh, the stories these walls could tell, madam. But you won't hear them from me. The wanton orgies. The pleasure chamber with its shameful secrets. You won't hear about the women, either. Three of them to a bed, sometimes. The wife of the Lord Mayor once. Ah . . . she was a rare one . . ."

As they slowly conquered the stairs he regaled her with lurid stories, interspersed with protestations of his utter discretion in all things.

One should never tell Crankshaw a secret. That much was clear.

Propositioning Rafe had seemed a simple matter when she was making her plans. He wouldn't have to reform entirely. A spy had to use all weapons, including seduction.

However, she never could have imagined the details of his debauched life. Three women in one night? Had he taken precautions against contracting diseases or conceiving unwanted offspring?

For that matter, were there failsafe precautions against such things? It seemed she had more research to do. She hadn't been fully aware of the sordid realities of rake-hood.

"And you know," said Crankshaw, his breath coming in gasps. "It's not only Lord Rafe these walls would speak of. His Grace was quite the rakehell as well."

As if to prove the point, the duke rolled her nipple between his fingers, making it go as hard as a marble.

"Wait," said Mina. "Are you telling me that His Grace used to be a rake?"

Her uncle's Duke Dossier hadn't mentioned anything of the kind.

"One of the most infamous in all of London," said Crankshaw proudly.

"Interesting."

"Here we are, madam," said Crankshaw as they entered a large bedchamber. "About-face." He helped her turn the duke so that he faced away from the bed. "And . . . heave-ho."

Mina and Crankshaw half lifted, half pushed

the duke onto the side of the bed. He lurched backward and grabbed Mina on the way down. She landed flat against his chest.

This was beginning to be a habit with him.

He wrapped his arms around her possessively. "At last we've achieved the bed."

"Kindly release me." She attempted to squirm out from under his arms.

He settled her more firmly against his long length and stroked a lock of hair away from her cheek. "You have soft, shiny hair."

"I see nothing, madam," said Crankshaw, staring into space. "I hear nothing."

"While you're seeing nothing, could you please fetch a basin of cold water and some ice from the ice house, if you have one?" she asked. "The duke requires a rude awakening."

"An excellent idea, madam." Crankshaw bowed and left the room.

"I'm so glad I still have it," said the duke with an alarming grin.

"Have what, Your Grace?"

"My devilish charm."

"Did you think you'd lost it?"

"When we danced you appeared to loathe me. As if I were a horrid turnip."

He knew who she was. So much for him forgetting she'd ever been here.

"Your Grace, I—"

"But now you're in my bed, therefore I've still got it." His grin was self-satisfied. "And what's more, you're in my arms."

"About that," began Mina. "It's late, and I really should be—"

"When thus reclining on my breast, those eyes threw back a glance so sweet, as half reproached yet raised desire, and still we near and nearer pressed." He clasped his arms tighter. "And still our glowing lips would meet." He kissed her lips softly. "As if in kisses to expire."

"Lord Byron? You're quoting Lord Byron." Now Mina was truly concerned for his sanity. His conversation thus far had been terse. Unemotional. He was not a man given to reciting love verses.

But that man was buried somewhere inside him, and all it took was a sharp blow to the head to bring out the poetry, the warm teasing . . . the passion.

Before her mind could come up with any more dangerous revelations, Crankshaw returned with a tin basin sloshing with water and chunks of ice. "This ought to bring him round, madam." He made a move as if he were preparing to upend the basin.

"Wait!" She was still entwined with the amorous, amnesiac duke and didn't relish a dousing.

She snuggled closer to him and lifted her lips to his ear. Again, the mouthwatering scent of his almond cologne nearly undid her. "Your Grace," she whispered.

"Mmm?" He kissed the tip of her nose.

"If you let me leave the bed, I'll divest myself of this cumbersome cloak."

His arms sprang open. She rolled away and hopped down from the bed.

"Now," she ordered.

Crankshaw stepped forward.

The duke's head swiveled. "Not now, Crankshaw. The lady's about to lose her cloak. Leave this instant and I won't sack you."

Crankshaw trembled. "I can't do it, madam. His Grace has a very long memory, once it's properly restored."

"Oh for heaven's sake. Give it here." She held out her hands and Crankshaw handed her the basin. "This will be cold, Your Grace."

He caught her skirts and attempted to pull her closer. "Ice can be used in love play. But only a sliver of ice, drawn slowly over a nip—"

She dumped the basin of icy water over him from head to abdomen.

"Bloody Hell!" he roared, springing to a seated position.

He shook his great shaggy head like a hound, spraying cold water across her chest. "Why'd you do that?"

"I-I'll just be downstairs if you require me, madam," said Crankshaw hastily. "All you need do is use the bellpull."

He scurried from the room, abandoning Mina with a dripping wet, highly enraged duke.

Chapter 11

"It was necessary," Mina said tartly, wiping water from her cheeks with her sleeve. "You were reciting Lord Byron."

"That's no reason to freeze a man's bollocks off." He leapt out of bed.

Mina retreated a few steps.

He ripped off his sodden robe and flung it over a chair.

Bare chest, glistening with water. Beads of water like diamonds glittering on the dusting of hair that trailed down the center of his chest and bisected his abdomen.

She noticed all of the details she'd missed before because she'd been too far away in the shrubbery under his window.

Grabbing a towel from the shelf near the washbasin, he rubbed it over his head, leaving his black hair standing on end like a farm cat's fur after being groomed by its paws. He lifted his arm and swiped the towel over his armpit. He had black hair there as well.

The wet fabric of his undergarments clung to narrow hips, emphasizing muscular thighs, long legs, the shape of his . . . . cock. Her mind couldn't think of any less objectionable word to use.

Her eyes couldn't look away.

There it was, not jutting out proudly but hanging down between his thighs.

The duke followed her gaze. "He's very cold," he said testily. "Which causes him to shrink. *Temporarily.* If you don't mind . . . a little privacy?"

This was without a doubt the most exciting and unexpected night of her life. Her thirst for knowledge and adventure was being satisfied. She was learning so many things.

She turned her back on the duke and stared at his rumpled bed instead.

Mistake. His bed made her think about what had happened there, after he'd moved away from the window and away from her awestruck gaze. The *finishing*.

She decided to stare at a squat, solid mahogany chair. Nothing too provocative about a chair. Except that it was so very sturdily built that it would no doubt support the weight of two people at once. Say, a duke and a . . .

"I dumped the icy water over you because you were fondling my bosom, Your Grace," she blurted. "Without my consent, I might add."

"Oh." The sound of a towel rubbing over taut, naked flesh. "I apologize. I don't recall that part. It was wrong of me."

"Very wrong." But it had felt right. Especially when he'd rolled her nipple between his fingers. That part had felt beyond right. The poor un-fondled nipple on the left was begging to be awakened into a tingling awareness.

"I think I thought I was dreaming," he said. "But we did . . . didn't we kiss? In real life?"

"I have to go now." She really should leave before he remembered everything.

"Wait." Sound of heavy footsteps. "Damn. I've the very devil of a headache. It hurts to walk. It hurts to think." That low, gravelly voice of his coming closer. "You can turn around now."

She turned around. His chest was safely hidden in a gray flannel wrapper. A pity his eyes weren't covered. His amber gaze penetrated straight through to her pounding heart and seemed to read her licentious thoughts.

"I must go," she repeated.

"One moment, Miss Penny. It's all coming back to me now. My idiot of a brother climbing through the window. The cowardly blow to the back of my head." He stared down at her. The ice had traveled from the basin to his eyes.

Thorndon was back.

She shivered. "You'll have a prize-winning bump on your head tomorrow to be sure."

"What I don't understand is why you didn't run after my brother. There's obviously something between you two, yet you stayed here with me. Why?"

EMOTIONS PLAYED ACROSS her expressive face like a strong breeze over a field of grain. She wasn't a person who hid her thoughts or feelings well. Drew read obstinacy in the set of her jaw. A tremor of fear in her lips.

Intelligence and evasiveness in her eyes.

"You might have been seriously injured," she said at last. "I stayed to make sure you were all right."

"It would take more than a candlestick to break my thick skull. If you haven't noticed, I'm solidly built."

"Oh, I noticed. I helped Crankshaw haul you up the stairs."

"And I notice that you haven't denied what I just said. You share some common cause with my brother—you speak his language. What is it that you want from him?"

Her mouth clamped tighter. "I have to go home. I can't be seen here by anyone else."

"Why are you here?" He walked to the fireplace and rested his hands against the chimneypiece, absorbing the heat from the fire.

"Why are *you* here?" she countered. "I thought you were staying at your club."

"I want to stay close to my sister, Lady Beatrice." His head throbbed with pain and his mind was crowded with questions. Miss Penny hadn't even known he'd be here. She hadn't come to see him. She'd come to see *Rafe*.

Darkness obliterated the glowing coals for a moment. "Why Rafe?" he asked, staring at hot coals instead of her, so that she wouldn't read the jealousy in his eyes.

Not jealousy. He couldn't possibly be jealous. He'd been hit over the head. He wasn't thinking clearly.

"It's complicated," she replied.

"I'm sure it is. Nothing you do would ever be simple." Changing gowns midway through balls, holding dukes at pistol point, climbing through windows, none of that was ordinary behavior for a young lady. "So everything your uncle told me in that brief, baffling letter—which I read, by the way—is an assemblage of lies."

Now he watched her closely, searching her face for her reaction.

She squared her shoulders. "That's correct. He was hoping to influence your feeling about me before you met me and learned the truth."

"The truth that you're not a country-bred yet educated young lady with a flair for secretarial work, who is as skilled with a hunting rifle as she is with managing an estate."

"I'm not."

She was lying. He knew it by the way her gaze faltered. He knew it because she was equal parts sensible and sensuous. There was something of a country morning in the clearness of her eyes. The scent of sweet heather on her skin.

The straightforward way she talked. She didn't mince around a subject, coating it with layers of niceties to make it more palatable. She just came right out and said what was on her mind, as if she'd never been taught the art of prevarication, as if she wasn't accustomed to flattering powerful men, and wasn't about to start now.

"What did you mean when you said you could help restore Rafe to your uncle's favor?" he asked.

"As the president of the Society of Antiquaries, my uncle takes certain gentlemen under his wing and grooms them to take on leadership roles in the . . . society. He has no sons, you see, and he

likes to think his influence helps these men realize their potential."

"I didn't know my brother had an interest in
antiquities."

"Oh yes, Lord Rafe visits my uncle frequently
to converse on the topic."

"I hope you noticed that my brother's not so
charming anymore," he said roughly. "He's gone
to seed. He called you a strumpet."

"Five different ways. Yes, I noticed."

Something she'd said while they were in the
shed made him want to know more about her
past. "You said that he was kind to you at a time
when you felt very alone?"

"I was orphaned at the age of ten. My parents
died while they were traveling abroad. I was sent
to live with my guardian, Sir Malcolm. He had lost
his wife, Emily, and his daughter, Rebecca, very
recently. He wanted me to be a replacement for
Rebecca. He gave me her room, her possessions. I
even used her hairbrush, with strands of her hair
still caught between the bristles. But I could never
be her, and he could never be my father."

"It must have been lonely."

"You have no idea. He was trying to protect me
but he locked me away, restricted my movements;
he wouldn't allow me to have any friends. It was
a prison. A benevolent one, but a prison nonetheless. You can't know how it feels to be helpless.
You're a man, free to roam. A duke. The world
rolls out the red carpet."

He did know what it was like to be locked
away, to be helpless.

Her words brought back the dark hold of the ship. The metal manacles biting into his wrists. The gnawing hunger in his belly that intensified every day until he was more beast than boy.

"I'm not unacquainted with loneliness, Miss Penny. I've lived in seclusion in Cornwall for the last five years."

"Yes, but my solitude was forced upon me, whereas your seclusion is by choice. Why do you choose to stay in Cornwall?"

Cornwall was the perfect place for him. There he could be numb and frozen with no one to judge him. There he was useful. "I prefer my own company."

"I saw that." Her gaze dropped below his belt and a saucy spark flared in her eyes. She was referring to what she'd seen in the window, and nimbly changing the subject.

Miss Penny didn't want to be interrogated and neither did he.

"I didn't know I had an audience," he said.

"You didn't seem overly concerned about passersby."

"The window looks out over private gardens which you were trespassing upon."

"I wanted to explore. My guardian and great-aunt haven't allowed me to do much of anything since I arrived in London several months ago. The ball tonight was my first social event of the Season."

"So you thought you'd venture forth on a solo midnight perambulation. In my rosebushes."

"If you had spent two months receiving deathly tedious lessons in deportment and decorum, you'd want to roam as well. And sample some brandy. And maybe even kiss a duke."

"I doubt I'd want to kiss a duke. Infuriating creatures. They should all be damned to a specially created duke hell."

She grinned at his repetition of her words from the shed. "Ha," she said. "Precisely."

His lips threatened to turn up at the edges. He sent them back down with a stern admonition. Thinking about kissing Miss Penny—however sweet her lips, however disarming her conversation—was absolutely off-limits.

She wasn't a girl, she was a powder keg waiting to explode and take him down with her. He wanted to regain his control and equilibrium, not slip further into chaos. None of what had happened tonight was supposed to happen in his carefully regulated life.

When he was with her he felt the ground begin to shift beneath his feet—she threw him off-balance with her unpredictability and her passionate kisses.

She wasn't part of his plans.

He wasn't to kiss her, think about kissing her, dream about her, pleasure himself after dreaming about her or . . . *damn it to Hell.*

As soon as his head cleared, he'd escort her home. "I gather the decorum lessons didn't take."

"Not when she kept me imprisoned with only her grim self and a host of stuffed hedgehogs dressed as nobility for company."

"Er . . . hedgehogs?" It could be the throbbing ache in his head, but he was having a difficult time following the conversational path.

"Stuffed hedgehogs. She says they expired of natural causes, but it's still gruesome. Their little faces look almost alive, except that she's replaced their eyes with gleaming bits of glass that are so very lifeless."

"An interesting hobby."

"She calls it taxidermy. You'd have to see them to believe it. If they were alive it would at least be more diverting. We could frolic about and knock things off shelves. As it is, I'm kept as immobile and trapped as they are, posed this way and that, garbed to her tastes. The only places in London I've seen have been her town house, one ballroom, one garden shed, a study, and a . . . bedchamber."

"Some might consider a bedchamber with me inside it to be the most exciting sight in town."

"Ha." She chuckled softly. "The funny thing is that my uncle might agree."

"He would approve of you being in my bedchamber?" he asked skeptically.

"Maybe not the bedchamber part. But he would be happy I was with you. He's practically besotted with you."

"With me." Now she was making even less sense.

"He thinks you're the, let's see, what were his words? 'The pinnacle of British manhood— dignified, statesmanlike, admirable, and, above all else, honorable.'"

The scornful curl of her lush lips gave him a burning desire to disabuse her of the notion that he was anything so boring and staid as statesmanlike. "I used to be wicked, you know."

"So Crankshaw informed me."

He shouldn't want to impress her but he couldn't seem to stop himself. His life might be slightly dull and predictable now, but it wasn't always that way. In his early twenties, he'd been a hedonistic rake, indulging in every way known to man to obliterate thought, to dull the pain.

If she'd known him then, he would have been everything her thrill-seeking heart desired.

"No, really. I was bad. Thoroughly disreputable." He moved away from the heat of the fire and closer to the laughing glow in her eyes. She didn't look all that impressed. "I was dangerous to a lady's reputation. Ask anyone who knew me then."

Still not impressed. He summoned the smoldering, half-lidded gaze that used to send ladies' hearts audibly pitter-pattering. "I owned this town. When I walked into a room, you could hear hearts shattering like glass struck by a bullet."

Her oval face tilted to one side and her sparkling silver eyes assessed him. "I, for one, can't quite picture it, Your Grace."

And there was a challenge if he'd ever heard one.

And a clever, blazingly pretty woman in his bedchamber issuing the challenge.

But he couldn't be goaded into losing control. He'd only kissed her earlier because he'd still been half asleep and she'd launched a surprise attack. And then he'd decided to scare her into leaving. He'd thought that if he kissed her thoroughly enough, he might find the cracks in her bold and brazen façade.

He was the cracked one. Fatally flawed. His mind scrabbling for higher ground.

Something about this woman wrecked his hard-won control.

When she'd stared at his bare chest earlier it had slayed him, absolutely devastated him. He'd had the forbidden desire to lift her in his arms, show her how strong he was, use his strength in the service of her pleasure.

The forbidden desire was back, and more powerful than ever.

"It's all in the past, Miss Penny. I'm not the man I used to be."

"And I'm only interested in present amusements. I want to see what I've been missing since I left London when I was a girl. The city's growing in fits and bursts. New people arriving every day, ships disgorging goods from across the globe."

"London has a squalid side," he cautioned. "People live in abject poverty. They only have thin gruel to eat. Made from oats boiled in brackish water. Lumpy and nearly tasteless."

Miss Penny stared at him with a puzzled expression. "It almost sounds as though you speak from experience."

"It's time I escorted you home." He mustn't indulge forbidden desires or wallow in nightmarish memories. And he certainly shouldn't be attempting to impress her.

She crossed her arms. "I'm not going anywhere until we talk about this." Her fingers dipped into her bodice.

He swallowed. Miss Penny's breasts, delectable as they were, equaled one giant headache, not an earthly paradise he'd do anything to explore.

She handed him the rolled-up letter.

"How did you find this?" he asked. "I hid it away."

"In the hidden compartment beneath the desk in the study. I assumed you had seen it, because it must be the reason that you're here in London, otherwise you would have stayed in Cornwall forever. Am I correct?"

"I was planning to come to London at some point to see my family and find a bride, but yes, you're right. The note forced my hand."

"You don't know who wrote it, as I heard you question your brother on the subject. I may be able to offer you some assistance in the matter. I have an interest in the discernible relationships between handwriting and writers. I've already formed some opinion about the person who wrote the note."

The smile she flashed him was warm and guileless. She truly wanted to help him.

"I don't want to involve you in my family troubles, Miss Penny."

"I'm already involved, Your Grace."

Drew got the feeling that Miss Penny never backed down. And if she did have some manner of expertise in handwriting, she could possibly shed some light on the letter. "Very well, Miss Penny. What have you surmised?"

She carried the note to a small table and laid it down next to a lamp. "The strokes of the letters are close set, heavy, and slashing. There is nothing open or soft."

He bent over her shoulder as she illustrated her points with a slender fingertip.

Her hair smelled faintly of chamomile and roses, soothing and sweet. When she concentrated, a deep little line appeared between her brows.

He wanted to smooth it away with his lips.

What the devil was wrong with him?

"This note is about taking control and displaying power," she continued. "And attempting to project power is about feeling powerless. I would conjecture that this person is not evil, but he feels wronged—by the world and possibly by you personally. I think that you should start making a list of people who could be holding a grudge against you or against Lord Rafe."

"Impressive." More than impressive. Nearly uncanny. He'd used the very same words with Rafe in the carriage. "I came to the same conclusion myself. The author of the letter could know secrets about our family."

The secret details of his kidnapping that only Drew knew—that he'd never told anyone.

His mind briefly touched the idea that it could have been written by his own kidnapper, and then recoiled. No. The man had been sent to a penal colony in Australia.

Drew's nightmares were in the past.

"Secrets such as . . . ?" she prompted.

"The nature of a secret, Miss Penny, is that it's something one doesn't speak of."

"But we're in this together now, Your Grace. We've formed a temporary alliance. You can trust me."

He could trust *no one*.

"There is no *we*, Miss Penny. This is a family

matter and a potentially perilous one. I won't involve you."

Her jaw clenched. "Then I'll conduct my own investigation into Lord Rafe's affairs. Maybe I'll sneak back in while you're out and conduct a thorough search of these apartments. These rooms are potentially riddled with clues, and if we—"

"Mother of God . . ." He clasped his temple with his thumb and forefinger. "You're not going to relent."

"I found something else while I was searching Lord Rafe's desk. Love letters signed by a woman with the initial "F." Her handwriting is completely different from the other author's, however."

"It's a starting place at least," said Drew.

"Until we solve the mystery and determine where Lord Rafe has gone, and whom he is setting a trap for, I won't stop seeking answers."

Drew wouldn't mind some answers. "Explain to me again why you proposed matrimony to my disreputable brother?"

"It was going to be a marriage of convenience, based on our mutual interest in . . . antiquities. My uncle never allowed me to help him with the more exciting aspects of his hobby."

He noted that she used the past tense. For some reason this filled his mind with elation. "I assume that you are referring to hunting for antiquities, as the Duke and Duchess of Ravenwood do?"

"Something like."

"Rafe isn't interested in matrimony. He's far too—"

"Dissolute, irredeemable, unworthy. So you've

said. At the moment, all I care about is discovering his plans. He could be making a very bad, very dangerous decision. We have a mutual interest in finding him, Your Grace. We'll want to interview all of your servants, but since they're probably terrified of losing their positions, as Crankshaw was, I may have better luck convincing them to talk."

"Speaking of which, why aren't *you* terrified of me?" Had he lost his fierce and forbidding edge, along with his devilish charm?

Her eyes sparked. "You're all bark and no bite. Anyone can see that, Your Grace."

"Oh, I bite, Miss Penny," he growled.

"If you say so, Your Grace," she said with a flippant look. "I'll call on your sister tomorrow during visiting hours and find a way to interrogate the servants. I left my bonnet in the study. I'll retrieve it and be off."

"You're not climbing back out the window. You could break your neck. I'm escorting you home."

"I only live around the corner."

"If you think I'm going to allow you to walk the street by yourself, you're addled. I'm not so much a rogue."

"I'm an expert in slipping through shadows. I was as silent as a shade on my way here. I can't just stroll down the street on your arm, what if someone sees us? I'd be compromised."

"Not to put too fine a point on it, but I'd say you're already compromised."

"Yes, but no one knows about it except us. I'm not going to tell anyone, are you?"

"Certainly not."

"Then it's all settled. I allow you to escort me home, from a distance, and in return, you allow me to interview your servants and help search for clues."

That smile. Warmer than a jug of heated brandy and even more potent.

He wanted to keep touching her. Fit her body against his. Show her that he still had all of the skills of a wicked rake . . .

Blow to the skull.

That was the only possible explanation for why he was agreeing to let her search his house and interview his servants.

That, and she'd talked circles around him. Strong-armed him with those slender arms of hers, twisted him around her tiny finger.

He was all in knots.

He'd agreed because they had a shared goal— they both wanted to find Rafe—and Miss Penny was liable to do something reckless in her pursuit of the truth.

Or perhaps he'd agreed to her demands because he wanted to see her again.

Closer to the truth.

She was standing right across from him and he already missed her smile, her spark, that wicked wit.

"It's time I found more clothing, and escorted you home, Miss Penny," he said gruffly.

Chapter 12

DREW WALKED THE street, whistling softly. Just a duke on a stroll in the wee hours of a London morn, admiring the faintest pearl sheen of dawn over the rooftops.

Pretending there wasn't a meddling debutante creeping through the hedges and shadows at his flank.

This area of Mayfair wasn't exactly dangerous, being patrolled by night watchmen and populated with stately mansions locked up tight behind tall iron gates, but he hadn't felt easy about letting her leave alone.

For all her bravado, breaking and entering, and analyzing of handwriting, she was still a respectable young lady. And despite his long-past amatory exploits, he was still a gentleman.

A stream of curses was unleashed not too far from him.

He chuckled. So much for slipping through the shadows undetected. Miss Penny had a foul mouth on her. Where had she learned those expletives?

Going to investigate, he found her attempting to rip her cloak from the jaws of an emaciated, mangy street dog. "Let go of me you flea-bitten bull's pizzle."

Drew searched the bushes and came up with a large stick. "Here boy." He waved the stick at the snarling dog.

The cur let go of Mina's cloak and sniffed the stick. Drew threw the stick as far as he could down the street behind them and the dog ran off after it.

Miss Penny shook out her cloak, examining a large tear in the fabric.

"That dog didn't like you sneaking through its shrubbery."

"I didn't want to hurt the poor thing. It looked hungry."

"You were nearly undetectable before that stream of inventive blasphemy." Drew couldn't help chuckling again.

"I'm glad you think it's so hilarious."

Drew laughed harder. "Where on earth did you learn to curse like that?"

"My Uncle Malcolm has some unsavory friends, including several former sea captains."

"Miss Penny, you amaze me." He hadn't had a moment of peace since he laid eyes on her at the ball. He'd been too busy being charmed and disarmed.

It was past time for her to be safely home and out of arm's reach.

She shivered and he resisted the urge to slip his arm around her slender shoulders and tuck her against him. She made him feel far too protective.

He offered her his arm. "Everyone's asleep and we're nearly there."

She glanced up and down the street. "I suppose it's all right. I'll melt into the shadows if we see any sign of life."

He snorted. "How did that work for you the last time?"

She glared at him. "That dog came out of nowhere, I tell you."

SHE'D GOTTEN HER wish. She'd made him laugh. He had a rich, bass laugh that vibrated in the air, tickling her throat with the desire to join in.

She smiled. "Perhaps I should work on the whole melting-into-the-shadows bit."

"You could never melt into the shadows, Miss Penny. You're a scene stealer. A wave maker. A hurricane. A thief of hearts."

Thief of hearts? She kept her lips in a half smile but her heart broke into a grin.

Perhaps the cold-hearted Duke of Thorndon was not so inured to fanciful imaginings as he supposed himself to be. She'd glimpsed another side of him tonight.

The passionate, poetic side.

Silly girl. That was only because he'd been hit on the head. Not because you drove him to it with your beauty and wit. More like your bumbling and wantonness.

What she'd seen tonight, what they'd done, the entire unforgettable night—it was as though she were truly living for the first time. This was *her*. The new Mina.

Fearless and free. Wanton and wild.

No boundaries. No more prisons. Her uncle couldn't control her anymore—no one could.

Thorndon slowed his stride to match hers. Gracious, his legs were long. And his biceps solid. Their linked arms symbolized their new alliance. They were united in the common cause of finding Lord Rafe. If her suspicions were correct, Lord Rafe could be pursuing Le Triton.

Her heart skipped a beat thinking about this new information. If she could help Lord Rafe apprehend Le Triton, she would not only have revenge for the death of her parents, she would be able to prove her skills and usefulness to Sir Malcolm. He wouldn't be able to stop her from becoming an agent after such a triumph.

"We're nearly to my house, Your Grace," she said. "I'll go 'round the back and enter that way."

He released her arm. "Then I will stop here, Miss Penny."

"Until tomorrow, Your Grace," she whispered.

His face was shadowed but his eyes glinted with amber, like a glass of brandy held before a fire. "Light a lamp in your room so I know you've arrived safely. I'll be watching until I see your light."

His words sparked warmth in her heart. She wasn't alone. They would do this together.

For some reason his concern for her safety didn't feel like a restriction—it was sweet. It meant he . . . no, he didn't care. He only saw her as a responsibility, one he was well rid of and hadn't wanted in the first place.

He probably didn't feel any of this earth-shaking attraction.

He held out his hand. She placed her hand

in his. He brushed his lips across her knuckles. "Until tomorrow, Wilhelmina Penny."

"Thank you for the lovely evening, Your Grace," she blurted, and rushed away.

Thank you for the lovely evening? Good lord, what a ninny-ish thing to say. She kicked herself all the way through the back door and up the stairs to her room.

But what else could she have said? *Thank you for the anatomy lesson. And the bone-melting kiss. Oh, and by the way, thank you for squeezing my nipple when you were semi-conscious?*

WHEN SHE REACHED her room she quickly removed her cloak, bonnet and boots, and hid her satchel in the back of the wardrobe.

He was still watching beneath her window. She lit a lamp and set it near the window.

Secret signals just before dawn—her life was already so much more exciting.

Had he seen the glow in her heart, her mind? She'd lit up like a lamp when he kissed her.

Thinking about it made her glow again. If she opened her window the moths would fly to her, instead of the lamp, and beat their fragile wings against her cheeks.

Why had she enjoyed kissing him so much?

Perhaps being opposed to someone, by nature and by goals, made the kissing more heated.

She knew what he looked like lying in a bed. How his long arms stretched the width of the bed and his tall body the length.

She knew what his hands felt like covering

her bum, her breasts, tangled in her hair to draw her closer into a kiss.

She knew so many things. All of which she must promptly forget. Her mind should be occupied by formulating a new plan. The more she thought about it the more she realized that her dream of marrying Lord Rafe had been misguided.

But he could be a means of bringing Le Triton to justice. He'd said he was after the biggest prize of all, and he'd been extremely startled when she mentioned antiquities thieves.

If Thorndon hadn't been injured she could have run after Lord Rafe, and she might be chasing after Le Triton with him even now.

As it was, she required more information before setting off on any quests for vengeance.

She should stop thinking about kissing Thorndon, and start finding ways to make him useful to her goals.

That's what secret agents did.

She should study the Duke Dossier more closely. She found the notebook where she'd cast it, in the bottom of her traveling trunk, and opened it to the chapters devoted to Thorndon.

> *This is a road map, if you will, to the heart and mind of London's most eligible duke. Study it closely, Wilhelmina, and you'll be the Duchess of Thorndon within a month's time.*

Her uncle had spent most of the chapters enumerating the duke's agricultural experimentations with the rotation of crops and new methods of irrigation. He'd highlighted his concern for the plight of poverty-stricken cottagers.

Thorndon has few discernible faults. He manages his vast holdings with a firm, yet just, hand, and has increased profits tenfold since the death of his father, while improving the lives of his tenants in every regard.

He attends church most Sundays, takes an interest in the welfare of his cottagers, and keeps a pack of superior foxhounds.

Sir Malcolm made Thorndon sound like the dullest man on the face of the planet, while Mina knew the opposite was true. Thorndon was storm clouds and the lightning zing of attraction.

She shivered, remembering the disconcertingly delicious feeling of being pressed against a wall by six-odd feet of solid muscle.

There was even a section devoted to the duke's dietary preferences:

Thorndon prefers strong coffee, with no milk or sugar, to tea. One might see this as a metaphor for his life in general, as he daily subjects himself to a punishing regimen of physical and mental exercise and work that would exhaust a lesser man.

She could certainly believe that. She'd seen what all that physical exercise had done to his body in the prominent ridges of his muscles, the taut firmness of his abdomen.

Oh Lord. There she went again.

She was supposed to be searching for exploitable weaknesses, not giving herself palpitations by remembering all of his strengths.

Finally, she found something. Buried in the next-to-last paragraph and issued as a warning for a topic never to touch upon. This must be the trouble that Lady Beatrice had referred to.

> As a boy of fifteen, Thorndon was kidnapped and held for ransom for the space of ten days. His kidnapping, and the resulting trial, were a public spectacle with devastating effects on the duke and his family. The experience made him wary, mistrustful, and gave him a desire for solitude. It is a testament to his fortitude that he was able to escape before any monies were paid by his family. Never mention this topic, Wilhelmina. It is one of discomfort for the duke, and should never be alluded to in conversation.

He'd been kidnapped and held for ransom. No wonder the letter he'd received had made him drop everything and race to London. He was here to protect Lady Beatrice from suffering the same fate.

She'd accused him of being privileged, of having no knowledge of what it was like to feel helpless. She'd told him she'd been kept in a prison and that he had no idea what it felt like. How wrong she'd been.

Uncle Malcolm had given her a comfortable home even if he'd withheld the love and acceptance she so desperately craved.

The brief mention of the kidnapping raised

more questions than it answered. Why had he been held for so long, what had they done to him, and how had he escaped?

This new information made Thorndon more complex and interesting than your average arrogant duke, but it changed nothing.

They were only temporary partners, thrown together for a shared purpose: to find where Lord Rafe had gone and whom he was pursuing.

She absolutely couldn't be drawn to Thorndale for so many reasons, not the least of which was that her uncle had chosen him as the perfect gentleman to keep her out of trouble by locking her away in his lonely estate in Cornwall.

Thorndon was here because of the letter, but he was also here to find a wife. And a wife for Thorndon was a purchase to be made and then forgotten about and neglected, a ripple on the dark waters of his life.

Their temporary alliance was a new pathway to her emancipation. The duke wasn't so much an obstacle, as a powerful ally.

Powerful being the key word. He had the power to make her knees wobble, to steal her breath away with his skillful kisses, to set off fireworks in her belly.

She'd have to be constantly on her guard. Constantly wary of his ability to scramble her mind.

This was her very first mission. She could taste some of the thrills and excitement she'd been longing for, but she couldn't go too far.

A good spy never lost their head, or their heart.

Chapter 13

THE CLUB HADN'T changed since Drew's last visit. Somber oil paintings of illustrious members still lined the mahogany wall paneling. A lingering odor of cigar smoke, citrus wood polish, and Sunday roast permeated the hallways.

In this upper crust bastion of brandy snifters and dampened passions the fates of men and nations were decided by well-fed politicians who had never known the knife of hunger or the bite of bitter cold.

The stasis of it struck him not as comforting and familiar but as rather pathetic.

Your days are numbered, gents, he thought as he left his hat and gloves with the wizened old porter. *There's a revolution brewing. There are ladies like Miss Penny on the loose, flouting your rules and expectations for femininity. Don't expect your reign to last forever.*

The club hadn't changed, but Drew had.

He wasn't the same reckless devil searching for a temporary surcease of pain at the bottom of a glass. His life had purpose now and his actions were controlled.

The place brought back too many bad memories. He wouldn't be here at all if he wasn't searching for news about Rafe.

"Hello, Mr. Bickerstaff," he said to the headwaiter, an unsmiling, gray-mustachioed man who betrayed no surprise at seeing Drew after so many years.

Bickerstaff, unlike Rafe's garrulous manservant Crankshaw, was trusted for his silence and discretion—which was a good thing because the conversations he overheard could no doubt start wars, both domestic and international.

"Your Grace." The waiter bowed. "Your usual table?"

"It can't still be reserved after all this time."

"I will make it so."

"No need to oust anyone on my account. I'll sit anywhere."

"If you insist, Your Grace."

"I do. How are you, Bickerstaff? How is your family?"

A shadow passed over the man's already gloomy face. "My family, Your Grace?"

"Er, that is . . ." Embarrassed, Drew strove to recall anything he knew about the headwaiter, besides his famed stoicism and tact. "Wasn't there a Mrs. Bickerstaff?"

"Never, Your Grace."

"Oh. I'm sorry." He'd offended the man when he was trying to be nice, to show how he'd changed from the drunken rake to a sober, well-meaning duke.

Bickerstaff looked mortified that Drew would

apologize for anything. "Think nothing of it, Your Grace. My brother is married and has a family. My niece Elsa is a bright young thing and a comfort to me."

"Glad to hear that." He cleared his throat. "Have you seen my brother lately?"

"Lord Rafe hasn't visited in several weeks."

Drew detected a note of scorn in his voice when he spoke about Rafe, which wasn't surprising given that dealing with an inebriated Rafe would try the patience of a saint.

"Perhaps one of his friends is here?" asked Drew.

"The Duke of Westbury is in the dining room, Your Grace."

"Perfect. I'll join him."

Bickerstaff led him to the table.

Westbury reminded Drew of Rafe—fair hair, cloudy heart, and up to his bloodshot eyeballs in debt.

Drew didn't think he could be the author of the note, though. Miss Penny had said that the person who wrote the note held a deep-seated grudge. And Westbury, while desperate for cash, wasn't the kind to threaten young ladies.

Westbury raised bleary eyes from a glass of something inappropriate to the early hour. "Thorndon. Heard you were in Town."

"Westbury." Drew took the seat across from him. "Bickerstaff, bring the duke some of that excellent Madeira."

"Coffee," corrected Drew.

The headwaiter bowed and left them.

"Coffee?" asked Westbury. "Heard you were

sober as a schoolmarm but didn't believe the rumors. You used to drink me under the table most nights. Those were the days, eh? Brandy, barmaids, and bedsport."

Drew frowned. He wasn't here to relive his wicked past or to defend his present choices. "I'm no schoolmarm but I never drink brandy before lunch. A little coffee would do you good, Westbury. Keep you alert."

"Don't want to be alert. Prefer a hazy state of inebriation gathering to full-on fog by nightfall."

"Have you seen Rafe?"

"Not for weeks. Owes me fifty quid. If I'd seen him I'd remember, because I would've tried to squeeze it out of him."

Westbury was a cautionary tale about what would happen to the estate if Drew failed to produce an heir. Westbury had already lost most of his fortune at gaming houses and had been forced to begin selling off his properties one by one, causing hardship and havoc for his tenant farmers.

"I'll pay his debt if you answer a few questions," said Drew.

"Ask away. I've got all day." Westbury leaned back in his chair, squinting in the sunlight shining through the windows.

"Viscount Fitzbart was chasing Rafe down the Strand waving a pistol—do they have a long-standing feud?"

Westbury snorted. "One of them is always chasing the other with a pistol. They don't mean anything by it—thick as thieves, those two."

Fitzbart could probably be ruled out. "Has Rafe

spoken to you about any trouble he could be involved in, or any plans to do anything foolish?"

"More than the usual foolishness? No. As I said, I haven't seen him in weeks. Been hiding mostly. From my creditors. And my sisters. And their music instructor, whom I haven't paid in months. Don't know why the young lady comes back every week to attempt to force some musicality into my sisters. It's no use. But she's very persistent, Miss Beaton."

Bickerstaff arrived with a young waiter, who served Drew his pot of coffee.

Drew blew on the coffee until he could take a sip. "I danced with one of your sisters the other night."

Westbury perked up. "Don't suppose you tumbled madly in love and offered to marry the girl?"

Drew raised his brows.

"Didn't think so," said Westbury glumly. "They're good girls but they don't have any dowries thanks to me. I'll have to be the one to marry well. No respectable lady in her right mind would have me, though. Thinking of trading my title for an American heiress."

"Best of luck. About Rafe—"

"Heard you waltzed with Sir Malcolm Penny's ward and that she's pretty and heavily dowered."

"I wasn't aware her dowry was substantial."

"As enormous as she is purportedly petite."

Miss Penny was small in stature but she was fierce. Also troublesome, persistent, and irresistible.

He had to stop thinking about her. "I require practicality and fortitude over prosperity," Drew said.

Westbury sloshed the liquid around in his glass. "I always seem to have these conversations with my friends about young ladies and then they marry them. Had a talk like this with Banksford about his governess. Red-haired slip of a thing, no fortune to speak of, but he wed her. Promise me that you won't marry Miss Penny until I have a go? Give a man a fighting chance. What's she like? Demure and sweet natured?"

"Hardly. She's quite the firebrand." The memory of their kiss was seared into his mind. He couldn't stop thinking about it.

"Damned pretty is what I heard," said Westbury. "Laughing blue eyes and ample bosom."

"Some might see her eyes as blue but they're a far more complex color. And don't talk about her bosom."

Westbury grinned. "Oh, I see how it is."

"What's that?"

"Nothing, nothing at all."

"If you're implying that I fancy Miss Penny you couldn't be more wrong."

"My mistake. It's just that everyone else fancies her. Marmont was blathering on about how he danced with her twice and she'd soon be his bride."

Drew nearly spit his coffee onto the table. "That bloodless complainer? There's no way Miss Penny would marry him."

"He's even wealthier than you, you know."

"I don't think she's after a fortune. Wasn't very polite to me while we waltzed." Enough talk about Miss Penny. He couldn't seem to escape the topic . . . or his thoughts about her. About their kiss. "Has Rafe mentioned any mistresses whose names begin with the letter *F*?

"That would be Frances Flynn, but that ended months ago. Wish I could afford to be her new protector."

"Can you tell me where she lives?"

"Didn't think you'd be interested in your brother's former mistress."

"I'm searching for Rafe and she might know where he's gone. He appeared at the house last night, drunk as a lord, hit me over the head with a candlestick and fled into the night."

"Sounds like Rafe." Westbury chuckled.

"If you see him, or hear anything about him, contact me immediately. I'll pay the cost of the messenger." He reached into his pocket and handed the duke a banknote.

Westbury's eyes gleamed as he accepted the note. "Much obliged."

"Spend the difference on your sisters."

He wouldn't. He'd waste it all chasing the dice.

"Are you certain that you won't consider marrying one of them?" Westbury asked. "I have several sisters to choose from."

Drew finished his coffee. Westbury's sisters were perfectly nice girls. Cultured, comely, and obliging, but they lacked . . . fire. They wouldn't contradict his every word. Or hold him at pistol point.

"I have to go," he said abruptly. "Remember to contact me if you hear anything about Rafe."

"I will," said Westbury.

He wouldn't. He'd forget all about this conversation after five more glasses. It was useless to enlist the help of drunkards. Perhaps former mistresses would prove more helpful.

Frances Flynn could know something.

Miss Penny would be at his house right now, visiting with Beatrice and then contriving a way to interview the servants. He hoped she'd have better luck than he'd had this morning. None of the servants had known anything about Rafe's troubles except in the general sense that he lost large sums of money gambling and lived an extravagant life.

If anyone could cajole them into unguarded speech, it was Miss Penny, with the one-two punch of her sunny smile and sharp wit.

MINA AND LADY BEATRICE were seated on a wide wooden swing in the gardens that separated the two Thorndon town houses, having left Grizzy with Lady Beatrice's mother. The two older ladies had settled in for a cup of tea and a nice long gossip, so Mina and Lady Beatrice had decided to move outdoors, since it was such a fine day.

The air was fragrant with the sweet scent of roses and peonies. To the left was the bedchamber window where Mina had observed Thorndon doing . . . what he'd been doing. A thrill rippled through her body as she remembered the unforgettable sight. His muscles straining, body taut with tension and desire. Had he been thinking about her as he touched himself? It wasn't unimaginable. He'd observed her revealing dance as she attempted to fasten her scarlet gown in the garden shed. She could have given him inspiration.

Or it could have been the seductive gown.

After she'd changed back into her demure white dress, she'd left the red silk gown in the storage bench, having nowhere else to stash it without attracting Grizzy's attention. Perhaps Mina would find a way to retrieve it soon.

"Are you a person with a happy temperament and a bright outlook on life, Miss Penny?" asked Lady Beatrice. She wore a simple gown in a lavender hue that contrasted pleasingly with her copper hair.

"I suppose so," replied Mina. "I haven't thought much about it."

"You appear that way to me but appearances can be deceiving."

"I'd say that I'm a person who believes in action. If I'm moving forward, learning new skills, challenging myself, then I've no time to mope."

Mina was enjoying their conversation, though she knew she must find a way to steal over to Lord Rafe's town house to interview the servants and continue her search for clues.

The glass of Lady Beatrice's spectacles sparkled in the sunlight as she shifted closer to Mina on the swinging bench. "And do you take a charitable interest in those less fortunate than yourself?"

"I've lived at my uncle's estate for the last ten years and the tenants and surrounding villagers are quite prosperous. I have to admit I've never engaged in charitable works."

"An honest answer. But you would, if given the opportunity."

"Certainly. When we traveled to Town, our carriage passed by groups of people living in terrible poverty and it saddened me. It doesn't seem right that there is such a tremendous gulf between the lives of those born into humble origins and those born with a silver spoon in their mouths."

"Well said." Lady Beatrice nodded. "And what are your views on childbearing?"

"Pardon me?"

"Do you want to have children, Miss Penny? Not all women do. I probably never will as childbearing generally means taking a husband."

"Well," began Mina, not quite certain how to answer the question. She decided on telling the truth. She liked Lady Beatrice and wanted to be honest with her. "I do want to have a child but not just yet. I'm of the mind that a young lady's purpose in life is not solely to produce heirs or create harmonious households. I believe women can achieve other goals."

"Quite so. What of your parents—they died when you were young?"

"When I was ten, though we were never close. They were always traveling. I made a vow that if I have a daughter someday, I'll spend more time with her. I won't withhold my time or my affections."

"The death of both of your parents could have made you bitter, but instead you made a resolution to be more affectionate and loving." Lady Beatrice lifted a finger. "See? A bright outlook on life."

Mina smiled at her. "Why do I feel as though I'm being interviewed?"

Lady Beatrice chuckled appreciatively. "Because you *are* being interviewed. I consider you to be the leading candidate for the position of Duchess of Thorndon, and my future sister-in-law. Drew told me that he hopes to choose a bride quickly in order to return home for the harvest, and so I offered to assist him in his endeavor."

"Ah. I hate to disappoint you but Thorndon and I are opposed in both temperament and prospects. He's brooding where I'm boisterous. He prefers the countryside of Cornwall, while I belong in the beating heart of London. He is—"

"I know, you already told me, it was loathing at first sight for both of you. But it does seem, at least in the novels I read, that sometimes the people one loathes at first can become the most attractive after further acquaintance."

"You've been reading Miss Austen."

"I adore her books. After I complete my etymological dictionary, I plan to write a study of female authors. I shall have a whole chapter dedicated to her works. It's so sad that she died so young. I often wonder what fantastic heights her career could have risen to if she'd only been allowed more time on this earth."

"Have you thought about writing novels yourself?" asked Mina.

"Never. Mine is a didactic mind, one that parses and interprets and never delves into the realm of the heart."

"You're proving my point about the goals of young ladies, Lady Beatrice."

"Please call me Beatrice, won't you? I'm only a few years younger than you, I believe, and I hope we may become best friends."

"I'd like that very much. And please call me Mina."

They smiled at each other. Mina did hope that they could become friends. She'd never had a best friend before.

"There's something very fearless about you, Mina. When you walk into a room it's as though a breeze comes in with you lifting everyone's spirits and making things seem a little more alive."

"Thank you. You make me want to read more books and expand my vocabulary."

"People are so incurious. They don't want to know where the words they use come from, they just learn a limited number and use them over and over. I want to expand and waken people's minds."

"What does Lord Rafe think about your literary scholarship?" Mina asked.

"He doesn't even know about it. My brother's too inebriated half the time to remember his own name."

"Has Lord Rafe appeared different to you of late?"

"Different, how so?"

"Has he spoken about taking a journey?"

"He never confides in me. We barely speak to each other. He's just coming home from his nights of vice and debauchery as I'm rising for the day."

"Have his servants expressed any concerns about any mishaps or troubles he may have?"

"Drew told me about the note, Mina."

"He did?" He hadn't mentioned that last night, but she was glad that he'd taken his sister into his confidence.

"I'm aware that Rafe might be in some predicament," Beatrice continued. "I even talked to the servants and no one had anything of import to confess."

"Does the threat of kidnapping frighten you? My uncle told me that your brother was kidnapped as a boy."

"It's because of his past that Drew is taking this business so personally. He's vowed to protect me. Which is more than I can say of Rafe." Beatrice clicked her tongue. "I do sincerely hope that you're not still thinking about attempting to reform him. That's where optimism would become sheer folly."

"I'm not," Mina hastened to assure her. "Don't you believe rakes can be reformed? I heard that Thorndon used to be a rogue."

"Yes, but it wasn't a woman that reformed him, it was Thornhill House. Working on improving the estate and the sorry plight of his tenant farmers gave him a new purpose. My fondest wish is to finally be declared a spinster so that I may go and live with him at Thornhill and plunder his vast library."

"Isn't Thornhill House rather decrepit and rundown?"

"And haunted by shades," said Beatrice.

"That's appealing to you?"

"I have a dark turn of mind. I've always loved gothic tales and ghost stories. I hear that Thornhill House crouches on a tall hill overlooking a bay. Black stone shards pierce the sky on either side of the massive front doors."

"Sounds inviting," said Mina with a short laugh.

"Some ancient lord—not an ancestor of ours, because Thornhill was acquired by Papa as payment for a debt—added pinnacles and crenellations wherever his whims suited him, attempting to create the impression of a medieval cathedral." Lady Beatrice's eyes shone behind her spectacles. "I'll wager that it's altogether glorious."

"Wasn't there some great tragedy that occurred? A great number of people crushed to death, I believe." The Duke Dossier had mentioned a brief history of the estate.

"One of the owners in the seventeen hundreds undertook extensive renovations and he wanted to complete a new family chapel before his bride arrived. He pushed the workmen; he wouldn't let them sleep or eat. The last stone was finally set in place in the family chapel. His bride arrived and they moved the wedding to an earlier date. But the workers had hastened too much. The chapel ceiling collapsed and killed him, his bride, the clergymen, and most of the assembled guests. His brother inherited the estate and sealed up the house. It sat vacant for decades, until my father acquired it."

Mina shuddered. "A chilling tale."

"They say a ghostly bride wanders the halls at night, wailing for her lost wedding night. I'd like to go and meet her."

"Surely you don't believe in shades."

"I believe that stories don't spring from nothing. Someone saw something."

"It sounds quite lonely to me."

"I think Drew is lonely there. It's as though he used his new life as an excuse to disengage from the old—he's cut us out of his life. It hurt me so much when he never returned my letters or came to visit."

"It must have been so difficult."

"But he's here now and this is my chance to reconnect with him. All Thornhill requires to make it a home is me . . . and you, Mina. Your brightness—your passionate nature. I sense a coldness in him, a perpetual state of frostbite, as though he's lost feeling not in his toes but in his heart. The house gave him purpose . . . but you could teach him how to love."

The warming of Thorndon's cold heart was not her goal and never would be, therefore it was best to simply move on to another, less perilous, subject. "Have you told the duke that you wish to live with him at Thornhill?"

"Many times but he won't listen. He thinks it would be too limiting and that I wouldn't have recourse to stimulating society or suitors. He thinks that if I don't marry I'll regret my choice later in life. But marriage wouldn't make me any happier, especially if the gentleman wed me only for my fortune, as he must, because who would love *this*." She waved a hand at the side of her face that sagged.

"Don't say that, Beatrice. You're lovely."

"I'm not, you don't have to lie just to make me feel better. All my childhood there were the doctors, the specialists, the treatments. Everyone watching me, observing me. Sometimes I wonder what my life would have been like if I'd been born poor. No doctors or supposed cures:

no hope, in other words. No false hope. I think it would have been simpler but we can't change the past, can we?"

"I wish I'd said good-bye to my parents before they left on their last journey and never came home. I wish that I'd been able to meet other girls my own age and to strike up friendships."

"It's never too late to change, and we're both young. Our whole lives ahead of us." Beatrice plucked a velvety red rose from the trellised side of the swing and brushed the petals against her cheek. "What will you do with your life?"

"I've always been on the periphery of things, always hidden away. I want in," Mina said. "I want inside the beating heart of life. I want excitement. Intrigue." She wanted to be worthy of the name Penny.

"And you shall have it."

If Beatrice wanted to believe that Mina might fall in love with Drew, and that he might fall in love with her, then Mina would allow her to have her fantasy. It was the most expedient way of framing her request for time alone in Lord Rafe's town house.

"Beatrice, I wonder if you might . . . cover for me. I would like to visit the other town house." She glanced at the window where she'd seen Thorndon.

Beatrice's eyes sparkled behind her spectacles. "You have a romantic tryst planned with Drew. He told me that he was visiting his club but he would be back in time to speak with you."

"I wouldn't call it a romantic tryst, but I do have something to speak with him about."

"Say no more. I'll take care of everything. I'll tell Mama that I've taken you up to my room to show you my collection of female writers. She won't disturb us. I'll stay inside my room reading a book and give you time alone with Drew. Mama will be perfectly content to gossip with your great-aunt for hours."

"Great-Aunt Griselda does love to gossip."

"Are we to expect a proposal after your tryst?" asked Beatrice with a mischievous smile.

"Certainly not. It's not that I want time alone with him, it's . . ." What explanation could she give? "Oh, never mind."

"You don't need to justify it—I completely understand. It's our secret." Beatrice hopped off of the swing. "I'm off to mislead Mama. I'll be over to fetch you in a little less than an hour."

"Thank you."

"Here." Beatrice tucked the red rose behind Mina's ear. "For luck."

A red rose like the one Rafe had given her, the color of her silk gown. A symbol of her dreams and her destiny.

Beatrice went back to her house and Mina slipped around the back of the other house. She'd like to interview Crankshaw—the man had to know *something*—and then she'd do another search of the premises.

Crankshaw answered Mina's knocking. "Madam," he bowed.

Mina entered the house. "Crankshaw, my name

is Miss Wilhelmina Penny and I want to offer you some explanation for my presence here last evening."

"Were you here last evening? I didn't see you here, madam." He winked at her.

"You can drop the act, Crankshaw."

"What act? I am the soul of discretion."

"Is there somewhere we can speak in private?" she asked.

"Of course, Miss Penny. This way, please." He led her into a small parlor.

She closed the door. "Lord Rafe may be in some difficulties, Crankshaw. I'm a . . . friend and I hope to be able to aid him. His Grace and I will be searching these apartments for information today."

"How might I assist?"

"Can you recall anything out of the ordinary happening in the past weeks? Any departure from routine or unexpected visitors?"

"Madam, Lord Rafe has many unexpected, un-announced visitors of the female variety, and this house is filled with extraordinary objects, the sight of which would make any respectable person blush. For example, there is a lacquered cabinet filled with the strangest assortment of, er, implements, col-lected from around the globe. And there is the—"

"I'm not interested in Lord Rafe's customary oddities, Crankshaw." She knew from previous experience that the servant would divulge every thought in his cluttered mind if left unchecked. "I'm asking you to recall anything different from the routine, from his habits."

Crankshaw stared at the ceiling for several
moments. "No, Miss Penny. I can recall nothing
except the habitual depravities. Which I never
speak of for fear of offending the sensibilities of
my audience."

"Then perhaps you would be so kind as to interview the rest of the servants. Someone might
have seen or heard something. Ask them about
any remnants of papers in the fireplaces, something Lord Rafe might have burned, any snip-
pets of words or any behavior that struck them as
more strange than usual."

"Does His Grace know about your assistance
in this matter?"

"He does."

"Then it will be my great honor to assist. You
shall have your report by this afternoon."

"You may give the report to the duke."

"Very good, Miss Penny."

"Now I should like to search Lord Rafe's study
again."

"Of course."

He must have a hiding place—all spies did—
and it wouldn't be as easy to find as a false bottom
to a desk or a loose floorboard.

This would be something cleverly hidden.
Something only another person with a knowledge of espionage could find.

Chapter 14

WHEN DREW RETURNED home he found Miss Penny walking slowly around the perimeter of the study, lost in concentration. He watched her for a moment just for the pleasure of it. She wore a conventional gown of dotted yellow muslin. He liked the way it moved with her as she walked, molding the enticing shape of her limbs.

She mumbled to herself as she trailed her fingers over the books on the shelves. Her hair was caught up in curls on top of her head with tendrils wending a spiral path from her ears to her neck. A blue ribbon cinched the hourglass curve of her waist.

An hour earlier he'd presented his card at Frances Flynn's door, giving the sophisticated beauty time to array herself on a low couch in a practiced state of dishabille that had been calculated to heat his blood.

His blood had remained icy as he questioned her about Rafe's whereabouts and activities. She'd told him nothing he hadn't already known, so he'd left, eager to return to the house. To *this*. Miss Penny searching for clues.

She stopped walking and turned toward the

bookshelves, providing him with a very appealing view of her generously rounded bum.

She plucked a book from the shelf with a flourish, as if she expected something to happen.

Nothing happened, except that he imagined pressing her up against the bookshelf from behind, savoring the way the soft curve of her bottom cradled his hard . . .

"Good day, Your Grace," she said, turning toward him. "I didn't expect you back so soon."

I can't stay away.

She had a red rose tucked behind her ear. He wanted to taste it—the rose, the curve of her ear, follow the trail down her throat, inside her bodice . . .

The sight of her immediately destroyed his calm, chipped away at his ice sculpture of a heart.

"Good day, Miss Penny," he said in as bland and businesslike of a tone as he could manage.

He was impervious. He felt nothing. They had a mutual goal—that was all. "I conducted a thorough search of this room earlier today. You won't find anything."

"Not thorough enough, Your Grace."

"Is that so?"

"You weren't searching in the right places."

He stopped short, several paces away, even though he wanted to be closer.

"What do you expect to find?" he asked.

"I'm not sure yet, but I'll know it when I see it," she said, resuming her slow walk along the bookshelf.

"Where's Beatrice?"

"Reading a book. We left my great-aunt and your mother in the parlor for a long gossip session. Beatrice told them that she wanted to show me her collection of female authors." She paused and glanced at him over her shoulder, her eyes like polished silver. "Beatrice thinks that I want time alone with you. Can you believe that?"

"But of course. She probably thinks you want to steal a kiss."

"I'm not after kisses. I'm here for secrets." She slid another book from the shelf, then replaced it.

Too bad, thought Drew. *I'm here for kisses.*

"I spoke with Crankshaw," she said, "and he couldn't recall anything out of the ordinary, but he's going to interview all of the servants to see if anyone noticed anything. He'll give you a report tonight."

He followed along as she slowly made her way from book to book, studying titles and selecting volumes to remove and replace, seemingly at random.

What was she searching for?

"I visited my club and spoke with Rafe's friend the Duke of Westbury. Found your turtledove."

"Oh?" She stopped walking and gave him her full attention.

"Frances Flynn, Rafe's former mistress, and one I knew nothing about. Apparently he ended it with her months ago. I visited her at her house."

"And was she beautiful and sophisticated?"

"Very."

"I suppose she was wearing a scarlet gown."

"She wasn't wearing a gown at all, only a lacy negligee and a thin silk wrapper."

"Oh." She blinked. "How scandalous."

"Very."

"And did you want to steal a kiss?"

Was she jealous? He studied her face. "I wasn't there for kisses. I was after secrets. Unfortunately, she had none to tell. It seems we've come to a dead end. Until the author of the note sends another communication, we've exhausted all avenues."

"We haven't come to a dead end, Your Grace." She smiled. "We're just getting started. You'll see."

We're just getting started.

It usually started with a kiss. Books helped. He wasn't precisely sure why, but he'd always found that well-stocked library shelves were a surefire method to enflame a female's passions.

"You know these are my books, not Rafe's, right?" For some reason he wanted to make that very clear. "He's not a great reader. He prefers gaming hells to libraries."

"Interesting." She studied the shelves. "Then we'll be looking for a book that's out of place. Something you never would keep in your library. How tall is Lord Rafe?"

"About my height."

"I'm searching on the wrong bookshelf. It would be on the next one up. And it will most likely be brightly colored, so as to differentiate it from other books."

"What the devil are you talking about?"

"The book that will open the secret chamber hidden behind the wall."

"I hate to disappoint you but there's no secret chamber. I have the working drawings for this entire house. It was designed by an architect who didn't have a secretive or imaginative bone in his body."

"Shhh." She held a finger to her lips. "Let me work."

He trailed behind as she chose books at intervals, this time rising on her toes to remove them from the shelf above her head. They were nearly to the end of the last row of shelves.

He overtook her easily and braced his hand on the shelves, cutting off her path.

She stopped, inches from him.

"There's no hidden chamber. See? End of the line," he said.

"That book. The red one your hand is resting on. What does it say?"

He moved his hand. *"Memoirs of a Woman of Pleasure."*

"And did you purchase it and place it there?"

"I most certainly did not," he said indignantly. "I may have been a rake but I didn't keep lewd books out in the open on my library shelves."

She giggled.

"Have I said something funny?" he asked.

"I knew it would be a bawdy title—that's Lord Rafe's sense of humor. That's the one." She stood beside him, her shoulder touching his upper arm, her eyes bright and clear with interest. "Your Grace, attempt to pull that book off of the shelf."

He pulled the top edge of the book toward him. "It won't move," he said, puzzled.

"I knew it!"

Miss Penny moved a few steps and ran her fingers along the edge of the narrow section of shelving. "It must be fixed to the mechanism that will open the door. Angle the book down and toward you and pull again."

He followed her instructions and a small crack opened up between the edges of the shelf sections.

He stared, dumbfounded. "That's not possible."

"Confronted with the evidence of sight and he still says it's not possible. Here, exchange places with me, Your Grace. You pull on the edge of the shelves while I work the book."

They switched places. She pulled down on the book with both her hands. "Now," she said.

He grabbed the edge of the shelf and pulled and the entire thing slid toward him, revealing a dark hollow beyond. "Well, I'll be twice damned. There's a secret chamber."

Chapter 15

"**I** TOLD YOU SO," Mina crowed. "I may not be completely stealthy, but I do know a likely location for a hidden room. My uncle has a similar one at Sutton Hall. Many houses have them to protect precious documents or jewels."

"Not this house," said the duke, gazing into the darkness behind the shelf with a disbelieving expression. "This was not in the floor plans."

"Lord Rafe must have had the room modified while you were gone. Does the study appear smaller to you?"

He glanced around the room. "Now that you mention it, the room does seem slightly off center. But why would he have this built, and why wouldn't Crankshaw have informed me of it when I asked him if anything strange had happened?"

"Perhaps Mr. Crankshaw is more discreet than he appears."

"I doubt that."

"Let's explore, shall we?" She was dying to go inside. This was where Lord Rafe would keep confidential documents. The entire mystery of his mission could be solved in the next minutes.

The duke hesitated outside the entrance to the narrow space. "I'll fetch a lamp."

"There's one over there."

He followed her gaze, his eyes gone dull and lifeless. Something was wrong.

"Miss Penny. I . . ." His throat worked visibly.

"You look pale. Is something the matter?"

His face closed like a door being slammed shut. "Nothing's the matter. I'll fetch the lamp."

It was dark inside the small space, but she could see the outline of a desk and what looked like a box on top of the desk.

He returned with the lamp and held it high, illuminating the narrow elongated chamber. "Nothing to see here. Just a desk and a chair. We should go find Beatrice. We've been alone together too long."

"No one's worrying about us, Your Grace. My great-aunt and your mother are gossiping and they think I'm reading books with Lady Beatrice."

He eyed the hidden chamber. "Maybe we should bring two lamps with us."

He was acting very strange. It was almost as if . . . could he be scared?

Suddenly she realized that this fear of a small and an unknown space could be related to his kidnapping.

"I see a wooden box inside the room," she said gently. "We must open it."

"Must we?" he asked, his face a study in conflicted emotions, none of them his customary arrogance.

He hunched his shoulders, staring at her instead of at the room. "Very well then." He took a deep breath. "Let's go explore."

"Wait." She wedged a book under the door. "That's usually the first mistake people make with hidden chambers. Now we won't be trapped inside."

"Excellent," he said shakily. "Though a secret chamber behind a bookshelf might make a perfect location to steal a kiss."

"Or the perfect location for your brother to hide information about his clandestine activities."

Though another kiss would be equally thrilling.

Although the duke didn't look amorous at the moment. He stood so still that he could have been a statue. The hand that held the lamp trembled.

She moved closer to him and placed her palm on his chest. "Your heart is beating so fast."

"I'm excited to see what the room will reveal."

"So am I."

He was obviously fighting for control over his emotions. He clasped her hand where it lay against his heart and threaded his fingers between hers until they were holding hands. "Are you ready for an adventure, Miss Penny?"

"Always, Your Grace."

They walked into the room hand in hand. He set the lantern on the desk, never letting go of her hand. The light from the lantern and the dim light from the study showed all sides of the room.

Thorndon appeared even larger in the tiny space, his head nearly reaching the low ceiling. The enticing scent of his cologne teased her senses.

Perhaps they would have time for just one stolen kiss in the dark. Or she could reach her arms as far around him as possible and give him a hug. It might help calm him.

It would have the opposite effect on her. Her body thrummed with the awareness of how near he stood. How their hands were linked.

She slid her thumb along his knuckles in a soothing rhythm.

"It's very Spartan and spare, like a monk's cell," he observed. "Not very Rafe-like."

She led him to the far wall and rapped upon it with her knuckles. "Walls intact. Nowhere else to hide anything." She bounced up and down on the floorboards, one by one, the duke following at her side. "No loose floorboards."

"Then it's just the box," he said.

That's where Rafe would keep his coded messages. They would be coded because agents were extremely cautious about what they entrusted to paper.

The duke's face was ashen and his breathing was ragged. He clutched her fingers so tightly it almost hurt.

"Let's take the box into the study and examine it there, Your Grace."

He relinquished her hand and passed her the lamp. He pounced on the box and carried it out of the room and over to a table near a window. He stared out the window for a few moments, his back to her, shoulders rigid.

"Your Grace?" She touched the back of his shoulder. He flinched. She sensed that he was fighting for control over his breathing, unwilling to betray any weakness.

He turned. His brow was beaded with sweat. She longed to ask him about his reaction but she could see from the closed, forbidding expression in his eyes that he wouldn't appreciate any prying.

"Are you going to open the box?" he asked, his voice harsh.

He watched intently as she opened the box and lifted out a leather-bound book. There was no lock. She spread it open. It was a coded diary. Each day had a date in English, but the entries were written in a cipher consisting of numbers and letters.

"That's Rafe's handwriting but what does it mean? It looks like gibberish," Thorndon said.

"Not gibberish. It's coded. In order to decipher it, we'll need to find the key. Are you familiar with the work of General Sir George Scovell?"

"Not specifically."

"General Scovell was a linguist who cracked the *Grande Chiffre* French code in just under two days."

"Sounds like a hero of yours."

"I've read everything by him and about him. When the Great Paris Code was sent to French army officers in eighteen eleven he had a much more difficult task. But eventually he understood enough of it to decipher critical French dispatches and aid Wellington's victory at Vitoria."

"Are you saying that my brother writes his diary in French military code? How are we going to crack that?"

"*We.* You said we."

"I did, didn't I?"

She was becoming addicted to that sly smile of his, the one that lifted a corner of his mouth and left the other one stern.

"I suppose we're in this together now, like you said. We've formed a temporary alliance." His breathing returned to normal. Whatever had happened in his mind, whatever dark, fearful place he'd gone to, he was back now.

And they would solve this mystery together.

"This is written in your brother's own cipher," said Mina. "My guess would be that he used a book from your library as the key. If we can find the book, we can crack the code by determining the pattern of pages, columns and words. For example, Scovell developed a common cipher for our forces to use by sending the same dictionary to each headquarters."

"You certainly know a lot about ciphers."

"It's a hobby of mine. I like puzzles, codes, and anagrams. Anything I can take apart and put back together. Words, timepieces, weaponry. It's interesting to find the hidden meanings, or to find new uses for ordinary items."

"Weaponry?"

"For example, the pistol you saw in the garden shed: I modified its mechanism to fit my small hands perfectly."

"Not a very normal occupation for a debutante."

She gave him a quelling look. "Do I appear to be an ordinary debutante?"

"Not in the least."

"I like anagrams in particular. As a girl I was

always dissecting words and putting them back together in different ways. I've already anagrammed your Christian name, Your Grace." She'd found an iteration that fit him perfectly. "Andrew becomes *Warden*."

He frowned. "I don't like that one. Andrew could be . . . *warned*." His eyes glinted. "Or *wander*."

"*Warden*," she said, though he did make her think of wandering down forbidden paths.

"And Wilhelmina?" he asked. "With so many letters you must have some interesting results. Let's see . . ." he said, staring out the window.

"That's easy. My favorite one is: *Ahem, I'll win*."

He smiled. "Very appropriate."

"I anagrammed Lord Rafe's full name."

"Raphael. And what hidden meaning did you uncover?"

"*Ale harp*," she pronounced.

The duke laughed. *Finally*. She wanted to help chase the darkness away.

"It fits him," Thorndon said. "I believe it was Dryden who said that anagrams are the 'torturing of one poor word ten thousand ways.' "

"And now we're going to have to torture all of the books in your library in order to find the key to this coded diary."

"There are too many books. How are we to narrow the search?" he asked.

"Sort through the books to see if any of them have any marks, any letters underlined or papers stuck between the pages. Or perhaps you can think of a book that had a special significance to your brother?"

"I told you he wasn't much of a reader."

"May I keep the diary for now, Your Grace?"

"You obviously have a talent for this sort of thing. Please do keep it. Perhaps you may be able to determine the pattern of the cipher, even without the key."

"Thank you." Her heart warmed at the thought that he recognized her talents and asked for her help. He really should stop being the exact opposite of what she'd imagined him to be.

"And perhaps my sister can assist you. She certainly loves torturing words until they reveal their origins," he added, making it even more difficult for her to distance her emotions.

A gentleman who recognized the talents and capabilities of young ladies, didn't feel threatened by them, and actively sought occasions for encouraging those talents to be put to use.

Oh dear. Mina was going to have to work much harder to protect her heart. He was launching quite the attack on her defenses.

She couldn't lose her head, or her heart. He was a means to an end.

She was glad to have the opportunity to crack the code. If this diary held the information she thought it did, it wouldn't be safe for anyone else to read it. She fully expected to find that Lord Rafe was after Le Triton.

"We ought to go and find Lady Beatrice now," Mina said. And then she'd go home with Grizzy—she couldn't wait to begin attempting to decipher the code.

They walked back through the corridor. "What's that room with the closed door?" she asked.

"A storeroom."

"In the center of the hallway? Seems a more likely place for a sitting room." She tested the knob. "It's locked. Do you have the key?"

"I searched that one already this morning. There's nothing there."

"That's what you said about the study. I think we've already established my usefulness at finding things you may have missed—it shan't take but a moment."

"It's just a storeroom where Rafe keeps odds and ends." His gaze shifted away from her.

"You don't want me to go inside. Why?"

"I misplaced the key. We can't go in."

"That's no impediment." She knelt in front of the door and plucked a hairpin from her hair. She wedged it inside the lock and jiggled the mechanism until she heard the telltale click. "There. It's unlocked."

DREW WAS UNLOCKED . . . unmoored. His mind still murky. He'd nearly had one of his attacks. The dark specks had started dancing before his eyes, his breathing had grown ragged and then . . . and then she'd placed her palm on his chest.

Her hand over his heart, warming his skin through layers of linen.

The dancing specks had receded. Vision had returned. Her hand over his heart like sunshine on his face.

Their bodies linked.

Her hand warm, melting the ice over his heart. He shook his head, pushing away these dangerous thoughts.

"It's just an ordinary sitting room," she announced.

If Miss Penny didn't examine the room too closely, there would be no harm done. He walked past her. "You're right. Just a storeroom that used to be a sitting room. Ordinary chair. Ordinary lacquered cabinet. Some unremarkable lamps."

"You're acting strangely."

"I'm not."

"There's something you don't want me to see in this room."

"Oh look," he said. "It's a perfectly mundane clock on a completely normal chimneypiece. It says a half hour has passed since I joined you. Should we be getting back to the other house?"

He should have known that wasn't the right tack to take. But if he let her explore, she'd notice the unusual features of the room that he'd discovered during his search this morning.

The reason he'd locked the door. He hadn't wanted her stumbling upon the evidence of Rafe's depravity. Even Drew had been shocked by the contents of the room, and he wasn't easily shocked.

"Beatrice won't come to fetch me for another fifteen minutes. She thinks I want to become better acquainted with you."

"I'd like to become better acquainted with a plate of ham. I'm famished. Aren't you? Let's raid the larder."

She narrowed her eyes. "You're hiding something." She walked around the room. "There's not another secret chamber because there wouldn't be anywhere to put it. And it's sparsely furnished. Red silk on the walls is a bit much. Rather garish, actually."

She dropped her reticule on a low, velvet-cushioned chair.

He cast about for a topic to distract her from opening any of the cabinets. "Speaking of red silk, when I entered her apartments, Miss Flynn was posed like one of the famous portraits of Nell Gwyn, the infamous mistress to Charles the Second, in a red silk negligee. Have you seen the portrait?"

"I should like to visit museums and view scandalous artworks but, as I mentioned, my great-aunt kept me under lock and key while she attempted to drum decorum into my head."

"How did that work for you?" he asked, keeping his expression bland, though he wanted to laugh.

"It didn't. As evidenced by the fact that I'd very much like to share a meal with Miss Flynn."

"Young ladies of good family don't dine with courtesans."

"Why not? It seems to me they might have a lot to teach us about men. About how to control them."

"I don't think you require lessons in controlling men. You seem to know exactly how to wrap everyone you meet around your finger. Take me, for example, I'm not the sort of gentleman to hunt for secret rooms. I prefer hunting hare and pheasants. I have my daily routine, which I never deviate from, and it doesn't include cracking codes or stealing kisses from troublesome young ladies . . ." As he talked, he led her out of the room, relieved that she appeared willing to leave.

She paused in the doorway. "I left my reticule."

"Allow me to fetch—"

"I'll get it." She darted back inside the room and bent over the elongated velvet chair. "How very odd. This chair has mechanical gears along this side. Why would a chair have gears?"

"I've no idea." And that was the truth. He'd noticed the modifications to the furniture but hadn't investigated. As soon as he'd seen the contents of the cabinet, he'd known precisely what this room was used for—and it wasn't used for anything that should be viewed by young ladies.

"I think I hear Beatrice coming," he said.

She ignored him, intent on studying the levers on the side of the chair. "I'm quite adept with mechanisms of all kinds. This appears to be a gear that might raise or lower the chair. An ingenious idea, if one thinks about it. A chair that could work equally well for both tall and short people."

That wasn't exactly the use Lord Rafe put the chair to. "You have your reticule, shall we go?"

"I wonder what happens when I pull on one of these?" she mused.

Drew held his breath, hoping nothing depraved happened. He exhaled. Nothing had happened.

"How odd." She sat down on the chair. "A gear must have a purpose."

"I wouldn't sit there if I were you, Miss Penny. We really should be going."

"It's remarkably comfortable." She leaned her head back against the cushions and laid her arms against the rests. The chair began to move, as if the pressure of her wrists had activated a spring.

Metal bands emerged from underneath the chair arms and legs and closed over her wrists and ankles before she had a chance to move. She stared up at him. "Your Grace. This chair just trapped me."

Drew groaned. "I was afraid something like that might happen."

"Why would a chair have mechanized metal restraints?"

Drew could only conjecture, and what he conjectured was that his brother was a no-good bastard. "Let's free you from those manacles, Miss Penny."

She attempted to free herself but the bands only tightened. She lifted her ankles and thumped them against the metal bands.

Another mechanism ground to life. The top of the chair began to tilt downward, and the bottom to elongate and lift until her legs were higher than her head.

"Get me down from here," yelped Miss Penny.

He sprinted to the chair and attempted to stop it from tilting any further but it just kept going. "I can't stop it."

As the chair rose higher, her skirts slid downward, revealing frilly petticoats and white drawers. He was a man, not a saint. The sight of Miss Penny stretched on the chair with her skirts over her ears was undeniably arousing. She was so perfectly proportioned, all feminine curves and alluring hollows.

Her abundant golden hair had tumbled loose from its pins, and the ends brushed the carpet.

While the sight heated his blood to boiling, the predominant emotion he felt was fury. He was going to kill Rafe. Drew could only imagine what depraved things went on in such a chair. How could he have something like this in the house so close to their mother's house?

"This is a very impolite chair," said Miss Penny, her voice brave but muffled by her skirts. "Please make it stop."

"I'm trying," said Drew, gritting his teeth as he attempted to bodily restrain the chair from moving.

Chapter 16

❧

THE CHAIR STUTTERED to a halt. "Thank you," Mina said. She couldn't see Thorndon because her skirts were over her eyes.

Her skirts were over her eyes.

Which meant he could see her petticoats, her drawers, her ankles . . . damn this impolite chair!

She pressed her thighs together.

"I didn't do that," came the duke's deep voice from somewhere nearby. "I think it reached its maximum tilt. I'll have you down in a moment, Miss Penny. I do apologize. My brother's indecency knows no limit."

"You did attempt to warn me." Why hadn't she listened?

"I swear to you, I didn't know about this infernal chair when I warned you away. I was only thinking of the other things."

"What other things?"

"The contents of the cabinets. What the devil?" he swore under his breath.

"What is it? Your Grace, is something the matter?"

"The lever on the side of the chair, the one you tried earlier. In my agitated state I may have . . . broken it off."

"You may have *what*?"

"Don't panic, Miss Penny. Don't panic. If anyone should come and see you like this I'd be taken to task."

"And forced to marry me by special license."

"Oh my God." Strong fingers slid beneath the metal surrounding her wrist and attempted to force it open. "I'll cut these damned restraints with clippers if I have to."

"Take a deep breath, Your Grace. It sounds to me like you're the one who's panicking."

Panicking at the idea of having to marry her. But then she would never wish to marry him, either. "The lever you broke didn't control the restraints, though it may have made it possible for them to be activated by the weight of my arms and ankles. So there must be another way to open them."

"There is another lever. But it's . . . it's . . ."

"Yes? Wherever it is you'd better try it."

"It's in a sensitive location," he said.

"I don't care. Do what you have to do."

Her breath went shallow and her heart beat wildly as his fingers brushed her inner thighs. Luckily, all the blood in her body was rushing to her head and not to . . . other parts.

"I wish I could do this in a more delicate manner but it's . . . there. I've got it," he said.

Nothing happened except that she experienced a longing for him to touch her again. Where his fingers had accidentally brushed. Her nerves were fraying. "This is the most ridiculous chair. I can't believe anyone would take themselves seriously while using it."

"It's a damned death trap," said Thorndon, fumbling around the sides of the chair, accidentally brushing her thighs with his fingers. "Pardon my language, Miss Penny. But if we don't find a way to free you soon, this could become extremely embarrassing for both of us."

"We're well past embarrassing, don't you think? It's becoming very hot and difficult to breathe under these petticoats. Would you mind lifting them away from my face?"

He rolled her skirts up and tucked them gingerly between her thighs.

She sucked in the sweet air, giddy with relief. The sudden illumination from a nearby lamp made her eyes smart, and rendered Thorndon an indistinct blur, looming over her.

Then a sensuous mouth appeared above a black silk cravat. "Are you all right?" he asked.

"I can breathe better now and my modesty is more protected," she responded.

With her hands stretched over her head and her feet higher than her face, he could not fail to notice her bosom spilling over her bodice. Mina had never felt so vulnerable . . . so exposed. She must be a sight. No doubt her face was as red as a beet.

"I'm going to set you free. I promise." He ran his hands along the sides of the chair. "I don't see or feel any more gears to try."

Perspiration slid down her forehead. "Have you tried directly under the chair?"

He immediately dropped to his knees and ducked underneath the chair.

"There's a series of buttons," he called.

"Good. Try the first one."

The sound of gears beginning to grind. She was saved! Wait . . . no she wasn't. Her ankles were being drawn farther apart. "Not that one!" The slit in her drawers. Everything would be exposed. *Everything*. "Do not, on pain of death, look at me."

"I would never do that. The person who's going to die is Rafe. When I find him, he'll answer for this."

"Press the same button again." Her ankles moved closer together and she breathed a sigh of relief.

"I'm trying the middle one now," he called.

The chair arms began to rotate, taking her arms up with them and over her head. "Not that one either," she groaned.

Her hands moved back down.

"Last one," he said grimly.

"Wait," she said. "Don't press it yet. If it controls the restraints, I could tumble out and hit my head. We'll have to think of a way to do this. You could pile cushions beneath my head."

"My arms are long enough to reach the button and be ready to catch you if you start to slide."

Of course they were.

A flood of relief swamped her mind as the restraints snapped open and began to recede back into the chair. She slid down the velvet cushions.

"I'll catch you, Miss Penny," Thorndon said.

She slid the rest of the way into the cradle of his arms, and settled against his chest, her weight supported by his body. She rested her head against his chest, breathing heavily.

He stroked her hair. "It's all over now. You're safe."

Safe and surrounded by his strong arms.

She clung to his chest, her shoulders shaking with . . . laughter. She had no idea where it came from. It just welled up inside her and had to come out.

"Are you crying, Wilhelmina?" he asked, tilting her chin toward him.

"I'm not . . . crying." She was laughing so hard now she was nearly crying, though. "It's just so . . . perverse, isn't it? They say curiosity killed the cat. Well, in my case, curiosity strung the cat up arse over elbows."

He laughed, a rumbling sound that struck a chord in her heart. "I'm glad you're unharmed." His arms tightened around her. "No more exploring my brother's secret chambers."

"You tried to warn me and so did Crankshaw." She wiped her eyes with her sleeve. "He said there were things in this house that would make me blush."

She rested her cheek against the hollow between his neck and shoulder. She had a view of his starched collar and simple cravat.

Shadow of a beard across his sharp-angled jawline.

His hand moved to her back, sliding over her spine. Soothing her and at the same time awakening a deep need to be closer. Much closer.

Soon they would separate, disengage. Soon he

would become distant again, but right now he was all around her. Strong. Caring.

Honorable. Too honorable to even look at her while she was trapped on the chair, yet she knew the taste of him, the things his lips did to her, the wicked desires he inspired.

"Being stretched upon that chair may have given me ideas, Your Grace."

His hand stopped moving. "No more ideas, Miss Penny. Are you able to stand?"

"Not yet." A small lie, though her legs did feel quite wobbly. "And please call me Mina."

"Not a very British name."

"My mother was half Swedish. They thought I would be a boy and had already chosen the name Wilhelm."

"And I'm Drew."

"I couldn't possibly call you Drew."

"Why not? I've seen your frilly undergarments."

She tilted her head up. "You have, haven't you? Did seeing me on the impolite chair give you any . . . ideas?"

"Of course it did." His voice lowered. Roughened. "I'm only a man. And you're so beautiful, Mina. I don't think you know how truly beautiful you are."

"I'm seeing this room with entirely new eyes," she murmured. She pointed at a velvet-padded wooden stool in the shape of an inverted V. "That's not an ordinary stool is it? No one would sit on a pointed edge like that. So it's for something other than sitting upon."

"Probably." His voice held an amused edge.

She liked the way his throat buzzed under her ear when he talked. She wanted to keep him talking.

Her mind flew through the possibilities. "You . . . fit your knees into those hollows in the lower cushions, your belly goes over the cushioned hump, and your head hangs down nearly to the floor. Which would . . . put your bum in the air. Oh dear."

He chuckled. "An astute supposition. That's a spanking stool."

"Why would anyone want to be spanked?"

"There are some that say that chastisement causes blood to rush to the region which creates lascivious sensations. There are pleasure houses catering to such tastes."

Her education continued. "Oh, of course. I've heard of such places," she said breezily, though she hadn't, and never could have imagined them. "I might like to be spanked," she said boldly. "But only very softly."

An audible hiss of breath sounded above her head.

He shifted beneath her, bringing her into a sudden awareness of the effects of her teasing.

"I might like to spank you," he said. His hand moved lower, to the small of her back, and lower still. He cupped her bum with his palm.

She squirmed on his lap, moving forward to give his hands better access. Excitement pulsed through her body, gathering in the tips of her breasts, the pit of her belly, the juncture between her thighs.

She remembered how he'd held her by the

wrists in the shed and how the feeling of being under his control had been both dangerous and arousing.

"To willingly lose control when you know that it's safe to do is exciting for some," he said. "Not for me."

"You never lose control, do you?" She played with the soft hair at the nape of his neck. Traced the outer edge of his ears. She wanted him to kiss her so badly.

She wanted to make him lose control.

"I've worked hard to cultivate utter control over my emotions and my life," he said.

"I know something about you." She tilted her lips to his ear. "A secret."

His face turned until their lips were nearly touching. "What's my secret?"

"You were afraid to go behind the bookshelf."

His body became even more rigid beneath her. "No, I wasn't."

"I could see that you were scared." She placed her hand over his heart, as she had earlier. "Does it have something to do with your kidnapping?" Her uncle had warned her never to speak of it, but she wanted to know more.

"Has anyone ever told you that curiosity killed the cat?" he asked, attempting a lighthearted tone.

"Tell me what happened," she said. "Don't shut me out, as you tend to do. Don't remain cold."

He remained silent for a few heartbeats and she thought he wasn't going to answer the question, but then he drew in a breath. "I was kidnapped when I was fifteen, taken from Eton, and held for

ransom in a small ship anchored near London."
His voice emotionless and flat, as though he were
reciting someone else's history. Someone long
dead and buried. "So the threat to Beatrice is personal. I'll never let the same thing happen to her.
Never."

She shuddered. "It must have been so frighten-
ing," she said.

FEAR SQUATTED IN the center of your chest and
choked the breath out of your body. Fear had the
taste of watery oats and sour milk.

The thing about fear was that it never really left
you. It was your companion for life, always there,
waiting to take control when you weren't vigilant
enough.

The other thing about fear was that you never
admitted it to anyone. Not if you were a man.

Not if you were a duke.

"You don't have to talk about it if you don't
want to," she said.

"I never talk about it."

"I understand."

She did understand and she wouldn't push him
to admit his weakness. She'd just been through the
experience of being trapped, her limbs splayed
out, and her skirts falling over her eyes.

She'd been vulnerable, and she'd been scared.
He'd heard it in her voice, though she'd also been
brave. Making a joke of it, trusting him to help
free her.

"Miss Penny, the sight of you in those manacles." He swallowed. It had brought everything

back. He'd been desperate to free her, clawing at the irons like an animal. "It reminded me of the kidnapping. I'm so sorry that you had to endure being trapped for even a few minutes."

"You were trapped for days," she said.

"Ten days. One of my wrists was chained to a ring in the wall. The other left free. I scratched marks on the rough wooden walls of the ship for every day of my captivity."

"Who kidnapped you, and why?" she asked. Her eyes held only curiosity, not pity.

He couldn't believe he was telling her this. But she'd been so brave and she listened so intently. The desire to unburden himself was overpowering.

Not everything. He couldn't tell her everything, but he could admit one small slice of his fear, just a swallow, and then he'd restore order to this room, this conversation, and to his life.

"My captor was a tenant farmer seeking revenge on my father after he lost his leasehold. He was desperate. He kidnapped me to put food on the table for his six children."

"How did they capture you?"

"I was at Eton attending the celebration for King William's birthday. There were speeches, cricket, and a procession of boats. Large crowds on the banks of the river. A messenger approached me and said that my mother had been taken poorly and I was to come with him immediately. I didn't think too hard about it. If Mother was sick, I must go to her. I climbed into the carriage willingly. He stuffed a gag in my mouth and placed a blindfold over my eyes so that I didn't know where he was taking me."

He stopped talking. One small admission—not a damned book.

He glanced down at her and their gazes met. The connection and the release of it crashed through his mind like a chunk of granite cliff breaking off and falling into the sea.

It felt *good* to talk to Wilhelmina Penny. More than good . . . it felt necessary.

And that scared him more than entering the shadowy chasm behind the bookshelf. She wanted to know more about him. She might even learn to care for him.

And he knew what happened to people who cared for him. He disappointed them. Left without a word of good-bye and stayed away for five years.

He withdrew, retreated, abandoned them because everything in London, even his family, reminded him of the dark memories.

Walls the color of a bleeding, beating heart.

Memories of his weakness, his vulnerability. He'd needed help and no one had come.

He could feel one of his attacks coming on, the drumbeat of dread advancing from the past.

This is why he couldn't talk about it—couldn't show his vulnerability.

He might lose control. He had to warn her.

"Ever since I escaped I've been damaged, Mina." Call her Mina now. Not Miss Penny. They were here together in this giant bleeding heart. They had to get out. "I don't feel things in the same way other people do. I felt nothing when my father died. I don't know how to grieve."

He'd had to find ways of shielding himself, of managing the irrational fears that gripped his mind.

He'd given his warning and now this connection had to be severed.

"If you ever want to talk more about it, one of my talents is listening," she said earnestly. "I've had a lot of time to think about grief and the absence of grief. When my parents died, the chief emotion I felt was anger. They were always traveling—and I was hurt and angry that they'd died before I had a chance to really know them."

"But you're not damaged, Miss Penny. You're all shining eyes and open heart. You wear your heart on your sleeve."

That was why he had to end this. She hadn't built defensive walls around her heart and he hoped she would never need to.

And she was uniquely adept at threatening his defenses.

He set her off his lap and rose to his feet. He extended his hand. "It's time to go and find my sister and forget you ever saw this room."

"I don't think I'll ever be able to unsee it," she said with a bright smile. "And you know I'm not going to leave until I look inside the lacquered cabinet."

"Please don't." They had to leave now.

"Just a little peek." She tossed a cheeky grin back at him as she walked to the cabinet and opened Pandora's box.

She stared at the contents. Then she turned toward him, jaw slack. "Why? Why would Lord Rafe use one of *those*?" She pointed at the row of ivory and polished wood phalluses of assorted sizes and shapes. "Doesn't he have one of his own?"

"I assume so. At least he did when we were boys and went swimming together in lakes."

"Then *why*?"

"My guess would be that he entertains multiple visitors at once and requires reinforcements." Or they could be for Rafe's use—but he wasn't going to mention such unmentionable subjects.

The sight of her staring at a row of hard, shiny phalluses was something he would never be able to unsee.

This was so far beyond inappropriate. The erotic accoutrements, the press of her palm against his heart, the desire to confess his buried secrets, share his pain . . . he had to lock it all tightly away.

She threw him off-balance and then, conversely, she seemed to be the only thing that could save him.

"Pardon me, Your Grace." Crankshaw hovered outside the door.

Mina slammed the cabinet shut.

"Yes, what is it, Crankshaw?" Drew asked.

"I apprehended a raggedy urchin preparing to throw this through your window." He held up a paper-wrapped brick. "Afraid the little rapscallion slipped through my fingers and made his escape before I had a chance to question him."

"How old was he? What clothing was he wearing?" Mina asked.

"About ten, I'd wager. Proper little guttersnipe. All wrapped in tattered, greasy rags with his face covered in soot."

"Well, give it here," said Drew, holding out his hand.

"I caught only a glimpse of the words. I saw nothing. No details." Crankshaw handed him the brick. "It's an attempt at blackmail. Not that I would presume to give you any advice, but don't hand over any cash, Your Grace. No good can come of it."

Crankshaw left. Drew set the brick on a table, unwrapped the paper, and spread it out beside a lamp. Mina moved to stand beside him.

Your brother is engaged to marry a HARLOT. The price of her name is two hundred in silver. Meet me behind the orchestra when they light the lamps at VAUXHALL GARDENS tomorrow evening. Come ALONE.

"Lord Rafe is engaged." Mina sat down in an armchair after checking to make certain that there were no visible gears.

"Troublesome, to be sure," said Drew, "but I was expecting something worse. I don't know, my mind ran away with me. Criminal activity, murder, I imagined it all."

MINA HAD IMAGINED many things, but marriage hadn't been one of them. Lord Rafe had been *her* escape route. Her future. Her claim to a life of adventure.

"This is extortion," Drew said, pacing in front of the fireplace. "Plain and simple. Now I know what Rafe's about to do—make an injudicious match. Someone, the woman's servant, or possibly a relative, found out about their plans and thought they'd extract some money from me. Once I have the name of the woman, I can stop the marriage. It's worth the price."

"Extortionists are never satisfied with only one payment when they think they can force another. And something else is troubling me. Why did Lord Rafe leave London?"

"Maybe he left to escape his fiancée," said Drew.

"Then why did he say he's going after the real threat? I think we'll find answers when we crack the code in his journal." She still believed that Lord Rafe was pursuing Le Triton. Capturing Sir Malcolm's mortal enemy would be the perfect way for Lord Rafe to restore himself to the inner ranks of her uncle's elite spy force.

It was likely that Lord Rafe's betrothal was only one piece of the puzzle. He'd become engaged to someone useful to his spy work in order to wheedle information from her.

"The author of this note is the one threatening to kidnap my sister," said Drew, his voice hard and merciless. "I need answers about Rafe but I also need to know that Beatrice will be safe."

Mina nodded. "I don't think the author intends any actual harm. The venue was chosen carefully.

Vauxhall Gardens. It's a public gathering place where the high and low classes mingle without raising any eyebrows. I would be surprised if the extortionist revealed himself—he will probably send a trusted messenger. And so should you."

"Send someone else to make the exchange? I don't think so. I want to contain the knowledge of this affair."

"Send me," she said, the idea striking her as the perfect way for her to gather more information about Lord Rafe's motivations for leaving.

The shock on Drew's face was almost comical. "You must be joking."

"If I give them the money and accept the information, you can be watching from the shadows. You'll trail the person as they leave—find out where they go, whom they speak with."

"I can have my manservant do that."

"Your manservant will be watching over Beatrice. You said we were in this together now. We're linked like a chain of daisies, one stem split and the next threaded inside until there's a chain."

"A daisy chain. Interesting choice. Are you sure you're not a country lass?"

"Absolutely not." She had to make him understand that this was the life she had chosen and she wasn't afraid of danger. "Since I arrived at Sir Malcolm's home he's wanted me to lead a quiet, secluded life and to be happy and content with being his secretary. I thought you'd be just like him, but you're not. You listen to me. You asked my opinion about the author of the first letter. I think you value my assistance."

"Well you did find a secret chamber behind my bookshelf and a mysterious coded diary. You're obviously far cleverer at that sort of thing than I am."

"It's distressingly charming and refreshing to meet a man who doesn't think that I should be sitting in the parlor with an embroidery hoop. Why are you so liberal-minded about such things?"

His lip quirked. "It could have something to do with the fact that you pressed a pistol to my chest the first night I met you. You're a lady not only equipped to defend herself, but ready to lead the charge."

"Why thank you."

"Also, I sensed from the moment I met you that nothing I said would hold any sway over you and that I may as well go with the current instead of fighting it."

"Very astute of you," she said.

"Now, if you don't mind, I've had enough secrets for the moment, Mina. Let's go and find my mother, my sister, and your great-aunt and tell them we're all visiting Vauxhall Gardens tomorrow evening."

"Do you think we should bring everyone with us?" she asked. She'd imagined a more intimate evening. Maybe she would even sneak out to meet him there wearing a costume and a mask.

"I do," he said firmly. "I need to keep Beatrice with me at all times. And obviously you and I require more than one chaperone."

Chapter 17

IT'S AN ENCHANTED FAIRYLAND.

Mina tried not to gawk at the glittering sights of Vauxhall Gardens like a country maiden at her first fair. Tried, and failed. She hadn't quite shed her country skin yet—she was awed by everything she saw: the performers reenacting famous battle scenes, the orchestra playing from the second tier of the round building decorated like a jeweled crown and topped by the royal arms and crest.

Red, violet, and blue lamps hung in the trees, clustered together to form bouquets of flowers with leaves of luminous green.

Patterned metal lanterns sent golden stars and moons dancing across the archways and the faces of the revelers.

She sat on a bench next to Beatrice and the duchess in a private supper box, open at the front and hung with paintings of rural scenes and men playing cricket. Drew had seen an acquaintance and left for a chat before supper was served, leaving his manservant, Corbyn, to stand sentry outside of their box.

Grizzy had stayed home, complaining of a sick headache, but she'd made sure that Mina was prepared for her first public outing with the duke and his family.

"It's an honor to be invited by the duke and his mother," Grizzy had told Mina as she supervised her toilette. "You'll be the envy of every marriageable lady at Vauxhall. The queen of the evening."

Grizzy had chosen a gown with a silver-threaded overlay meant to sparkle in the lamplight.

Mina had her mother's oil-of-roses perfume behind her ears and in the valley between her breasts. Not that anyone would come close enough to her bosom to smell the candy-sweet scent with a lemony finish.

Especially not Thorndon. There could be none of that.

He was still the man her uncle wanted to force her to marry.

Yet he was so much more than that.

He knew what it meant to feel helpless, to feel trapped and alone. He was far more fascinating and complex than your average arrogant duke.

Which changed nothing.

Douse the desire. Squelch the sympathy. They were on a serious mission tonight.

Drew had the silver in a leather pouch. Mina had her pocket pistol. During the lighting of the lamps, they'd hand over the money in exchange for the information.

The danger of what she and Drew must do tonight, the exciting prospect of answers and subsequent action—she'd been dreaming and scheming about intrigues such as this her whole life.

Moving with freedom among the unfamiliar and intoxicating sights of London.

Ladies in vivid silk gowns with wavering ostrich plumes in their hair promenaded on the arms of gentlemen in cutaway tailcoats and white trousers.

In the distance the famed gardens extended, filled with exhibitions and novelties, tightrope walkers and pantomimes. Lovers sought shadowy walkways and secluded groves.

"The problem with Vauxhall is that these oil lamps strung in the trees aren't bright enough for me to read by," said Beatrice.

"You bring a book with you everywhere you go," complained the duchess. "I don't think it's too much to ask for you to forego your precious reading for one evening. Who knows, if you removed those spectacles and lifted your nose out of your novels every now and then, you might even find a husband. Oh, is that Viscount Fitzbart? Perhaps he knows where my second son has disappeared to—I haven't seen Rafe in days. Excuse me for a moment." She rose and hastened after the viscount.

"Where can Rafe be?" asked Beatrice.

That was the question of the evening. Mina searched for Drew in the crowd, as if the sights of Vauxhall paled without him by her side.

"Do you think Rafe left London for a spell?" asked Beatrice. "I wonder if he took a foreign mistress? He could be in the graceful arms of a French actress."

"Perhaps." Mina was fairly certain that Lord

Rafe's sudden journey had nothing to do with a mistress and everything to do with espionage.

She caught sight of Drew in the distance and her heart flip-flopped. He stared at her as he approached, holding her gaze, a secret smile on his lips meant only for her.

"I ordered a Burgundy instead of that diluted arrack punch," said Drew, returning to the table and sitting across from Mina. "Where's Mother?" he asked Beatrice.

"She chased after Fitzbart—thought he might know where Rafe's gone."

"I already questioned him. He knows nothing. Ah. Here's the wine."

A waiter held out the bottle for Drew to inspect.

Mina accepted a glass and took a small sip. The earthy fullness of it surprised her. She drank more. "Cherries," she said. "Cinnamon." She sniffed the glass. "Worn leather."

"Leather?" laughed Drew.

"Saddle leather. Warmed from body heat."

He swallowed more wine. "I can taste the cherries but nothing so fanciful as leather. Maybe a hint of coffee? Coffee ground with rose petals."

"Strong, yet delicate."

He raised his glass to her. "Like you, Miss Penny."

If you like the taste of roses, you might try my bosom. Wayward mind, wandering down forbidden walkways.

He stared at her with something hungry and untamed in his eyes. He'd said that he was frozen and he didn't feel appropriate emotions. But his gaze was heated.

It made her conscious of every movement she made—the angle of her fingers on the stem of the wineglass, the press of her breasts against the edge of her corset.

Her reaction to him was impossible to suppress and defied all logic. It wasn't something she could control. She longed to touch him.

Tip the brim of his beaver hat up until it toppled off his head. Tear off her gloves. Bury her fingers in his thick, dark hair.

His hands had been between her thighs when she'd been trapped on the chair.

Huge, roughened hands.

She'd wanted them to wander.

He'd become the forbidden, exciting prize and she wanted to drag him off into the shadows and have her way with him, or let him have his way with her, or a combination of both.

"What are you thinking about, Miss Penny?" Drew asked.

Getting lost with you in the woods and never finding our way home.

"I approve of this wine," she replied.

Beatrice watched them with a satisfied little smile on her lips. "Who needs a novel when a romantic scene is being enacted before my eyes?"

Mina dropped her gaze to her glass. Had she been so obvious?

"You're causing quite a stir, Mina." Beatrice nodded her head at a nearby supper box where a group of ladies was watching them. "If looks could kill, Lady Millicent would be a murderess. It makes me so happy. Carry on, you two." She waved a hand at the bottle. "More wine. More compliments."

Drew cleared his throat. "There's a group of the new Metropolitan Police Service in their long blue coats. I heard they were organized last year by Robert Peel as the first professional police force. They have a new headquarters that backs onto Great Scotland Yard Street."

"Is that so?" Beatrice giggled softly. "Very neat change of subject, brother dear."

Mina approved of the new topic. "Will they replace the Bow Street Patrols? What kind of weapons will they carry?"

"I'll go ask them," said Drew. "I see a man by the name of Langley whom I knew before I left London. It appears he's risen to the rank of inspector. I'll report back." He rose and made a short bow. "Miss Penny." He narrowed his eyes. "Beatrice."

He walked toward the group of policemen.

"I frightened him away," said Beatrice. "Don't worry, he'll be back."

"I'm not worried."

Lady Millicent left her seat and headed in the direction Drew had taken. Now who was the obvious one?

Silly, frivolous thing to love, being the girl the duke had chosen, the one whose wine he poured.

Mina knew he hadn't chosen her. She was the thorn in the beast's paw that he couldn't shake loose, here by dint of persuasion and subterfuge.

But no one else knew that.

She looked like the chosen one. The queen of the night, as Grizzy had crowned her.

In a few more nights, he'll be all yours, ladies.

Though there was something possessive in her that wanted to claim him.

Eyes off. He's mine.

The two positions grappled in her mind, vying for dominance. It didn't matter if she wanted to grab him and kiss him every time she saw him. He was the road to respectable rustication and convenient abandonment, and she was searching for the road to daring international intrigue.

Stories from his boyhood, the strong circle of his arms, his wicked kiss . . . none of it brought her one step closer to setting her plan for her future in motion.

But it did bring her closer to finding Drew. The real Drew, the one she sensed underneath his gruff, taciturn exterior. There was pain in his eyes and a depth she could detect but couldn't reach. He obviously couldn't trust anyone because of the kidnapping.

But he'd trusted her enough to tell her some of the details. And he trusted her to be with him here tonight, to help him hand over the money.

There was a tightrope stretched between them and if either one of them lost control they would both fall.

It felt as though everyone in the other boxes along the colonnade, every member of the orchestra, every person promenading in the gardens must be aware of the tension between them.

"MISS PENNY, IS IT?" asked a cultured female voice.

"Yes." Mina turned to find Lady Millicent standing near her. Drew had taken Beatrice to see a fountain with a light show, but Mina had lingered in front of the orchestra, enjoying the dulcet, lilting tones of Miss Doyle, an Irish soprano.

"I'm Lady Millicent Granger." She pronounced her name as if the whole world should know and acknowledge her consequence. She was a beauty, to be sure, with fine green eyes, radiant skin, and honey-colored ringlets piled fetchingly atop her head and dotted with strands of lustrous pearls.

"How do you do?" asked Mina politely, immediately on her guard. This was the lady who had always been horrid to Lady Beatrice, the one who'd set her eye on Mina's prize.

Not my prize.

"Oh, simply divine." Lady Millicent smiled. "Are you enjoying the gardens?"

"They're magical, are they not?"

"It's all paint and paste. Merely a clever illusion of grandeur," said Lady Millicent. "I shouldn't want to see it in the harsh light of day."

Worldly. Sophisticated. Elegant. Lady Millicent was everything Mina aspired to become and yet . . . her eyes were cold and her smile felt more like a sneer.

"It's my first time," Mina explained.

"Oh, believe me, I'm well aware of that. I've been doing some research, you see. I know all about you, Miss Wilhelmina Penny, ward of Sir Malcolm, of Sutton Hall, formerly of Berwick Street, London."

"Er . . . research?"

"Know thine enemies, Miss Penny. One of my mottos."

"Are we enemies, Lady Millicent?"

"We are." Lady Millicent kept her voice pitched low, so that only Mina could hear. "Don't think you can arrive fresh from the countryside, with no education, no accomplishments, and claim the greatest prize on the marriage mart. I've worked too hard for this. I was born to become a duchess, and who are you? A nobody."

"Do you feel threatened by me, Lady Millicent?"

"Ha. Of course not. I only want you to know that I recognize your tactics. If I had known that Thorndon would arrive in London so suddenly, I certainly would have befriended the sister. Don't think I don't know about what you're doing to-night."

For a brief moment Mina thought she might be referring to the exchange of coins for information, but then she reminded herself that Lady Millicent would have no way of knowing about any of that. "Whatever do you mean, Lady Millicent?"

"Befriending Beastly Beatrice to insinuate yourself into the duke's inner sphere."

Mina's body went still. "Don't call her that."

"Everyone knows she only has half a pretty face and half her wits as well."

"You need to stop talking now," said Mina.

"Or what, you'll slap me in full view of everyone? My, wouldn't that cause a scene."

Mina's fists clenched. Lady Millicent was goading her, taunting her. She wanted her to make a scene.

Stay calm. Walk away.

Mina drew herself up to her full height, though

she was inches shorter than her statuesque opponent. "If you were a man, Lady Millicent, I would throw down my glove and challenge you to a duel. Since you are a lady, I shall turn the other cheek and walk away."

Lady Millicent burst into laughter. "A duel? You can't be in earnest."

"I'm deadly in earnest. I've a pistol in my reticule."

Lady Millicent laughed harder. Heads swiveled toward them. A lovely brunette lady wearing glowing pink silk approached. "What's so funny, Millie?" she asked.

"Miss Penny wants to challenge me to . . . a duel, Chloe!" gasped Lady Millicent between giggles.

"Hush," said Mina. People were beginning to stare.

"Says she has a . . . pistol in her . . . reticule!" More peals of laughter. Lady Millicent was deliberately causing a scene.

"Petticoats and pistols at dawn," said Chloe. "What shall we call her, Millie?"

"Let me see . . . I've got it! Beastly Beatrice and her defender, the Dueling Debutante. A match made in misfit heaven." They dissolved into giggles again.

Dueling Debutante. They'd spread the name throughout the *ton*, repeating the story of her challenge, embellishing it, making her out to be a hotheaded hoyden.

She *was* a hotheaded hoyden, she'd always been one, always had trouble controlling her temper.

So many things made her angry—being locked out, held at arm's length, laughed at . . .

Bursts of anger and humiliation sparked in her chest.

She must remain calm. She shouldn't let them goad her into a scene.

"I've always said you can take the girl out of the countryside," said Lady Millicent.

"But you can't take the countryside out of the girl," rejoined Chloe.

People stared at them. Mina's face heated. She would probably break out into red blotches soon. She always did when she was angry.

She didn't belong here.

She didn't fit into their world and they could sense her otherness, these polished ladies with sharp tongues.

The sound of their laughter echoed in her mind until she wanted to scream. Before she did something she would truly regret, she spun around and dashed away into the welcome darkness of the gardens.

She must be able to exist in this world, as her mother had, disguise her emotions, learn to be witty and elegant. She had to learn those things because that's what a spy did and she'd never be a good spy if she couldn't disguise her emotions.

She'd thought she was the queen of the night.

But she was really the court jester.

DREW SAW MINA run into the gardens by herself. It was nearly time for their assignation with the extortionist. What was she doing?

"Stay here with Corbyn," he said to Beatrice.

"Gladly, brother dear," replied Beatrice with a knowing glint behind her spectacles. "Run after Miss Penny. And please don't come back for at least a half hour, is that clear?"

"Not very subtle, sister dear. You're trying to push us together."

"It's selfish, really. I'm doing it because I don't want to lose you again. I think Mina's your best hope. If anyone can melt that cold heart of yours, it's Mina."

Drew walked swiftly away and broke into a run when he was hidden from the central grove by tall trees whose branches met overhead in shadowy archways.

He caught a glimpse of silver through the trees.

"Why did you run off like that?" he asked when he reached Mina.

She wiped her cheek with an ungloved hand. "I wanted a stroll through the trees."

Her gown was shot-silk in a silvery color that matched her eyes. There were ruby eardrops at her ears.

He had to touch her or he would die.

He caught her fingers in his hand. "Something upset you."

Give me a chance to defend you, to loosen some of this knot of tension coiled in my chest.

"It was nothing, really. Someone made a snide remark and I lost my temper. I'm not as cool and detached as you are."

"It's not in your nature. You're passionate. I like that about you." He liked how she attacked life and how she didn't hide her emotions—he liked it too much. "Was it Lady Millicent? I saw you speaking with her."

She nodded. "She feels threatened by me, so she lashed out. We all lash out when we feel cornered."

"Why would she see you as a threat?"

"Think about it, Drew. We're here together in public. It looks to her as though you're showing a preference for me."

"Oh, I see. I suppose it could appear that way." Because he'd invited her to Vauxhall with his family. Because he couldn't take his eyes off of her.

He liked the way she made his sister's eyes shine and brought her out of her shell.

When his mother looked at Mina, he could practically see the visions of plump infants parading across her mind, chubby little fingers grasping her finger, a babyish voice calling her "Grandmama."

When Mina was nearby he couldn't look at anything else. He found himself smiling for no reason. He'd caught himself in the glass before he left this evening with an unfamiliar curve to his lips.

How had she circumvented his defenses so easily, and so swiftly?

He was accustomed to control in all things. Control over his body, particularly his lips. He decided when to smile—and it wasn't a decision made often.

She forced him to smile, to see the joy and absurdity in life. It was her boisterousness, her unpredictability. It should have set him on guard but instead it made him smile.

There was magic left in London. Full-bodied French wine on the tongue. A symphony carried on a summer's breeze.

Mina's eyes filled with wonder as she drank in the sights.

"I'm rash and impulsive," she said. "My uncle was always trying to force me to be more circumspect. Oh, I wish I didn't care what people thought of me. You don't give a damn, do you?"

"I wouldn't say that. When they call me half mad, it stings, even though there's some truth there. I'm not whole, Mina. I haven't been since the kidnapping. When I was a rake, London approved. They understood me then, they were able to classify me. I was fulfilling the right role. But now that I live in seclusion they think I'm mad for giving everything up—everything that they aspire to. They don't understand something so they vilify it. London craves villains."

They couldn't comprehend why someone would give up the things that everyone else wanted in life—the easy access to opulence, the sycophancy, the power.

It wasn't a true power. He'd given up trying to change things through Parliament.

Now he worked from within the agricultural system, one cottager at a time.

"Lady Millicent chose her words carefully, to wound me, but I allowed her barbs to reach their target."

"You're not impervious, you're sensitive and you feel things deeply. It's nothing to be ashamed of."

"I want to say the right things, to make the right impression, but awkward speech just flies from my lips sometimes. You have a laconic way of speaking, almost as if you think your words aren't that important. That whatever you say will be the right thing to say. But then titled gentlemen are born with an innate sense of worth, of their right to be in the world, and to occupy a large space in the world."

"I try to always say exactly what I mean. My words may be sparse but they'll never be false."

Her gaze moved to the treetops. "You'll probably hear my new nickname soon. Everyone will call me the Dueling Debutante. I may have insinuated that I wanted to challenge Lady Millicent to a duel."

Drew snorted. "Oh Lord. Mina. You do know how to make an impression."

She grinned ruefully. "I'm not denying the suitability of the moniker. But I feel stupid for playing into her hands. I must learn to be more controlled and detached."

"Please don't." He touched her chin. "Don't ever change. You have such an expressive face. Your every emotion scrolls across it like a magic lantern show."

"Lantern show," she repeated.

"You're lit from within, Mina." He traced the line of one of her eyebrows.

He wanted to kiss her so badly. Wasn't that what dimly lit, unchaperoned garden paths were for?

A loud whistle sounded in the distance. They were alone.

"They're lighting the lamps," he said.

A thousand oil lamps, touched by cotton-wool fuses, the flame passing from one lamp to the next, illuminating the trees.

Dimming the stars.

His heart touched by her fuse, consumed by her flame.

He stroked her lower lip with his thumb.

"Drew." She clasped his hands. *"They're lighting the lamps."*

The money. The name of Rafe's fiancée. The reason they were here.

"Devil take it, Mina," he said. "We have to hurry."

Chapter 18

MINA TUGGED HER cloak over her eyes, covering her hair, her gown. Everyone's eyes were on the glittering lamps, the magical effect of so many lights bursting to life nearly simultaneously.

"I shouldn't be allowing you to do this," Drew said as they approached the back of the round orchestra building.

There was a sheltered grove of trees not far from the building. That would be where the extortionist waited.

"You're not allowing me to do anything, Drew," she insisted. "We came to the decision together, remember? We agreed that I'm the logical choice to hand over the coins since no one will see me as a threat and everything will be swift and easy. He said to come alone. If he thinks that you've alerted the watch or brought your guard, he'll run and we won't have the name."

"I changed my mind. This is too perilous for you. I will make the exchange."

"You'll follow him out, remember? Observe his actions. See if he talks to anyone, which direction he heads. Or did you want to trade roles?"

Drew kept shaking his head back and forth, his brow creased. "This isn't right."

"Stop worrying, please. You'll be watching. If anything goes wrong, you can rescue me. Not that I'll require rescuing. And please don't reveal yourself unless you absolutely must."

"You'll stay behind that tree until I return," he said, pointing out a large oak tree nearby.

She liked it when he used that rough and caring tone like granulated honey.

"I promise, Drew. I'll be waiting for you to return."

"I still don't like it."

"I know it's difficult for you to relinquish control, to trust someone." She brushed her fingers over his collar. "But we have an alliance now. We work as a partnership. I seek freedom from my uncle's control, you want to protect Beatrice, and we both need to find Lord Rafe."

His chest rose and fell with his breathing. "If you change your mind, Mina, all you have to do is signal me and I'll come forward."

"I'll whistle, would that be a good signal?"

"Yes. Whistle and I'll come running."

"Don't come running, that will startle him. Walk slowly and steadily toward us, talking all the while."

"Very well. I feel better about this plan."

"Don't worry. Everything will go smoothly." He handed her the heavy bag of coins and took his place behind the tree. She moved into the circular grove of trees. It was quite dark here.

Several people moved nearby, couples walking arm in arm. She hovered in the shadows, the bag of coins in one hand and her pistol, only loosely covered by the velvet of her reticule, in the other.

A tall man garbed all in gray approached. A shiver passed over her.

" 'e sent a girl?" the man asked with clear disbelief.

"What's your name, sir?" she asked bravely.

"D'you think I'll tell you that, girl?" She couldn't see his face clearly, but she judged him to be about thirty years of age and accustomed to hard labor. His face was weathered and his nose reddened from drink.

"No, but it can't hurt to ask."

"I could just grab that sack of coins and be gone."

"You could, but I'd shoot you in the back of your knee as you ran." She revealed the nose of her pistol. "I assure you that I know how to use this." Her hand was trembling so badly that the pistol visibly shook.

Fear closed her throat. She hadn't expected to be so afraid.

She'd been training for this, planning for it and now, faced with walking into a truly dangerous situation, everything seized up inside her and she could barely breathe. It was because she knew too much.

She knew about the agents who had died in the field. Died for their king and country.

"You'll shoot me in the middle of Vauxhall?" the man scoffed. "I don't think so."

Control yourself. Project strength and confidence. "I'll maim you and then I'll take back the coins and melt into the shadows, leaving you lying on the ground bleeding. No one would suspect a young lady of being the one with the pistol. Now, do you have the information, or don't you?"

He spat on the ground. "What guarantee do I have that you'll hand over the coins?"

She held up the bag of coins in one hand and her pistol in the other. She shook the bag and the coins clinked together.

His eyes narrowed with greed.

She avoided glancing in Drew's direction, but knowing that he was there gave her strength. "You give me the name and I'll give you the coins."

"I have my orders. I'm to hand over the note at the same time you hand me the coins."

"Orders from whom?"

"D'you think I would tell you that?"

"All right. On my count, then. And don't think I can't shoot you in the time it takes me to read the note. One. Two."

She held out the coins. He raised a scrap of paper.

"Three."

They made the exchange.

She glanced at the paper. *Olivia Lachance, proprietress of the Princess Eve.*

The man backed away, eyeing her reticule, then briskly walked away.

Drew moved after him stealthily, keeping to the trees.

Mina collapsed against a tree trunk, letting out a ragged breath.

Until now, her dabbling in espionage had all been conducted at a distance, from the safety of Uncle Malcolm's guarded stronghold and training grounds.

Solving puzzles, finding the codes within the ciphers, recognizing patterns, piecing together information, experimenting with weaponry, all worthy pursuits and all . . . safe.

Very, very safe.

She couldn't be afraid. A spy knew no fear.

Some of the dedicated spies her uncle handled had been indoctrinated from a young age at a secret spy boarding school. The Duke of Ravenwood had attended the school. She'd heard it said that he entered school a normal, healthy boy, teasing and laughing and charming, despite the recent death of his father, and that he'd become a hardened man, tough and ruthless, without a conscience or a soul.

She'd seen her mother through ten-year-old eyes. To Mina she'd been a laughing, vibrant vision of loveliness sweeping into her life and then twirling back out again. But she knew that her mother and father had been spies in wartime. She'd read her diary.

Her mother had killed an enemy during the war. It had been kill or be killed.

Could Mina become that person? And if she couldn't become tough and hard, then who would she become? The thought sent panic spiraling through her mind. She'd been so focused on one idea: becoming a spy like her mother.

The tree branches above her swayed in a sudden wind like grasping fingers.

She couldn't be afraid. She simply couldn't. If she were scared of danger, then the entire premise of her future would collapse as easily as a stack of cards.

Her reticule fell to the ground. She leaned her head back against the tree trunk. The air was cool but there wasn't enough of it in her lungs and her cheeks felt hot.

She undid the buttons of her pelisse. Where was Drew? Why hadn't he come back yet?

A fresh surge of fear swamped her mind until Drew entered the grove of trees.

She'd never been so happy to see someone in her life. He was tall and strong. Her accomplice. She didn't have to do this alone.

"Drew," she said, and wrapped her arms around him. "You're here."

"Where else would I be?"

She buried her face in his coat, trying to calm her breathing. She couldn't admit her fears to him.

"Mina, are you all right?" He lifted her chin. "Are you hurt?"

"No, no," she said. "Only a little bit shaken."

"You were so brave. I can't believe you did that."

"Where did he go?"

"He didn't talk to anyone. Left by the main gate and boarded an ordinary ferry. No one joined him. I think he was alone."

"He's not the extortionist, only a hireling. And

a rough one, at that. I could smell the ill will on him. He would have harmed me if he could. The man who hired him isn't evil."

"And yet he hired evil to deliver his message." She handed him the paper.

"Olivia Lachance, of the Princess Eve," he read. "A business establishment? We have a name and that's what matters. I'll soon discover where to find this Lachance woman."

ANOTHER PIECE OF the puzzle. "Mina." He caught her eye. "You were wonderful. The way you threatened him with that pistol. You controlled him."

"Did you doubt me?"

"I doubted myself for putting you in danger. If anything had happened . . ."

"But you trusted me."

"I trusted *us*, but accidents happen. Mina, if anything had happened." He framed her face with his hands. "I would never have forgiven myself."

"Seems to me there are lots of things you've never forgiven yourself for, and this will be one of them."

"Putting you in danger."

"No, not that." She smiled. "You'll never forgive yourself for kissing me again."

He groaned. Pressed his forehead to hers. "Mina." He couldn't stop saying her name. He loved the way it sounded. Mina.

So close to *mine*.

He made the decision from some other part of

his brain. Or maybe it wasn't his brain. Maybe it was his body that made the decision, because she looked at him and said he was about to kiss her.

She'd read his mind.

He drew her deeper into the shadows. Pressed her up against a tree. Covered her with his body.

He wanted to show her what she was up against. A tree. His body.

She made him so aware of how short life could be. How alive he felt when she was in his arms.

He kissed her commandingly, one hand in her hair and one hand braced against the tree bark.

She kissed him back, moaning softly, a sound deep in her throat. She tilted her head and he kissed the column of her neck, her throat, her lips again.

Her tongue like warm, wet silk, her taste somewhere between Heaven and Hell, prayer and curse.

One of his hands closed around her generous bottom, the other held her head so that his tongue could do as it wished.

When he was kissing her, his mind dimmed like the sun fading behind a cliff.

"Drew," she sighed against his lips, and it was the most soul-stirring, arousing sound he'd ever heard.

He knew he should stop, but what stopped was the rest of the world, unspinning, slowing, and finally grinding to a halt until the only motion was the two of them kissing, exploring.

Sap running through his veins.

He was a tree and she was ivy twining around

him, climbing him. He was rooted and firm, his body one with the earth, his heart in the clouds.

"You want danger. You want excitement and adventure," he whispered. "I'll be your adventure. Explore me, Mina."

MINA RAN HER hands over the angles of his face, the rough stubble defining his jaw, the roped muscles of his neck. He was a safe harbor and a perilous path.

She'd wanted to make him lose control enough to kiss her again, and she'd won.

She wanted to keep winning, over and over again.

His tongue inside her mouth—another victory.

Strong hands gripping her bottom, clasping her against the evidence of his arousal—give her a gold medal.

She'd imagined kissing a handsome gentleman at Vauxhall Gardens. There hadn't been any of this rawness, a sensation as though she'd been rubbed with sandpaper and her nerves, her emotions, exposed.

Kissing him right here in the park, with people promenading so nearby and the threat of discovery ever present.

It was the sweetest, wildest thing she'd ever done, and she wanted more.

More of his lips, firm yet supple. More of his tongue, teasing and skillful.

More of his body, hard and huge.

Her back against the ridges of the tree. A knot

in the tree, a gnarl pressing into her lower back, releasing the coiled tension there.

There was so much mystery to him. He wouldn't open up to her with words and so she'd force his body to tell her things. She'd force his hands to speak all of the things she wanted to know.

There was a story behind the pain in his eyes. Strength in his arms.

Urgency and longing in his kiss.

Would she be able to unlock this guarded fortress of a man? She might find a way to open him, just a little at first, and she might find a way to make him admit that he needed her.

"Mina," he groaned. "I've been dying to kiss you again."

"Yes," she said simply. "Give me more."

She wanted him never to stop, and at the same time she wanted to end this because it was too much, it felt too good, and her desire almost frightened her.

She wasn't scared of anything. She was bold, brave Mina. Newly wild and newly free.

She knew what he looked like under these respectable clothes, the powerful chest, narrow hips, and strong thighs.

She'd watched him pleasure himself. She'd wanted him to touch her, to awaken her senses to passionate awareness.

The time for new sensations, new discoveries had arrived.

"Touch me," she whispered.

"Where?" he asked, his breathing labored. "Tell me where."

"Where you touched me before."

"Your breasts?" he asked.

"Yes." She arched her back, thrusting her bosom into prominence.

"Yes, please," he growled.

"Yes." She felt wicked. Bad. Up against a tree, begging for him to touch her. Panting. "Please."

He pulled her bodice and chemise down, exposing her breasts to the night air and to his eyes.

"So lovely." He cupped her with both of his hands, his thumbs grazing her nipples, and she nearly fainted from the pleasure of it.

He lowered his head and took her nipples into his mouth, teasing them to aching awareness with his tongue.

Every other reason for being in London coalesced into this one purpose: prolong this sensation.

Find an antidote to the restlessness coursing through her body.

His thigh was lodged between her legs. Tentatively, she rubbed against him, welcoming the friction. Tender and swollen. Her lips . . . the peaks of her breasts . . . the sensitive place between her thighs.

Her heart.

Waiting made everything sweeter. Everything worth having was worth waiting for. But now was not the time for discretion or denial.

"Don't stop kissing me. Don't stop," she commanded, fully aware that she was begging and not at all concerned about it. He made her wanton and she was going to dive in and not worry about whether she would ever resurface.

He caught her wrists with one of his large hands and moved them over her head, trapping her against the tree trunk. She thrust her hips forward to feel him, to connect with him.

"Mina." He kissed her neck, murmuring in her ear. "You smell like roses. You're so sweet. I want to eat you up." He nibbled at her earlobe and she shivered.

He pushed her hair away from her neck and bit her, softly, gently.

She bent her neck to the side inviting his lips and his teeth to claim her.

It felt heavenly. She moaned. Low and throaty. "Devour me."

Soft nips with his teeth along her neck and his body, long and hard, covering her, pressing her back against the tree.

Night air against her cheeks. Breeze playing over her nipples.

Wanting building inside her, a desire to find fulfillment, an ending to the chapter.

Fireworks lighting her chest, blossoming in her mind. Popping overhead in bursts of red, green, and gold.

There was such a newness inside her. Such a sense of limitless possibilities.

"Mina. Fireworks."

"I feel them, too," she said.

"Over our heads."

She glanced up. "How long have we been here?"

He dropped her arms. Backed away.

They exchanged a tense glance.

"We have to go back. Your mother."

"My sister."

She lifted her bodice. He adjusted his trousers.

"I'll just be . . . a moment," he said, breathing heavily. He rested his back against the tree.

They stood side by side.

"We can't keep doing this, Mina."

"I know."

He touched her cheek. "No, really. This is wrong. Our every encounter veers into forbidden territory. We have to stop."

"You're right."

But she didn't want to stop. She would have laid down on the grass right here in Vauxhall Gardens with him and been truly bad.

Truly wanton.

He had this powerful hold over her. She must fight against it.

"It won't happen again," she promised.

"It can't."

Fireworks sprayed stars over their heads. The smell of smoke filled the air.

Children shouted and people clapped.

She refastened some of her hairpins. A soft, restless feeling pulsed between her thighs.

"Are you ready, Mina?"

So ready. Make me explode.

They walked back through the dark grove and onto the lighted path.

Tonight she'd been seduced.

More than the kiss, even, it was the hungry way he'd stared at her while she drank the wine. The way he'd jumped down from the carriage and claimed the privilege of handing her down.

The look in his eyes when he'd praised her bravery. Grinding her grand resolutions to powder.

He cares. No, he doesn't care. They had a shared goal, that was all.

She cared. No, she would never be so foolish as to fall for a man who stood in opposition to all of her dreams. She would never lose her heart so easily.

She'd been carried away by the contrast—the overwhelming fear and then the sudden relief and comfort of Drew's strong arms. His intoxicating kiss.

Mixing up the desire for adventure with desire for him. A dangerously narrow distinction.

She was courting danger . . . she was courting him.

She wanted him, desperately. She was inexperienced but she was willing to learn.

She wanted everything he could teach her. Everything had seemed so clear cut and now everything was blurred.

Chapter 19

❧

"GOOD EVENING, WILHELMINA."

Mina nearly jumped out of her skin. Uncle Malcolm was waiting for her in the doorway of the front parlor when the duke's carriage dropped her back home.

"You startled me, Uncle," she said.

"Come in here."

He knows everything. He'd had her followed. He knew what she'd been doing.

Don't confess to anything.

At least she'd been kissing the man he wanted her to marry.

He entered the parlor and indicated that she should sit in a chair near the fire. He took the seat across from her.

Something was very wrong. His face was shuttered, his eyes hard.

Sir Malcolm shook his head slightly. "You look . . . like your mother tonight."

"Do I really look like her?"

"Too much."

For the first time she wondered about her uncle's relationship with her mother. Had he admired her? There was something about the way he'd said those words.

"I wish . . . I wish she could see you tonight," he said.

Now she knew something was very wrong. Her uncle never talked like this, he never gave her compliments.

"I know it wasn't easy for you to come and live with me. I hope I didn't do wrong by you."

"You gave me a safe upbringing," she said carefully.

"I know you want to be here in London, that you view going back to Sutton Hall as an imprisonment, but something's changed. You can't stay here any longer."

"What do you mean?"

"You're returning to Sutton Hall with me. Tonight. There will always be another Season."

"First I had months, then weeks, and now minutes?" She struggled to keep her voice even but dread swamped her mind.

"An old enemy has resurfaced after nearly a year. I'm going to be leaving London sooner than I thought I would, tomorrow morning, as a matter of fact. I won't leave you with only Griselda. She's too feeble and her headaches are becoming more frequent. The doctor told me that she requires absolute bed rest and silence."

"Let me stay, please. I can care for her."

"You're not the most silent of creatures."

"If you fear for my safety, set a guard on me."

"The only place you'll be truly safe—from my enemies and from yourself—is at Sutton Hall. It's impenetrable."

If he was alluding to his espionage activities

this must be a grave threat, indeed. "It's Le Triton, isn't it?"

He sighed. "You know I can't talk about that. You're . . . you're all I have." A rare crack in his armor.

"You've protected me too long, Uncle. You can't stuff me full of cotton batting and keep me on a shelf like one of Great-Aunt Griselda's hedgehogs. I tried so hard to become what you wanted me to be—a substitute for your own daughter. I suppressed my true nature and tried to be content with all of the restrictions. I wanted to be useful to you. I became your secretary, always thinking that if I worked hard enough you would . . ." her voice faltered.

What—what had she been hoping for? Kindness, understanding . . . affection?

His face remained closed. "Are you finished?"

Stung, she nodded.

"You're far too clever, Mina. Clever enough to get yourself killed. Now not another word. Write Griselda a farewell note and we'll go now."

"No." The word rose from some buried well of anger and helplessness to explode from her mouth.

"What did you say?" Her uncle's eyes narrowed.

"I won't go."

"I'm your guardian and I'm sworn to protect you. I say you go to Sutton Hall."

She recognized the steel in his eyes, the coldness in his words. Her mind spun through all of the avenues she might try. But there was only one path she could see that would remove her from his power—break the hold he had over her.

"You can't make me go." She rose from her chair. "Because I have a new protector now. I followed your instructions. I'm engaged to the Duke of Thorndon. Aren't you proud of me?"

His eyebrows rose. "You're lying. I can feel it."

"I'm not. You don't control me anymore. I'll go and live at his house with his mother and sister until we can be married. His sister invited me to stay with them."

"When did this happen?" her uncle asked suspiciously.

"Tonight. We kissed in the dark paths of Vauxhall and then he proposed."

"Proposed marriage?"

"Of course marriage. What else? We're madly in love."

"I don't have time for your games. You're coming with me now."

"Go and visit the duke tonight—he'll tell you that it's true."

If she could find a way to reach Drew first, plead her case, he might agree to help her.

Grizzy's ancient doorman tottered into the room. "Sir Malcolm, the Duke of Thorndon is here to see you."

"It seems the duke has come to us," said her uncle.

Drew strode into the room. "Forgive the intrusion, but you forgot your shawl in my carriage, Miss Penny." He held out her ivory pashmina.

"Your Grace," said Sir Malcolm. "I believe we have much to discuss."

"Indeed?" asked Drew.

"Indeed." Mina moved toward him quickly. She'd whisper in his ear as she accepted her shawl.

A hand clamped around her elbow and directed her, none too gently, toward the door.

"This is between gentlemen, Wilhelmina," said Sir Malcolm.

"But—"

Her uncle pushed her out of the room. The door closed with an ominous click.

Dismissed. Locked outside. Her future a matter between gentlemen.

She bit her lip so hard that it bled.

If Drew chose to corroborate her lie, then she might be allowed to stay in London.

But why would he? She'd made sure to antagonize him from the moment she met him. And all of those inappropriate kisses, most of which she had initiated. He didn't think of her as a respectable, sensible candidate for his marriage of convenience.

She'd dug her own grave.

When he told her uncle that she'd lied, there would be no option but to go back to Sutton Hall or run away with no money, no means of supporting herself.

Sir Malcolm's network of informants and spies would find her within hours.

Her entire future hinged on Drew trusting her to have had a valid reason for lying about their relationship.

Her entire future was in his hands.

Chapter 20

MINA PACED UP and down the hallway. After what seemed like years the door to the parlor finally opened.

"You may join us, Wilhelmina," said Sir Malcolm. She couldn't tell anything from his voice or his expression—he was unreadable as ever.

She walked into the room, her heart leaping into her throat.

Drew had a forbidding expression on his face. He had his arms crossed over his chest, her shawl still draped over his arm.

Her heart sank. He hadn't covered for her. How could she have expected him to go along with such a wild and unprincipled scheme? He prided himself on his iron control over his life.

Had she really expected him to throw caution and control to the wind and lie to her uncle's face?

"Go to your room and gather your things, Wilhelmina," Drew said. "You're coming to live with my mother until our wedding by special license."

Wedding?

She searched his face. He gave her a nearly imperceptible nod, a small glimmer of warmth.

She couldn't believe it. He'd lied for her.

She wanted to fling herself into his arms and

pull his head down to her level for a glorious thank you kiss. But instead she merely inclined her head in an elegant manner befitting a future duchess. "Of course, my Duke."

"Take the long way home," Drew instructed his coachman after he handed Mina into his carriage. He wanted some time to talk to her before he brought her home.

"Imagine my surprise, Mina, when I returned a shawl and gained a fiancée," he said, settling onto the seat across from her.

She wrapped her shawl tighter around her shoulders, her eyes hidden by the shadow cast by her bonnet brim. "Why did you corroborate my lie?" she asked.

He'd done it for many reasons, none of them practical. He couldn't confess to the reason that remained topmost in his mind. When he'd returned her home that evening, he hadn't wanted to leave her.

He wanted to keep her by his side.

It was as simple as that. Right now it was all he could do to remain seated across from her, instead of moving next to her. Taking her into his arms, where his heart told him that she belonged.

He must choose his words carefully. He wasn't thinking clearly. "When your uncle asked me if we had become betrothed this evening, I didn't know what to say. We have shared several passionate embraces, and most would say that was grounds for an engagement."

"Oh no. Drew." She twisted the edge of her

shawl in her hands. "I'm not trying to trap you into marriage. I hope you didn't agree out of some chivalrous notion that since we've kissed we must wed, because I don't feel that way."

There may have been some chivalry involved. Some pride and some possessiveness. She brought that out in him. "All of this—the kissing, the search for Rafe, and now this fake engagement. Won't any of it have consequences?"

"Perhaps for me," she replied softly, "but your life can go on exactly as it was before you met me. Once this is over, and we break things off, you'll be able to find your sensible bride and bring her to Cornwall."

He didn't know what he wanted anymore—for life to go back to the way it was before, or something else.

A new way forward. A possibility he'd never imagined.

"I don't blame you if you're angry with me," she said, her voice quiet and subdued. "I know you don't like to be caught off guard or to lose even an inch of control."

"I didn't lose control, I seized it. There were two ways to turn—left or right. Good or bad. Moral or immoral."

"Agreeing to a fake engagement with me was the moral choice?"

"You told me that going back to Sutton Hall would be like dying for you. After speaking with your uncle, I fully understand why. He doesn't understand who you are at all. He thinks he can shape you, mold you into something he wants you to be." He placed his hand against the seat cushion, wishing he could touch her instead. "He's obviously deluded."

She frowned, and then her face cleared and her eyes brightened. "You understand. You really, truly understand."

"Don't sound so shocked. I'm not without perceptive abilities."

"You know that he stifles me with his overprotectiveness, his rules and restrictions. And you're offering me my freedom. It's extraordinary. When I first met you I thought you were just like him. But you're the complete opposite." She met his gaze. "Drew. You have no idea how much this means to me. Thank you."

The emotion lighting her eyes was reward enough. Though it was all a sham, and probably an enormous risk that could have unforeseen and damaging consequences, it all felt worthwhile in this moment.

He'd helped her, he'd been useful to her, and he'd fought for her freedom.

She was grateful. She was smiling. It made him happy.

"I told him that his letter and my brief acquaintance with you had confirmed that you were the perfect choice of wife for me. I told him that we would be married by special license and I would hasten you back to Cornwall immediately, where you would stay under lock and key until you bore me an heir."

Her eyes widened. "You did not."

"Words to that effect. It seemed to be what he wanted to hear."

A slow smile spread across her face. "You're brilliant. You were speaking his language. How did you know that would be the perfect thing to say?"

"I know men like your uncle. They see the world always in terms of what it means to them, not what it means to other people. You were either going to become my wife, because then you would be mine to protect, or you'd be hidden away back in the countryside, where he could protect you. I told him that we didn't want the union made public until all of the details were in place. It buys us time to continue the quest."

But what came after the quest was over?

The carriage traveled over cobblestones, jostling her against the cushioned wall.

She pressed her nose to the window. "We're close to Berwick Street. The house I grew up in is Number Seven. I haven't been back yet. I didn't want to see it. But now I want to, just for a moment."

Drew rapped on the carriage ceiling and the wheels slowed.

It was a fine evening, crisp and cool. The air didn't smell as clean as it did by the ocean, but the coal smoke wasn't overpowering because of the brisk breeze.

They walked along the street, the gas lighting casting pools of golden light. There was no one out. Everything was silent, as if the world was holding its breath.

He took her hand because he had to touch her.

"This one," she said.

A town house like any of the others on the street. Stone, wood, bricks, and glass.

"This is where I grew up. My parents left me here when they traveled, which was most of the year. They were always traveling on the Continent. Once they even visited America."

"What were their names?" he asked.

"George and Lilly. My mother loved to wear red gowns. I had one of her gowns altered."

"The scarlet gown you changed into?"

"The very one. I believe you said it looked like a rose mated with a bawdy house sofa."

"I didn't know it was your mother's gown."

"No one would. The seamstress made far too many modifications, added too many frills. But the fabric remained the same. A memory from my childhood. She was always laughing, always chattering, she never stood still. In my memory she's just this swirl of red, like a brushstroke on a canvas eternally caught in motion."

That's how he felt about Mina. That she was this swirling force that touched everything around her with renewed life. "And you wanted to be just like her when you grew up."

"Of course I did. During their infrequent so-journs in London they held the most decadent and notorious at-homes with all of the dissipated artists, writers, wits, and adventurers. I used to sneak out of my bed and watch from the upstairs balcony. I saw Lord Byron drinking wine and reciting poetry."

"I can tell you from personal experience that Byron was a donkey's arse."

"And yet you quoted his poetry to me."

"I had suffered a blow to the head."

"You must admit that his words hold power. The power to move our hearts."

She had the power to move his heart. And that scared him. It was impossible to be in her presence and remain impassive. "I'll admit it," he said. "But you have to admit that his private life was a disaster. Much like Rafe's life is now."

He couldn't resist pointing out the similarities. It still galled him that she'd ever considered his brother as a marriage prospect.

"Before she left with my father on their final tour of the Continent, my mother gave me a gift that I've only recently begun to understand."

"A family heirloom?" he asked.

"Five words. It was the day my parents left. I was sullen all morning, plaguing my governess and refusing to do any lessons. My mother entered the schoolroom. I ran to her, threw my arms around her waist, and begged her to take me with them."

"You were ten years old?"

"Yes, too young to go with them but I didn't understand that. It was almost as if my mother had a premonition that she would never see me again. She dismissed my governess. I made a fuss and she let me cry and she didn't try to quiet me. She let me cry myself out and then she smoothed my hair back from my face, and she looked me in the eyes and said, 'Don't be a good girl.' That's it. That's what she said. And then she left and I never saw her again."

"What an odd piece of advice for a mother to give her daughter."

"I've asked myself so many times what she meant by that. Had I misheard? Had she actually said, "Be a good girl," which would of course be what most people would have said, but I'm sure that's what she said. And I think she was giving me her philosophy of life. Good girls are supposed to be rewarded—the good girls who know their place, the girls who don't make a fuss, the girls who stay inside. She was telling me to break the rules, to not care what people thought of me."

"Not an easy or popular philosophy."

"Especially with my guardian. He always promised me that I could go to London when I turned sixteen. Then it was seventeen. Then eighteen. I made a vow when I was stuck in the countryside facing the prospect of a dreary spinster life as my uncle's secretary, that if I were ever allowed to have a Season I would make it count. I would taste all the fruits of town, be they sinful or saintly."

"You're here now."

"I don't know what changed his mind. He went to Paris and the Duke of Ravenwood was there, and Uncle Malcolm came back changed. He told me I could have a Season. But when I arrived in London, my great-aunt pronounced me unfit for polite society, and she embarked on a series of etiquette lessons."

"The ball where I met you was your first appearance."

"Yes. I had finally arrived. I was going to make the most of it, taste it fully, drink it down. Wear red silk dresses, drink brandy, and face danger head on. And then tonight when I came home from Vauxhall, Uncle Malcolm told me I had to go back to Sutton Hall immediately. I just couldn't. There was only one circumstance that I knew would break his hold over my life. Becoming engaged to a gentleman of his choosing. Namely, you."

She surprised him, disarmed him and the thin ice was dangerous.

He needed his routine back. He wanted to know precisely what everyone would say and do at precisely what time.

Predictability. Routine. She was the opposite of that. It was as if she'd set herself on a direct collision course intended to knock him completely off his axis and into a state of chaos from which he might never return.

He had to regain control over his life. She was a girl who courted danger, lived for adventure.

She was everything he shouldn't want. And yet he was dying to take her in his arms. Kiss away her sadness.

That was the problem. She made him *feel*.

Feelings were dangerous. Emotions were quicksand.

Unreliable, shifting ground that sucked a man down into madness.

"A gentleman of his choosing," Drew repeated. "He thinks I'm some paragon of gentlemanly virtues, when I can't stop kissing you every chance

I get. That has to end, Mina. Especially now that you're coming to live under my roof. Your uncle would never forgive me if any harm came to you under my watch. You're under my protection now and I take that very seriously, no matter how brief my tour of duty."

"I'm not your duty. I'm temporarily under your protection, but don't worry, I can take care of myself." She patted her reticule. "Don't trouble yourself, I'll make certain that this episode doesn't impede your ability to find the perfect, sensible, retiring duchess to provide you with an immediate heir and a spare."

She averted her eyes, staring at her feet. "I'm utterly replaceable, remember?" There was a dull tone to her voice that wrung regret from his heart.

"You're not, Mina." He lifted her chin with his forefinger. "I didn't know you when I said those words."

Damn, she was beautiful. Eyes that belonged to the nighttime. Hair that glowed like lamplight. That lush lower lip the shape and color of a fallen rose petal. He wanted to envelop her in his arms. Crush her lips to his and kiss away her doubt.

The curve of her lips. The taste of her on his lips, like the Burgundy wine. Ripe berries and cinnamon. Sweet and hot.

Warm leather of a saddle after a hard ride.

He wanted to tell her that she was everything he desired, and that he would die to protect her.

"But conventional and replaceable is what you want," she whispered.

Not anymore, his heart insisted loudly. But he

had to repeat the lie to himself until he believed it again. He couldn't give her the love she craved.

If he allowed her inside his heart, all of his painstakingly erected walls would come crashing down, leaving him vulnerable and lost in the darkness.

"WHY, MISS PENNY," said Beatrice when they arrived. "I thought Drew was returning your shawl, not returning with you."

"Miss Penny's great-aunt is taken poorly," Drew said. "So you, dear sister, decided to invite her to stay with you and Mother for the remainder of the Season."

"Oh?" His sister's eyebrows winged. "*Oh*. To be sure. I'll inform Mama first thing tomorrow morning. Mina, you can have the guest chamber next to mine."

"Thank you," Mina said, smiling at Beatrice.

Beatrice grinned at Drew. She thought he was in love with Mina. Which he wasn't.

It was complicated.

"It's nothing serious with your great-aunt, I hope?" Beatrice asked.

"Only megrims, but she'll be confined to her chambers with a maid to tend her and the doctor has prescribed absolute quiet and solitude."

"Mama will be thrilled. Not about your great-aunt. About you staying here."

Both mother and sister would be thrilled by this turn of events.

Fake engagements were tricky things. They had a way of going awry and ruining reputations.

Men usually survived unscathed but Mina might not be so lucky. But did she truly care? It was freedom she sought, after all.

"I'm so glad you're here," said Beatrice warmly, taking Mina by the hand. "We'll have a wonderful time together. Mama will want us to attend balls and go shopping at the fashionable places—see and be seen—do other silly things like that, but we'll revolt, won't we?"

Revolution was Mina's middle name.

"Absolutely. What would you like to do instead?" Mina asked.

"Show you my favorite bookshops. And introduce you to some of my new friends."

"What new friends?" Drew asked, immediately suspicious. A new friend could be suspect.

"You wouldn't know them. I joined the Mayfair Ladies Knitting League. It's a charitable committee. We knit garments and blankets for foundling children."

"Sounds like a worthy charity. I'd like to make a donation," said Drew.

"That would be most welcome, brother. I can't wait to bring you to meet them, Mina."

Mina looked doubtful. "I do have to say that I'm not the best knitter in the world. I never learned any domestic arts, actually. Can't embroider to save my life."

"Yes, but you're very good at picking locks and aiming pistols," Drew said.

"Are you?" Beatrice asked Mina. "You don't have to knit. We have very stimulating conversations."

Drew crossed his arms. "Come to think of it, I've never known you to be an enthusiast for domestic arts, sister."

"Go off to bed now, brother dear, and leave the ladies to plot their own kind of social season."

Laughter in Mina's eyes. She liked seeing him dismissed.

He cleared his throat. "I'll leave you then."

Walk away. Not nearly far enough away from those sparkling blue-gray eyes. He paused in the doorway. His sister and Mina sat at the table, heads bent together, two clever, powerful young ladies.

He turned his back, resolving to forget about Mina, if only for the space of a few hours of sleep. Dreamless sleep. Mina-less sleep.

"Thorndon?"

He met Mina's gaze. "Yes?"

"Thank you." A soft blanket of approval and gratitude in her smile.

"You're welcome." Gravelly voice. Cold heart.

Off to his lonely bed.

If he were a stretch of countryside, she would be the new railway track being laid.

He wouldn't be able to sleep tonight, that much was clear. Mina was too close. He needed distance.

First close the door of his mother's house. Next, walk the few steps to Rafe's front door. There was the shrubbery where she'd crouched and watched him. That was the rosebush that had scratched her cheek.

There was the window she'd climbed through.

Christ. Maybe he should sleep on a bed of thorns tonight. Maybe he needed a painful reminder that he'd chosen a solitary life because the ability to love, to cherish, had been stolen from him.

Though he was obviously still capable of desire.

He'd be hard as a rock in seconds if he allowed himself to relive Vauxhall. The luscious curve of her breasts in his hands.

Give me more.

He'd wanted to give her everything and take everything in return.

When he'd told Sir Malcolm that he'd take care of her, he'd meant it. She was under his protection now.

Everything changed as of this moment, although she didn't seem to see it that way. For her it was only a little lie, a temporary, secret arrangement.

What he'd said to her uncle, the promises he'd made . . . he didn't take those lightly. He'd vowed to protect her, and he would.

He was her temporary protector, and her temporary adventure—the means by which she could enjoy London outside of her uncle's control.

His heart chose that moment to remind him that he wanted her, and not just in his bed. He wanted her approval, her companionship.

He couldn't show her how much he thought about her, or dreamt about her. How she had him thinking about second chances.

She made him want to change, to transform. Crawl out from under his rock and greet the dawn of her smile. But he couldn't give her this much control. He must impose some order on his life. Attempt to find his routine even here, in London, where the sunshine was filtered through coal smoke and the rooster didn't crow his sunrise. Where the milk was too thin and there was no true silence.

Keep the solitude of his plant conservatory in his mind. The silence of plants growing, new life sprouting. Sunshine on his face.

The solitude of the sanctuary he'd created was the best method for keeping his balance.

If he lost control, if his hold on his emotions faltered, he'd be at her mercy. He'd plunge back down into the madness and darkness.

The only safe path was to stick with the plan. Find this Lachance woman. Continue the search for Rafe.

And repair the walls around his heart.

Chapter 21

THE NEXT MORNING, Drew found Mina with her head bent over a heap of books and a jumble of papers in his mother's parlor.

She scratched something out with her pen and stared down at her work, frowning.

"I'm off to search for Miss Lachance and the Princess Eve," he told her. "I think the Princess Eve is some sort of public house, or gin shop that's opening soon—I'm not sure where."

She glanced up from her work, a shaft of sunlight turning her eyes nearly iridescent. "A public house proprietress for a duke's brother?"

"An improper match—one that merits blackmail. It would be an embarrassment for the family. Although if Rafe is truly in love with the woman, and there are no other impediments, I won't stand in his way."

"Olivia Lachance could be working both sides," she suggested.

"If they're keeping their engagement secret, why would she want her scheme exposed?"

"Then someone else?" asked Mina. "A jealous lover. Or a servant. Someone who knows their plans and thinks to capitalize on your wealth. I wish I could go with you to search for answers, but I promised to accompany Beatrice to her knitting-society meeting this morning."

"If the Princess Eve is a gin house, it's no place for young ladies," he said.

"You know I don't care about that. I don't want to only see the approved places. I want to make up my own mind about what should or shouldn't be a place for me."

"Trust me, gin shops are bleak and filled with misery. Usually a filthy old shack that smells of juniper-laced desperation. Gin will rot a person more quickly than any other spirits."

"If you deprive someone of something it makes it illicit and more thrilling than if you'd offered access, even restricted access. My uncle forbade me to do so many things and now I want to do them all at once, glut myself on the dangers of Town. I want to shed my country ways."

"So you *do* have country ways." He couldn't resist teasing her a little.

"I'll admit that I've led a sheltered life and I haven't fully broken out of my shell yet. I'm like a sketch done in charcoal right now, and I want to fill in the rich hues."

"The scarlet gowns. The amber brandies."

A smile lifted her lips. "I filled in a few colors last night along the dark walks of Vauxhall. I learned quite a bit about . . . fireworks."

No more fireworks. "I brought you more books to try," he said abruptly, setting the stack of books he held on the table near her. "These all had markers placed in their pages, or writing in the margins. Are you having any luck with the diary?"

"Not really. We must find the key—the text Lord Rafe used to create the cipher. I can't remember if there were any books in *that room*? I was too distracted by other things to notice."

"There weren't any books there," he said hastily. Erotic play-chambers were definitely off-limits from here on out. "I'll help you when I come back this afternoon. Where is Beatrice?" Now that he'd delivered the money to the extortionist and received no other threats, he wasn't as concerned for her safety, but caution was still advisable.

"Reading in bed, where else? I promised that I would go with her to this meeting of lady knitters at the Duchess of Ravenwood's private house. I wish the duchess were going to be there but she's on an archaeological expedition—I've always wanted to meet her."

"I think you and she would be fast friends."

"You've met her?"

"I attended one of her antiquities exhibitions once, many years ago. Take my manservant, Corbyn, with you when you go out. And when you meet Beatrice's new friends, see if any of them strike you as the sinister type."

"The lady knitters?"

"One never knows the nefarious machinations of a knitter's mind."

She smiled. "Perhaps after the lady's society meeting I could join you. Or we could sneak out of the house at night together? I could finally have an occasion to wear my red silk dress." At his silent—and truth-be-told terrified—look, she shrugged. "I didn't think so. Well, promise me that you'll observe Miss Lachance carefully."

"I will."

"Do you want to borrow my pistol?"

"I have my own. A matched pair of engraved and gilded flintlock dueling pistols by Manton," he said.

"Manton's craftsmanship is superlative. I've always wanted to visit his workshop."

"Why do you know so much about weaponry?"

"Oh, it's just a hobby of mine. We'll reconvene later today then."

He had his marching orders: Find Rafe's fiancée, help Mina crack the coded diary, locate Rafe, and ensure Beatrice was safe.

As he left he added another item to the list: do not, on any account, abandon all control and fall madly in love with Miss Wilhelmina Penny.

"THIS IS THE Duchess of Ravenwood's former home, which she's currently letting for a song to her good friend Miss Viola Beaton," explained Beatrice as she and Mina exited the carriage.

Drew's manservant, Corbyn, an unsmiling, towering older man with gray-streaked black hair and wary brown eyes, watched them until they entered the building.

Mina and Beatrice were ushered into a cozy sitting room by a fresh-faced young maid.

"The duchess is still in Egypt, isn't she?" asked Mina.

"She won't be back for at least six months," Beatrice confirmed.

There were knitting baskets, one beside each of the gathered ladies, piled high with colorful balls of yarn and gleaming knitting needles, and several half-finished blankets, hats, and sweaters were draped over chair backs.

Something was odd about all of this.

Mina knew a lot about the Duchess of Ravenwood, enough to know that she wasn't known for knitting. She was an infamous archaeologist known for dressing in male clothing and for convincing the Duke of Ravenwood to abandon his rakish ways and settle into matrimony.

She also knew the inside story—that the duchess had also convinced him to give up his career as Uncle Malcolm's best and most brutal secret agent. Apparently, these days Ravenwood accompanied his wife on her archaeological expeditions.

Mina had always wanted to meet the unconventional and powerful Duchess of Ravenwood, but she'd have to wait for another chance.

"Fern, we have a new initiate today," Beatrice told the maid.

"Very good, my lady. I'll fetch the committee registry." Fern bobbed a curtsy and left.

"Beatrice," cried a petite woman with bright green eyes. She jumped up from her chair, sending balls of yarn tumbling onto the carpet, and ran to embrace Lady Beatrice.

"Viola." Beatrice bore the embrace stoically, and Mina could tell she didn't like to be hugged.

"And who's this?" Viola turned to Mina. "A new recruit?"

"Miss Wilhelmina Penny, may I present Miss Viola Beaton."

"It's very nice to meet you, Miss Penny," Miss Beaton grabbed her hand. "We'll have some tea and a long chat." She pulled Mina toward an armchair.

"I'm afraid I don't know how to knit. I'm dreadfully sorry," Mina said.

Several of the ladies chuckled.

"That's quite all right," replied Miss Beaton. "None of us knows how to knit. Well, that's not quite true. Miss Finchley knit all of these coverlets. Which truly are used for cover." She giggled.

There was some joke here that Mina wasn't getting. "Ah. How nice." She nodded at Miss Finchley, a brunette who lived up to her name by darting an amused glance at them and hopping to her feet to pour Mina a cup of tea.

She handed Mina the teacup. All of the ladies leaned in to watch her.

"Very fine weather we're having," said Mina.

"Drink your tea," whispered Beatrice.

The ladies were acting very strange. If she didn't know better, she might think they were slightly . . . inebriated. Their eyes were bright, their laughter ready, and there was a general air of merriment in the room.

Mina took a sip of tea and nearly choked as the liquid burned her throat. And not because it was hot. "She sniffed the contents of her cup. "This tea is laced with brandy." She knew the stuff now. She'd rather developed a taste for it.

"And this isn't a knitting league," said Beatrice.

"It's not?" Mina glanced at all of the balls of yarn.

"First, let me make the introductions," said Beatrice. "We're a small group today, as several members couldn't join us. You've met Viola Beaton, and Ardella Finchley, and this is Miss Isobel Mayberry."

"Very pleased to make your acquaintance," said Miss Mayberry, her brown eyes twinkling.

"So what are you, if not a group of knitters?" Mina asked.

"Each of us has talents and ambitions beyond those ordinary for females," said Miss Mayberry.

"We're professional-minded ladies." Miss Finchley's hands moved as she spoke, a fluttering accompaniment to her words. "I like to knit, but I'm also a chemist."

"Wait . . ." Mina glanced at Beatrice. "Is this the organization you mentioned to me at the ball? The secret society of professional ladies?"

"This is it," said Beatrice proudly. "I'm very excited to introduce you. Ladies." Beatrice stood up. "Miss Penny is an expert in improvised weaponry for the purposes of defense."

How did Beatrice know that? Mina had never told her about her skills.

"Are you surprised that I know, Mina?" asked Beatrice.

"We know all about you," said Miss Beaton. "You're quite legendary. When Beatrice told me that you were in London I couldn't wait to meet you. It was your unusual timepiece that helped the Duke and Duchess of Ravenwood escape from their captors in Paris. I heard all about it from the duchess."

How much did they know? Mina couldn't imagine that the duchess had revealed the truth about her husband's past life as one of Sir Malcolm's spies.

She'd have to question Beatrice in private.

"I do consider mechanical modification to be one of my talents," said Mina. "I have a flint-lock pistol with me, one that uses a flint striking ignition, but at home I'm working on an ignition device that will be able to fire reliably in all weather conditions."

"Ooh. And will it be named after you?" asked Miss Finchley.

"I hardly think so. My aim isn't for fame, but rather to aid those who use weaponry responsibly and for the prevention, rather than the perpetuation, of war."

Miss Finchley nodded her approval. "A worthy goal, Miss Penny."

"Truly though, anything can be used as a weapon if you are called upon to defend yourself," Mina continued. "Even these knitting needles, wielded with the right amount of force and velocity against a man's more vulnerable regions, could mean time to make your escape."

"Will you give us a demonstration?" asked Miss Beaton. "All of us are sometimes called upon to take risks and knowing how to defend ourselves would be most welcome."

"I'd be happy to. Why don't you tell me about your talents first, Miss Beaton?"

"You probably know of my father, Mr. Louis Beaton."

"The famous composer?"

"I finished his last symphony," said Miss Beaton proudly. "He's quite deaf now, and too feeble to write. By day I'm a music instructor to the Duke of Westbury's sisters, but by night I write powerful, passionate symphonies. I've entered one into a contest held by the Royal Society of Musicians."

"And of course you know that I'm working on an etymological dictionary," said Beatrice. "For which I require the use of my brother's library at Thornhill House."

"You must convince him to allow you to move there for at least a year," said Miss Finchley.

"The world must have your book," agreed Miss Mayberry.

Beatrice finished her tea. "And the bachelors of London certainly won't go into mourning if I declare myself a spinster."

Mina was beginning to like the Ladies Knitting League. "And you, Miss Mayberry?"

"She's the boldest one of us all," enthused Beatrice. "Tell her, Isobel."

Miss Mayberry was about to speak when Fern came running into the room. "Ladies, I'm very sorry but there's a man at the door. Lady Beatrice, it's your brother, the duke. He insists on coming in."

"Code alpha, code alpha," shouted Miss Mayberry.

The ladies sprang into action, grabbing knitting needles and balls of yarn and frantically beginning to knit.

Chapter 22

❦

"CODE ALPHA?" MINA whispered to Beatrice.

"When a man arrives unexpectedly we must hide our seditious activities." Beatrice thrust a knitting basket into Mina's hands. "Knit!"

"But I don't know how to knit . . ." Mina froze as Drew strode into the room, all wavy dark hair, chiseled jaw, and golden eyes.

Several of the ladies glanced up from their knitting and never looked down again.

Drew took in the scene in one swift glance. The ladies knitting, Mina with a basket in her arms, not knitting.

He cleared his throat. "Ladies."

"Your Grace," said Miss Beaton with an angelic smile on her face. "Are you here to make a donation to our cause?"

The sound of needles clicking industriously provided a counterpoint to their conversation. Mina hoped Drew didn't notice that some of the needles were being held upside down.

He made a clipped bow. "I already left a sum with your maid. I came on a different errand, however. Might I borrow Miss Penny for a short while?"

"Of course you may," said Beatrice. "Mina would be delighted, wouldn't you Mina?"

"Er . . . delighted." She happily relinquished her knitting basket. She understood that Beatrice wanted Drew to leave in order for the ladies to continue their meeting. She rose. "It was lovely to meet all of you."

"We hope you'll be back to give us that demonstration . . . the one with the knitting needles," said Miss Beaton.

The maid brought her pelisse and bonnet and she hurried Drew out of the house and away from the professional-minded ladies and their plans for infiltrating all-male societies.

"You can't burst in anywhere just because you're a duke," Mina scolded.

"I have an invitation you won't want to refuse. I found the Princess Eve and I was thinking you might want to see it."

"I thought you said a gin house was no place for a lady."

"It's not a gin house, it's a gin palace and there's a difference. I've never heard of a gin palace but apparently they're going to be all the rage soon."

"What's the difference?"

"The gin palace is housed in a very respectable old building in Hanover Square, and it's been renovated to the highest standards. They haven't opened to the public yet, but they will soon. The quality of the gin will be vastly superior, as will the refreshments, décor, and clientele. I thought you might like to accompany me." He ducked his head as he entered the carriage after her. "Because you're very observant. And I'm liable to overlook something obvious."

She smiled, her heart warming. He might not have admitted it to himself yet, but he needed her help.

He trusted her. They were truly a team.

"I'd be delighted," she said.

A YOUNG MAID WITH light brown hair braided into a crown on top of her head and frightened green eyes answered Drew's knock on the door of the Princess Eve. "May I help you, sir?"

"The Duke of Thorndon and companion. We're here to inspect the premises."

The girl startled, her cheeks flushing. "Oh, Your Grace, we weren't expecting you. We're not open yet."

"I know that, I just want to have a look around. I may be interested in making an investment in the place."

"What's your name?" asked Mina.

"Elsa, miss."

"It's going to be a grand success, isn't it, Elsa?" Mina asked. "Just look at those chandeliers."

"Oh yes, a great success. I-I'll just go and fetch someone to speak with you."

"No need for that," said Drew, leading Mina into the wide hallway. "Is Miss Olivia Lachance here?"

"Miss Lachance has gone away, Your Grace. I don't know when she'll return."

"How long has she been gone?" asked Mina.

"Two or three days, I believe."

"Well, which is it?" asked Drew. "Two or three?"

"I-I'm not sure, Your Grace. I really must find

someone else to speak with you." She curtsied and scurried away.

"Rafe left two days ago," said Drew. "They could have left together. To Gretna Green."

"I don't think so. He said he was going to set a trap for someone. That maid is nervous about something," said Mina. "She jumped when she heard your name."

"I agree. She knows something. Why does her name sound so familiar, as if I've heard it recently?"

"Elsa." Mina walked behind the handsome mahogany bar that lined one of the walls and rummaged under the counter. "Ah, here we are. A record book." She placed the book on the bar and opened it, thumbing through the pages. "Elsa Bickerstaff, barmaid."

"Bickerstaff." The headwaiter at his club. He remembered the bitterness in Bickerstaff's voice when he'd spoken about Rafe. The opportunities the waiter had to overhear the secrets of powerful men.

"We're going to my club," he said.

MINA WAITED IMPATIENTLY in the carriage for Drew to return. Of course she hadn't been allowed inside the club because it was a male-only establishment. The Mayfair Ladies Knitting League would surely have many things to say about that.

He'd been gone for a quarter of an hour at least.

He'd said that he suspected the headwaiter at the club of extorting him because Elsa was his niece. This Bickerstaff, and Miss Lachance, could be working together.

But if they were, then why would Bickerstaff reveal the name of her establishment? Wouldn't he know that was the first place they'd go for news of Lord Rafe?

Or perhaps Bickerstaff didn't know that Lord Rafe had disappeared.

Finally, Drew returned. When he joined her in the carriage, he sat next to her instead of across from her. The leather upholstery groaned under his weight. Mina slid toward him on the now sloping seat.

He draped his arm across the seat behind her. One slight shift and she would be flush against him, his arm around her.

Attraction sizzled up her spine. The urge to slide against him, fit her body into the crook of his arm, was nearly overwhelming.

The carriage began moving.

"Well?" she asked. "What happened?"

"I was right. Bickerstaff sent the letter. Poor man," he said, shaking his head.

"Poor man? He's an extortionist. He threatened to kidnap Lady Beatrice."

"An empty threat. I don't think he realized how truly terrifying it would be for me. He certainly didn't expect me to leave Cornwall and come to London. Beatrice had the right of it. She surmised that the author of the letter was hoping to conduct the whole affair from a safe distance."

"Why did he do it? Did he hold a grudge against Lord Rafe?"

"He holds a grudge against every arrogant, unmannerly lord he serves. He said to me, 'Do you think I want to be a headwaiter my entire life? Do you think I live to serve you and your privileged, puffed-up friends?'"

"You had him sacked, I assume. Or you called for the Metropolitan Police?"

"I didn't."

"Drew. Really?"

"In exchange for my allowing him to keep the money, he promised never to extort anyone again."

"You let him keep the money?" Mina smacked his shoulder lightly. "Why don't you just write him into your will while you're at it?"

"At first I was angry. I grabbed him by the collar and pressed him against a wall. That's when the whole story came out. He needed money desperately. His brother is dying of tuberculosis and doesn't have long to live. He'll use the money to provide for his brother's seven children. He showed me their portraits, all seven of them. Beautiful children."

"One of whom is Elsa, I take it?"

"She was the one who alerted him to Rafe's injudicious engagement to Miss Lachance. I made him promise never to resort to extortion again and that I'd hear about it if he did. I told him that I'd employ one of his nephews if they were likely lads."

"Drew." She shook her head. "You big soft lug."

"I'm not soft."

"Your heart is all soft and squishy."

"It's not."

He pretended to be hard and unfeeling but he

was remarkably solicitous of the sensibilities of others—even those who attempted to extort him.

"This could be a ruse, you know," she said. "He could have fabricated the entire story. He could be in league with Miss Lachance to extort you and entrap your brother."

"Possibly, but his words had the ring of truth. The emotion on his face when he spoke of his nephews, it was real."

"I'm reserving judgment until we find Lord Rafe."

His hand had settled squarely on her shoulder.

She shifted closer to him on the seat, suddenly aware of the enormous breadth of his thighs in his tight breeches.

"So where does this leave us?" Drew asked.

"With a code to decipher. I'm hoping that it will reveal where Lord Rafe has gone and the identity of the evil target he referred to in the study."

"Then I follow him," Drew said.

"*We* follow him." She nestled closer to him. He was just so warm and she had a slight chill from sitting in the carriage. "Because you'll never be rid of me. I'll needle you until you allow me to go."

"Because we're linked," he said, his arm circling her shoulders tighter.

MINA HAD PLED a headache and gone to bed early. When the duchess retired, Mina had snuck out, making her way stealthily to the other house.

They'd been sitting in the study, working on deciphering the coded diary for hours and hours. Mina's brain hurt. Her mind was a mishmash of numbers and letters. Her heart was even more mixed up.

Sitting side by side with Drew, working together on this puzzle, felt so very right. The closeness and camaraderie of it filled some hollow place inside her.

He looked so handsome, even when he was exhausted. His thick, dark hair stuck out at all angles and the stubble on his jaw had darkened into the beginning of a beard. He had purplish shadows under his eyes.

They'd been through every volume in the study. Books were piled everywhere.

She walked to the far wall of the room and back again. Sometimes movement helped her brain follow different paths.

"We're missing something," she said. "Something simple. Something easy. One more time, please try to think of a book that might have some significance for Rafe. Was there a story he loved as a child? A gift someone gave him? A school grammar he particularly hated?"

"Say that again," said Drew, his expression intent.

"Which part?" She was so exhausted she couldn't remember her own words.

"You said a school grammar he hated. Well, he hated them all. He hated them so much that he hid gruesome crime broadsides and gossip sheets inside of his schoolbooks and read them instead. He likes the penny fictions, or penny dreadfuls, as they call them. Sensational stories published and sold for a penny."

"The key's not a book," said Mina, excitement jolting her awake. "It's one of his penny fictions. Where does he keep them?"

"Beside his bed. He has a whole drawer filled with the things. Highwaymen, footpads, tales of intrigue, the bloodier the better. He likes gothic horrors. Vampires, witches, that sort of thing."

They hurried upstairs and into Rafe's bedchamber. Drew pulled open the drawer.

Mina rifled through the lurid pamphlets until she saw one that was so well worn the pages were nearly transparent. " 'Vanquished by the Vampire,' " she read aloud. " 'A Bloodthirsty Tale.' " The cover depicted a skeletal figure hovering over a supine woman with long, flowing black hair wearing a ruffled nightgown.

"That's got to be the one," said Drew. "Didn't he use those same words? He said he was off to vanquish a bloodthirsty foe."

"You're right, he did!"

Mina spread the diary open on Rafe's bedside table beside the penny pamphlet. "It will be simple now that we have the key. See here." She tapped the diary page. "The cipher has the number three, the letter *B*, and the number four all grouped together. I think that means page three, column B, fourth word down. And if there's another number in the grouping, it won't be a word, but an individual letter of a word."

She applied her theory. The word was *Paris*.

She inhaled sharply. "We've done it, Drew. We cracked the code!"

Chapter 23

&

Paris in chaos. House of Bourbon will fall. Le Triton must move inventory. Poseidon arrives Falmouth in one week. Lachance becomes my chance to prove myself.

"WHAT DOES THIS mean?" It made no sense to Drew but Mina was staring at the diary with a flash of recognition in her eyes.

"Falmouth is in Cornwall, is it not?" she asked him.

"Yes. A port town only a half day's ride from Thornhill House."

"Of course," she said. "We had it all wrong."

She straightened and walked to the engraved map of the world hung on Rafe's wall. "Le Triton's stronghold is outside of Paris," she pointed with her finger, "but the diary entry says the monarchy is about to fall and Le Triton must leave. The next location is Falmouth." She traced a line from France to the coast of England. "A port town."

"Falmouth is notorious for sheltered coves—the perfect location for smugglers." Drew had been called upon to assist the county magistrate in capturing and prosecuting smugglers on more than one occasion.

Mina stared at him, her eyes alight with excitement. "The Princess Eve isn't only a gin palace. It's a front for an audacious smuggling enterprise. And Lord Rafe became engaged to Miss Lachance as a means of obtaining information."

"So Miss Lachance isn't in league with Bickerstaff?"

"No. I believe that her connection to him is only peripheral—circumstantial—his niece happened to be her barmaid. The connection is between Miss Lachance and Le Triton."

"And who is Le Triton?"

"A notorious French antiquities thief and criminal and my uncle's nemesis. He's been slowly making inroads into the British criminal networks but this would appear to be his gambit to corner the British stolen antiquities market. I can't believe he would risk coming to England, but that's what the diary says, and your brother had inside information."

"And so Rafe has gone to meet this Le Triton with Miss Lachance? Why would he do such an idiotic, foolhardy thing? Does he want to impress your uncle so very much?"

"Because he's a . . ." She stopped abruptly as if she'd been about to tell him something and had a change of heart.

"Mina." He walked toward her. "There's something you're not telling me. Rafe's not sober or noble enough to embark on perilous journeys to capture dangerous smugglers."

She perused the map, her back turned toward him. "The diary entry says that the *Poseidon*, which is the name of Le Triton's ship, arrives in one week, which means that there are only three more days. It will be piled high with stolen antiquities—jewels, paintings, statuary, priceless treasures stripped from their rightful—"

"Mina." His hands settled on her slender shoulders and he turned her body to face him. She avoided his eyes. "This is my younger brother we're talking about, whom I'm sworn to protect and aid. You need to tell me why he's risking his life to apprehend a notorious criminal."

She remained mute but regret flickered in her eyes. She wanted to tell him, he could feel it.

"Mina. Talk to me. I have a right to know." He brushed the back of his knuckles against her cheek. "There should be no secrets between us. You already know more about me and my past than anyone else on this earth."

Her shoulders rose as she inhaled. Something changed in her eyes, softened. "I want to tell you," she whispered. "But it's against the code."

"What code? Mina, what is this all about? I know that you have something deeper in common with Rafe. At first I thought that you were in love with him but it's not that. It's as though you have a shared language, a shared history. It's not just about antiquities and artifacts, is it?"

"I can't tell you," her voice was anguished, her eyes pleading with him. "Please don't ask me any more questions."

"Don't ask you any questions." He dropped his hand and took a step backward. "You've been accusing me of shutting you out, of remaining cold. Well you're the one shutting me out now."

"You'll have to trust me, Drew. Trust that there's a reason I can't tell you what you want to know."

"Very well." He was alone again. This bond they'd been forging had been all on his side. She didn't trust him.

He strode toward the door. He had to pack. "I have to go after Rafe. The idiot will get himself killed. If I leave tomorrow I'll be there in time to meet the ship."

Mina ran to him and grabbed his hands. "Stop, Drew. You can't go after him alone. You don't know what Le Triton is capable of—he's ruthless. A brutal murderer who cares only for riches and power. He . . . he killed my parents."

"I thought they died while traveling abroad."

She tightened her grip on his hands and stared into his eyes. "My uncle is on a ship bound for France. I have no one else to turn to, Drew. We have to go together to help stop Le Triton. We go together." She brought his hands to her chest and clasped them to her heart. "As a partnership."

"We won't be much of a partnership if I don't know the truth about what we're doing."

Her heart beat wildly beneath his fists. Her jaw clenched.

She nodded. "You're right. I'll tell you everything."

ONCE MINA MADE the decision to tell him, some of the weight lifted off her shoulders. He'd proven himself to be a powerful, formidable ally. She needed his help on this mission.

He deserved to know.

"I haven't been lying to you . . . exactly."

"Never a good way to begin a conversation."

"There's another layer, a secret layer."

She began circling Lord Rafe's bedchamber, lifting paintings and examining the walls for small holes.

"What are you doing?" Drew asked.

"Shhh." She pressed her fingers to her lips. She flung the door wide. No one was outside listening. She shut and locked the door. "I was checking to make sure that no one was listening. What I'm about to tell you can never leave this room."

His eyebrows rose. "Sounds like this confession might be eased by a brandy and a warm fire."

"That might help," she admitted. She was so tense that she felt as though her shoulder blades might knit together permanently.

When the fire was crackling and the lamp trimmed, Drew led her to an armchair and placed a glass of brandy in her hand. Then he pulled another chair close to her and folded his long body into a seated position.

"Take your time," he said gently. "We have all night."

We have all night.

Did he know what those four words did to her? How they made her heart stutter and her insides melt?

A whole night for talking . . . for touching. She could keep her secrets hidden and give him her body instead. Demand that he take what she willingly offered.

She wanted him. He wanted her. But would he still want her after she told him the truth?

She sipped the brandy, welcoming the sting and then the softening in her belly, the loosening of tension.

What she was about to do frightened her. Once she confessed her deepest secret, he would know everything about her. And he could reject her, shut her out, refuse to partner with her anymore.

Remove himself physically and emotionally as her parents had done, as her uncle had done, leaving her alone again. Alone and longing for connection, to be a part of something larger than herself.

He could send her right back to Sutton Hall. She wouldn't stay, of course—she'd run away. But her fate, once again, was in his hands.

He'd lied for her, to give her freedom from Uncle Malcolm. She owed this to him.

She gulped the rest of the brandy in one fiery swallow. Best to have done with it, to brave the sting of his reaction in one quick sentence.

"My uncle is a spymaster who trains an elite force of agents for the Crown," she blurted, the headiness of the brandy spurring the rush of her words. "Your brother is one of Sir Malcolm's spies." She stared into the empty bottom of her glass instead of at Drew.

"Rafe is a spy?" he asked, his tone incredulous. "Drunken, disorderly, promiscuous Rafe?"

"All part of his cover. He masquerades as a

rake in order to extract information from criminal elements."

A snort. "Are you sure about that? Seems more like he might be masquerading as a spy in order to justify his life of debauchery."

"There was an incident. He was supposed to be investigating a gambling house suspected of being a cover for a ring of counterfeiters, but he ended up gambling away all the money and producing no information."

"Sounds like Rafe."

"He was disgraced. This is his way of redeeming himself, of proving to Sir Malcolm that he's worthy to be reinstated as an agent."

She stared harder, wishing she could disappear into the nothingness inside the glass, a swirl of Mina swallowed away. It was too much risk to take to confess her role in all of this. But now that she'd started, she couldn't stop. She must tell him everything and let him make his own choices.

"I proposed marriage to Lord Rafe because I viewed him as my path to freedom. I was going to offer him my intimate knowledge of my uncle's affairs in exchange for an espionage partnership like the one my parents had. They were both spies."

Now he would silence her. Send her away. Tell her that she was mixed up in something far too dangerous for a young lady.

"You want to form a spy partnership with my brother?" he asked.

She dared a quick glance at his face. Was that hurt in his eyes? "It was to be a marriage of convenience. Not unlike the one you are seeking."

"Except that you would be spies."

"Yes." She couldn't read his expression. He could be laughing at her, or he could be furious. He was so good at hiding his emotions, maddeningly so.

He poured both of them more brandy. "That's why you know about secret rooms behind bookshelves and coded diaries. That's why you carry a flintlock pistol in your purse."

She nodded. "I found my mother's hidden diary and I read all about her adventures. I begged Uncle Malcolm to allow me to become a spy but he refused to allow me even a small role in his secret world. He thought he was protecting me but it was a prison."

"Your mother died young."

"She died in service to the Crown. By the hand of Le Triton." Her fingers tightened around the brandy glass. "When I see him I'm going to make him pay for what he did."

"You're speaking of . . . bloodshed?"

"You don't know what he's done—the blood on his hands. So much blood. If I have the chance . . . if *we* have the chance to bring him to justice and avenge my parents' deaths, then yes."

"No." He shook his head back and forth. "No, Mina." He set his glass down and leaned toward her, resting his elbows on his knees. "I won't believe that of you. You have your whole life ahead of you. Bloodshed, darkness, evil . . . none of it has any place in your future."

This was when he would tell her it was too dangerous. Send her away. "I know it's difficult for you to understand, but I don't make this choice lightly. I've thought it through carefully."

"It's not difficult—it's impossible. Mina, you're too alive, you're too filled with light. You were meant to bring sunshine to this world, not darkness. The life of a spy is filled with danger and uncertainty."

"Oh, and you've never done anything reckless or dangerous in your life?"

"Many, many times. Too many to count. When I was a rake, I tried to use pleasure to blot out the pain. I drank myself into stupors, woke up not knowing what had happened the night before. I entered illegal boxing matches. Welcomed being thrashed nearly to death. Danger is a powerful addiction. I can't imagine you harming yourself in the same ways. When I look at you all I see is unadulterated goodness and light."

"Good and pure and helpless. Made to be protected and sheltered. You've fashioned me into some kind of conventional paragon of womanhood in your mind."

"You're mishearing me. I'm not idealizing you, I'm simply stating what I see. Why risk your life?"

"Men risk their lives all of the time during war. This is no different. I was born into a family of spies. I'm meant to fulfill my destiny."

"You were meant for a long and happy life. I thought you wanted to have adventures, to travel and meet poets and debate with radical thinkers?"

"I do. I want to make my mark on the world."

"The world I've retreated from."

"I believe our paths crossed for a reason. You're part of my adventure. I believe that together we can defeat Le Triton. I want revenge and I want adventure and I want . . ." Could she confess the last of it? "I want you."

His eyes the color of firelight, one hand resting on his thigh, palm upward, inviting her touch.

"I want you, too," he said.

"I can't sleep because I'm thinking about you, Drew."

"I was thinking about you when you saw me in the window pleasuring myself. I had a dream about you that night. We were lying together in a field of daisies. Damned daisies. That's what you do to me, Mina. You make me dream about daisies. Whole fields of them. Clean and sweet and sun soaked. But the things I did to you were depraved."

"I thought about you that night after I returned home and I touched myself as well. Dukes don't have a monopoly on self-pleasuring. There's nothing saintly or even ladylike about me, Drew. You've awakened something in me. You make me long for something I had no idea that I wanted. When I look at you I want to rip your shirt off with my teeth."

"Jesus, Mina." He closed his eyes. "Do you have any idea what you do to me?"

She stood on unsteady feet. "What do you want to do to me?" she asked.

"I want you to touch yourself for me."

Touch yourself for me.

His ragged, husky voice made her want to do bad, bad things. It vibrated along her spine like a bow dragged across the bass strings of a cello.

Was she brave enough to do anything about it?

She held his gaze and walked to Lord Rafe's bed. She climbed on top of the covers, lay back against the pillows, and closed her eyes.

Be brave, Mina.

Fingers trailing from her throat, down the center of her chest, over her belly. She glanced at Drew and her heart nearly stopped. The ravenous look in his eyes was back.

She wanted to force him to lose control, leap to his feet and kiss her again with that same rough, reckless abandon.

Reach down and lift the hem of your skirts now, slide them over ankles, calves, knees . . . thighs.

His sharp intake of breath gratified her, gave her the courage to keep going.

Her fingers hovered over the apex of her thighs.

"Lower your drawers," he ordered.

Did she dare?

She undid the tie of her drawers. She wriggled her way out of the undergarments and allowed them to fall beside the bed.

"Lie back on the bed," he said, his breathing harsh and quick. "Spread your legs."

The most daring act of all. She parted her thighs slowly, savoring the low sounds he made, the desire in his gaze. The thin fabric of her shift still partially covered her most intimate place.

He was giving the orders, but she held all the power. A new kind of power.

She could get used to it.

"Touch yourself for me, Mina."

"I suppose it's only fair," she whispered. "I saw you in the window. A pleasuring for a pleasuring."

"That's right," he growled with a roguish smile.

She loved his smile, how it quirked one of his lips higher than the other and crinkled the edges of his eyelids. His smile ignited something inside her. A round hollow in the center of her chest, glowing through her skin.

She was a heat source, a light source, and it was because of him.

One soft, exploratory swipe of her finger over that most sensitive place. She arched her back off of the bed. She was already at a fever pitch of arousal.

She'd been there since she'd met him.

It was exquisite to touch herself but she would die soon if she couldn't have his hands on her instead. A dangerous precipice to dance upon. She knew that she could fall.

She couldn't help herself. She wanted him too badly. "You say that you used to be wicked. But how am I to know that it's true?"

He straightened, rising like a cliff on the horizon, shoulders so broad and strong. "It's a fact."

"Then prove it."

"Prove what?"

"That you used to be a rake."

Chapter 24

*P*ROVE *IT*.

Prove he'd been a rake. Prove that he still had *it*—the talent for giving a woman pleasure.

Drew's throat constricted and his chest expanded with longing.

Oh, he could prove it—there was no doubt about that.

In order to do it right you had to listen. Pay attention. Pick up on small cues, infinitesimal shifts in a mood, a body. The angle of her hips, the rhythm of her breath, her sighs.

He wanted to prove himself to Mina, prove more than just his expertise with lovemaking. He wanted to be worthy of her trust, her partnership.

She was right. He'd been building her up into something perfect and untouchable in his mind, placing her on a pedestal. She was a woman who defied definition. She was her own unique species. He had no way to define her or classify her.

"Drew," she whispered. "You're thinking too much. You need to let go. Take a leap of faith. Stop thinking."

"When I used to be a rake, I didn't think at all," he replied. "I obliterated thinking with wine and whisky. I existed for pleasure, because pleasure drives everything else away, at least in the moment."

"We don't need wine." Her eyes half lidded, fingers moving gently beneath her shift.

"No, we don't." He paused at the foot of the bed. Damn, she was lovely.

Hair loosened, flowing over the bed in silken loops and whorls.

Curvy breasts spilling over her bodice, the hint of one darker pink areola.

White stockings ending midway up her thighs, cinched by pink ribbons. Legs spread. Fingers between her thighs.

One thin layer of muslin covering her sex from his gaze.

Blood rushing in his ears like surf against cliffs, heart pounding, cock granite hard and at the ready. He had Mina spread before him like a feast.

"What are you waiting for?" she asked. "You're my adventure. I choose you. And you know." She grinned. "If it's not you, it will be some other wicked rake."

The hell it would be. That was it. She was offering herself to him, offering him the chance to give her pleasure.

He could keep her at arm's length—or he could wrap his arms around her and give her all of the pleasure and adventure she could handle.

His mind screamed at him to keep a safe distance, push her away.

His heart abandoned all of his defenses and pushed him over the edge, plunging him toward her.

"I'm going to make you cry my name when you come, Mina," he said.

Her cheeks flushed to the color of a sunrise. "For someone who thinks he's as cold as ice, you're heating me through and through."

"Not yet though," he said. "Hands above your head. Clasp them together."

Her breath stuttered, eyes hazy. She obeyed him, moving her hands above her head and clasping her wrists together.

He reached for her waist and dragged her down the bed until her bottom was at the edge and her legs hung down.

He sank to his knees on the carpet, gently pushing her legs wider and spreading the folds of her wet sex with his thumbs.

She bit her lower lip. "What are you doing?"

"Preparing you for my mouth. I'm at the perfect height now."

"Your *mouth*?"

"I want to taste you. Satisfy you. Make you come with my mouth. Would you like that?"

"Oh." She raised her head slightly, arms held high above her head. "Yes, please. Carry on."

Petal-soft skin and mist-smile in her eyes. She wanted to be pleased.

She deserved to be bathed in pleasure, float away in it, and he could give it to her.

What a gift it was to be the one to give her this experience. He would make this so good.

He spread one palm over her belly so that he could feel her responses.

He lapped at the hood of her sex with his

tongue, dancing around the main course. She squirmed beneath his tongue and her belly trembled under his palm.

She had the most adorable rounded belly, not flat like his but with a few soft rolls of flesh that drove him wild.

He rose on his heels to have a view of her tumbled hair and hazy eyes, her full breasts pushed high by the position of her arms.

Had he really thought he was content to be alone? He'd been only half living. His senses dulled.

He felt so alive, his purpose narrowed to one task: make Mina cry his name in ecstasy.

He resumed his work, licking the folds of her sex, uncovering the sensitive bud at the center and flicking his tongue back and forth. Her soft belly rippled, thighs trembling on either side of his head.

She liked that.

His tongue danced again, finding the steps that made her roll her hips to meet him and her breath come in little gasps.

"Drew," she moaned.

His heart soared into the heavens. He redoubled his efforts; moving his hands under her hips, angling her against his mouth.

He dipped his tongue inside her. She tasted slightly salty and honey sweet.

A frustrated sound above him, a little breathy moan. She was close now. She didn't want him to stop licking.

He was hers to command.

Tongue stroking faster now, her body straining beneath him, striving for climax.

He was everything essential to her right now, her wild London adventure. He'd prove his worth again and again.

Her hands came to his head, fingers buried in his hair, clutching his skull. He rubbed his cock against the side of the bed in the same rhythm his tongue was using, aroused by the taste of her, the sound of her sighs.

She was close now. Stay right there, her hands told him. Don't stop.

A few more seconds of steady, firm tongue strokes and she came at last, undulating her hips, riding his tongue and digging her nails into his scalp.

"Oh," she moaned. "Oh. Drew."

He didn't stop moving his tongue until her hips stopped moving and she fell limp against the bed, hands leaving his head.

He rose and climbed onto the bed, fitting his body around her.

She was smiling. She turned sleepy eyes toward him. "That felt marvelous."

"And?"

"You were definitely a wicked rake. Still are, though you try to deny it."

He kissed her lips. "I'm not nearly finished proving myself yet."

Her breath hitched. He laid a hand over one of her breasts, testing the weight and curvature. So delectable, her nipples prominent through the thin cambric of her shift.

He'd been known for his stamina—how long he made lovemaking last—and tonight would be no exception.

Not that his stamina would be put to the test tonight—things would never go that far. No, it would be her endurance that was tested. How many times he made her come.

How many times she'd moan his name.

He propped himself on his elbow while he continued his slow, unhurried exploration. Pulling the bodice of her gown down, uncovering her breasts, fabric sliding over shell-pink nipples.

Her eyes were huge as she watched him. He lowered his head.

"Drew." A sweet little moan as his lips covered her nipple.

Sugary nipples under his tongue. He gave it the same treatment, fluttering his tongue and licking around the contours and then sucking gently.

The other nipple now, the same swirling and sucking, the same care and attention, giving everything to this moment, unhurried.

While he explored, he listened. The bliss of it when she arched into his mouth. The joy of her small hand settled on his head, not to push him away, but to become buried in his hair, to urge him on.

He rolled on top of her and wrapped his arm around her waist, holding her to him as he delved into her mouth and she answered, kissing him back with urgency.

A moan escaped his mouth and she answered with a soft sound that was music and fireworks and all the sustenance he'd ever need for the rest of his life.

He slid his fingers across the seam of her thighs. She shivered and her thighs opened slightly.

Not yet. All the time in the world to lose himself in the music of her sighs. There should be a symphony called Kissing Mina.

He slid his cock against her mound through the fabric of her shift.

"Drew." Her eyes flew open.

"Do you want me to stop?" *Please don't want me to stop. I want to make you come again. And again.*

"No, I . . ." Her hands grabbed fistfuls of bed-clothes. "I want . . ." She rubbed her pelvis against his cock in a wordless request.

That he could give her. "You want to come again."

"Y-yes."

"You will." He kissed her forehead. "Here's what you're going to do. I'm not going to move, you're going to move. You're going to find your pleasure."

He lifted his hips and freed his straining cock, pausing for a moment to squeeze the head to discourage him from being too eager.

He showed her what he meant, moving her shift aside and guiding her seam against his cock, indicating that he wouldn't move, he was hers to use.

"Find what feels the best. Use my body."

"Oh." She bit her lip. "Like this?"

Tentatively, she wrapped her fingers around his cock and rubbed it over her cleft.

"Just. Like. That," he ground out, fighting for control.

Sweet torture not to move, to hold perfectly still, cock swelling, harder than he'd ever been, as she moved more confidently now, using him with her fingers, and with the undulating movement of her hips.

He sucked on her breasts as she rocked against him, faster now, more pressure, her slickness cradling him, her body shuddering as she slid along the base and middle of his cock.

Every ounce of him wanted to take her, press inside her warmth and heat. It would feel better than anything had ever felt. Joined together with Mina, bodies slick with sweat.

Make her cry his name as he stroked inside her. Buried so deep. Lose himself.

Lose control.

He would never lose control completely. Not in bed, not in his life.

He could give her pleasure, but he would take none in return.

Her body clenched tight beneath him. She gripped his shoulders with her fingers and rocked her core against his cock in swift, uncontrolled movements.

"Come for me," he whispered in her ear. "Mina. Come."

She reached her peak in a shuddering series of gasps, bucking beneath him.

He collapsed at her side, smiling into her hair. He still had it.

She cupped his cheek with her soft hand,

rubbing her thumb over the stubble on his jaw. "That was . . . extraordinary."

A rush of pride and possessiveness filled his chest. "I'm glad you thought so." He kissed the tip of her pert little nose. "But you know that we can't keep doing these things. Not without consequences."

"I'm not one to follow orders, Your Grace. But you see"—she flashed a rakish grin—"taking orders from you in bed is my new favorite thing."

His cock responded to her words with an approving twitch. *Not your turn.*

He tucked his cock back inside his smalls.

"Don't." She grabbed his wrist. "Don't put him away. I want to explore."

A request no rake had turned down ever. "No," he said, with a Herculean effort of will.

"No?" she asked.

"I can't let you do that. Because . . ." Because he couldn't lose control.

"It would be improper?" she asked. "I think we're way beyond that, don't you?"

They were so far beyond improper.

"I know why you won't allow me to reciprocate," Mina said. "You won't allow yourself to surrender control with me." The expression in her eyes was frustrated, hurt. She shaped his cheek with her hand. "Don't you trust me?"

He couldn't surrender any more control. She'd already melted too much of his ice-cold center. The shell around his heart was cracking. He would end up abandoning her, hurting her, when this was all over. When they had to return to reality. He never let anyone inside his heart.

"I think I proved my point," he said. "And that's all that was asked of me."

Don't ask anything else. I have nothing else to give.

She stared into his eyes for a long moment. "You're afraid," she whispered. "What are you afraid of?"

He turned his head away. They were so different. She flung herself headfirst into danger and he'd replaced his fear with routine. Their futures diverged.

His place was at Thornhill House, sleeves rolled up as he tested the soil, propagated plants in his conservatory, designed new ways to irrigate fields.

She wanted to become a spy for the Crown, as her parents had been. She wanted to avenge their deaths.

"There's something you're not telling me, Drew." She turned his words back on him. "Something about the kidnapping. How did you free yourself? There was only a brief mention of it in the Duke Dossier."

He stared at her. How could she know that he'd freed himself? No one knew that. And what in Hell was a duke dossier? "The *what*?"

"Oh, I forgot that I never told you about that. My uncle compiled a background document on you. He called it the Duke Dossier and it detailed all four of London's eligible dukes, with you being the number-one choice. That's how I knew all about your treatises on crop rotation techniques."

"I wondered why you'd been reading agricultural journals."

"He probably had you watched for weeks, months, even. Was there any new addition to your household staff in the weeks before you came to London?"

He thought about it. "A new scullery maid."

"My uncle is very thorough."

"So you know everything about me. That puts me at a decided disadvantage, I'd say."

"You care about the plight of the tenant farmers of England, you introduced a bill on tenant rights that was laughed out of Parliament, you retreated to Cornwall where your estate now serves as a model for a true end to famine. You sounded very noble and rather boring, if I'm being truthful."

"Ouch."

"I didn't say that I found you boring. When I met you, I learned there was more to you than what my uncle wrote. For example, he neglected to inform me that you were a former rake. I suppose he thought that information inappropriate for a young lady."

"You discovered that part all on your own."

She lowered her skirts and covered her breasts with her bodice. "I certainly did." She rested her head on his chest.

He played with strands of her hair, the texture as soft and smooth as silk. He pulled the coverlet over them. "There's one thing I still don't understand. Why would Rafe write a coded diary and hide it in a secret room? No one else could have found and deciphered it but you."

"Or someone like me. Someone raised on spy craft. I'd say he kept the diary out of a sense of pride and perhaps as a legacy. If anything happens to him, he'd want there to be a possibility that someone, someday would know what he'd tried to do."

"He's always been a hothead. Never thinks things through. The idiot will get himself killed."

"He may even have left another coded letter for my uncle somewhere, using one of the ciphers common to our organization. He's doing all of this to prove himself to Sir Malcolm."

"You know we can't just run off together, Mina. You'd be ruined."

She raised her head and caught his eye. "Does it seem to you as though I'm concerned about my reputation?"

"I don't want to be the cause of your options being limited."

"Then we'll take Beatrice with us. She'll be thrilled. We can leave her at Thornhill House in your library and she won't emerge for a year."

"Mother won't like it. The Season isn't over and she still has hopes for finding Beatrice a match."

"Beatrice has no desire to wed. Find a way to convince your mother that Beatrice is miserable. She hates going to balls and dancing with shallow dandies. Allow her into your life for once. She's not only longing for your library, she wants to be your friend. She wants your love and your acceptance.

This is your chance to forge a real connection with your sister."

"She can ride this Season out. It will give me time to continue renovating Thornhill."

"If you truly care about your sister, you'll let her choose her own destiny. You'll let her be free to make her own choices."

"And if my mother demands to come with us to Thornhill?"

"Then bring her along. If you tell her that her younger son is in Cornwall, she'll drop everything and accompany us in a heartbeat. We can leave them at Thornhill House."

"We need reinforcements, Mina. We can't do this alone. That police inspector I spoke with at Vauxhall, Inspector Langley, is a stouthearted fellow, and his force is well trained and at the ready."

"Would they allow him to leave London?"

"I'm sure if I put it to his superiors that he could be a hero for England by intercepting a smuggler, they'd allow him to commandeer a stagecoach. They could arrive before we do and try to find Rafe."

"I like those odds far better."

Drew counted the days on his fingers. "Rafe has nearly a three-day start on us."

"Can we make it to Falmouth before the *Poseidon* arrives?" Mina asked. "The diary said one week but that was more than three days ago."

"Falmouth is the Royal Mail packet station and the roads are good. I have fresh horses stabled along the route."

"I'll bring my red silk gown," Mina murmured sleepily. "In case I need to look seductive and distracting."

"You don't have to wear the gown. Everything you do, every breath you take, seduces me. Every time you hold that pistol, every time you unleash an unladylike curse, it seduces me. I've no doubt that you could become a spy, and a damned good one. You can achieve whatever you set your mind to, but please take your time coming to that decision. You don't have to shape yourself in someone else's image. You want to become your mother, but perhaps that's not who you are."

"I don't have time to contemplate my choices, Drew. We only have three days." She raised her head and stared straight into his eyes. "Are you with me, or not?"

"I'm with you," he said.

"Then tomorrow we leave for Cornwall."

"And now it's time for sleep," he said gruffly. "We have preparations and a long journey ahead of us tomorrow."

Fumbling with clothing, restoring respectability.

He found one of her slippers under the bed and handed it to her.

Back to Cornwall, to his home. Taking Mina with him.

Hope threaded through his heart. Maybe . . . when she saw Cornwall, the wild beauty of it, she'd never want to leave.

He shook the wrinkles out of the coverlet on his brother's bed with more force than necessary to hide the direction of his thoughts.

Maybe she was everything he'd ever wanted. Maybe he could be the one who showed her that she was absolutely perfect the way she was— she didn't need to change or throw herself into danger at every turn.

"It's time for you to go to bed, Mina," he said. "I'll talk to Beatrice and my mother tomorrow morning."

"And I'll go and say good-bye to my great-aunt."

Chapter 25

WHEN MINA ENTERED Grizzy's bedchamber the next morning, her great-aunt was sitting upright in bed wearing a gray wrapper. Mina almost didn't recognize her out of her usual black silk gown and with her long gray hair falling over her shoulders instead of piled on top of her head.

She was so much smaller and less intimidating. A tray with an array of wires, brushes, bottles of fixative and dead butterflies was balanced on her lap.

"Good morning, Great-Aunt," said Mina. "I hear you're feeling improved?"

"Much improved, thank you, Wilhelmina." She brushed fixative onto a butterfly wing and the brilliant orange color danced to life. "I never did hear exactly how the duke proposed. Come and tell me all about it."

"We're keeping our engagement a secret for now."

"Oh of course, Sir Malcolm told me as much. But you can't keep it a secret for too long, Wilhelmina. People will start to talk."

"We're leaving for Thornhill House today."

"With the duchess, of course?"

Mina wasn't sure about that, but Grizzy would

never allow her to go if there was any doubt. "And Lady Beatrice," she said.

"I'm quite proud of you, Wilhelmina." Grizzy carefully set the butterfly onto a velvet cloth, and lifted another. "And so is your uncle, though I'm sure he didn't tell you in so many words."

When the truth came out, Mina would be such a disappointment to Grizzy.

"I know you think my taxidermy is unnatural," said Grizzy with a smile.

"It's rather odd."

"My husband, Albert, was a game hunter, and he was always traveling. When he returned home from his hunting expeditions, he always brought another carcass, another head to mount on the wall. I hated those animals hung on my walls. Each one reminded me of one of Albert's prolonged abandonments."

Mina moved to sit in the chair next to Grizzy's bed. She'd never heard her speak of her marriage. "Didn't he want children?"

"Desperately. But every time I increased, by the fourth month I lost the babe. After I lost my fifth child, the doctors said that I could never bear children, that I was too scarred. Albert left then, and he never returned. I hated him for leaving but I didn't blame him. What use was a wife who could bear no children? I allowed my grief to consume me. I stopped eating. I nearly died."

Mina's heart pinched. "How sad."

"Then he died," said Grizzy without betraying any emotion. "He was hunting tigers in Africa and one of the beasts had his revenge. They couldn't even ship Albert back for me to bury. Do you know what they sent me?" Her hands shook as she continued her work. "His heart, preserved in a box. That's what's buried under his headstone. A heart. A heart that never belonged to me."

The acrid scent of fixative filled Mina's nostrils. She got up, walked to the window, and opened it. "You should let some air in. It's not healthful to inhale those fumes."

"None of this is healthful," said Grizzy with a little laugh. "But it's my own small way of finding delight. These creatures that I preserve, their lives were cut short by the cycle of nature. I give them a lasting life."

She held a butterfly up to the light coming in from the window. "Some of them I give to museums. Others I keep in my home. My stuffed creatures do the things I never could do. My little hedgehogs get married, have children, go on grand tours of the Continent."

"So that's why you make clothing for them. I always wondered about that."

"I never traveled out of England. I should have insisted on accompanying Albert on his expeditions. Or I should have embarked on an adventure of my own. I never had a day of trouble in my life." Grizzy caught her eye. "Be bold and brave, Wilhelmina. Fight for what you believe in. I don't want you to regret the roads not taken, as I do."

"My mother gave me the same advice before . . ." She dashed away a tear from her cheek. "Before she died."

"And now you're leaving. Off with your duke to Cornwall."

"I swear to you that I will come back to London soon and you will get stronger and we will have an adventure together. I'll take you somewhere. Wherever you like."

"Nonsense. I'm too old. It's too late for me."

"You're a strong woman. You were broken and you rebuilt yourself. You'll do it again and we'll have our adventure."

Grizzy ducked her chin, hiding a smile behind her hair. "Yes, my dear. Perhaps we will. And in the meantime, my duke hedgehog will wed his duchess vole. Her veil will be decorated with these butterflies."

"I'm sure the wedding will be a grand occasion."

"Off with you, girl. You have a duke to dazzle."

"It's not like that. It's more of a convenient arrangement."

Grizzy waved her brush in the air dismissively. "Oh you can deny it all you want but you can't fool me. Every young lady desires a duke."

Mina rose and bent to kiss her great-aunt's cheek. She realized, with a lump in her throat, that she was going to miss Grizzy.

She had been a stern taskmaster, but now Mina understood her better. She'd only been trying to give Mina better opportunities than she'd been given.

And she was right about Drew.

Mina did desire him, but giving in to desire and chasing her destiny were two very separate things. The information Mina was learning about Drew wouldn't come together to form some big, earthshaking discovery about life and love.

She was dangerously close to falling in love with him. She realized that now. But he wasn't some puzzle for her to solve. If she took him apart and put him back together, his heart wouldn't be more open to her.

And their futures would still run in opposite directions.

WHEN MINA RETURNED, the preparations for the journey were nearly complete. Drew was supervising the placement of the luggage. She watched him from the parlor window, avoiding the moment when they would have to speak to each other.

After what had happened last night, she didn't know how she would be able to meet his gaze.

She'd be thinking about what he'd done with his tongue. The burst of pleasure that still reverberated through her body. The secret pulse between her thighs.

The twist of emotion in her heart.

He knew everything about her now and it was a relief to have the weight of those secrets lifted from her shoulders. But there was a new heaviness. A sense that she was losing a battle with her heart. That what they'd done had woven them together even more tightly, linked their hearts together into a chain.

A beautiful chain, but a chain nonetheless.

Crankshaw appeared at the door wearing his smart black coat and knife-creased white trousers. "Miss Penny, a word if you please?"

"Yes, Crankshaw? What is it?"

He joined her at the window. "I found a red silk gown in the garden shed, Miss Penny, and I thought it might suit you. I took the liberty of having it pressed, folded, and added to your traveling trunk."

"Er, thank you, Crankshaw."

"And, Miss Penny . . . I wanted to let you know that whatever mission you and His Grace are embarking upon, I'll be here cheering for you. Of course, I know nothing of Lord Rafe's dabbling in intrigues, or French smugglers."

Mina started. "Crankshaw. Did Lord Rafe confide in you?"

His face was a blank mask. "About what, Miss Penny?"

"You know . . . about"—she lowered her voice—"his clandestine activities."

"I've no idea what you're referring to, Miss Penny. My lips are sealed. I also took the liberty of including a kit with bandages, antiseptics, a bottle of whisky, and everything useful in the unlikely event of injury. Though I'm sure your journey will go off without even the slightest hitch."

She searched his face. There was a twinkle deep in his blue eyes.

"Crankshaw," she said. "You're the very soul of discretion. And I'm glad we have you in our corner."

"Why thank you, Miss Penny. I'm also pulling

for an announcement of nuptials in the very near future. We do so want a little heir to coddle. Now, if you will excuse me, I have my duties."

He bowed and left swiftly before she could protest about the heir part.

Sir Malcolm, Beatrice, Grizzy, and now Crankshaw. Everyone wanted her to wed the duke.

What they didn't understand was that wedding was out of the question. As was bedding.

At least that's what she told herself as she fixed a decorous, determined smile upon her face and marched out of the parlor.

No more hiding.

They had a rescue mission to mount.

"Isn't this exciting?" Beatrice said as Mina joined her beside the carriage. "I can't believe he's allowing me to go with you to Thornhill. You made it happen, didn't you?" She caught Mina's hands in hers. "Thank you."

"Is your mother joining us on the journey?"

"She has a charity auction to organize. She'll join us at Thornhill a few days later. I can't believe she's allowing you to accompany Drew with only myself as chaperone. She must be truly taken with you."

"Or truly desperate for grandchildren."

The duchess walked down the front steps. "I still don't see why you must cut your Season so short, Beatrice."

"Mama, I'm a wallflower, you know that. No one will miss me."

"I'll miss you." Her mother sniffed.

"I do hope your decision is made swiftly,

Miss Penny." The duchess caught Mina's eye with a decidedly frosty expression.

What had Drew told her? Mina nodded noncommittally.

"Ladies, it's a fine day for traveling," said Drew, appearing from behind his sturdy workhorse of a carriage. No gilded insignia or high-sprung wheels for him.

He wasn't flash . . . he was substance.

Substantial. Solid. Made of strong, durable material.

He was dressed for traveling in tall, worn black leather boots, buckskin trousers that hugged his muscular thighs, and a plain blue serge coat.

He handed Beatrice into the carriage first and Mina waited as she arranged her books and pillows to her satisfaction.

Drew's hand rested on her lower back, a casual gesture of possessiveness that sent a silent thrill through her body. She wanted to touch him in return but they had an audience.

And they weren't supposed to indulge in any more physical intimacy.

His mother noticed the gesture and a smile spread across her round face, lighting her hazel eyes with warmth.

"Do be careful on the road, Andrew," the duchess said. "You have very precious cargo."

"I know it," said Drew. He bent to give his mother a peck on the cheek.

His manservant arrived with the wicker luncheon basket and Beatrice found a place for it inside the carriage.

"The preparations are complete, Your Grace," said Corbyn.

"Is everything settled with Inspector Langley?" Mina asked Drew in a whisper.

"He's already departed in a stagecoach with four trusted officers."

The matched quartet of bay horses stamped their hooves, eager to leave.

"Miss Penny." Drew held out his hand. "Are you ready for an adventure?"

She placed her hand inside his palm. The instant frisson of awareness chased through her body, setting her nerves tingling.

His eyes held a flickering flame the color of sunflowers in shadow. An answering flame lit in her heart.

"Always, Your Grace."

Chapter 26

✑

Drew massaged his neck, soaking in the tub filled with hot water. He was stiff and sore from sitting for so long. The journey on the great mail coach road from London to Falmouth had passed swiftly in a blur of long hours sitting in the carriage, hasty meals at coaching inns while the horses were being changed, and restless bouts of sleep.

They'd stopped for the night at the White Hart in Launceston. They'd reach Thornhill by the next afternoon, leave Beatrice at the house, and be in Falmouth before sundown.

Inspector Langley had left before them in a hired stagecoach that would travel even more swiftly. He would reach Falmouth a half day before they would.

Drew thought about Rafe making plans to confront a ship filled with smugglers and his throat constricted. It was difficult to maintain an outward show of calm when he knew the dangers they were riding toward.

Beatrice remained oblivious and happy. She chattered excitedly when she wasn't reading her novels. Drew hadn't had any time alone with

Mina. He'd told her that they needed to talk, and he'd tried to find time alone with her, but she always slipped away.

He rubbed soap under his armpits, scrubbing away the grime from the journey. She'd probably be enjoying a bath now. He'd ordered hot water for all of them, and maids to attend the ladies.

Sitting in the carriage with Mina for hours on end and not being able to speak with her about anything deeper than superficial topics was wearing on his nerves.

Beatrice thought they were retiring to Thornhill House because he'd agreed to let her end her Season early and proclaim spinsterhood. He'd also misled his mother into believing that Mina had expressed a desire to see Thornhill House before she agreed to marry him.

His mother had hopes.

He scrubbed harder with the rough-textured soap, over his chest and abdomen.

There was a part of him that had hopes as well. Some irrational fantasy that he was bringing his bride home to Thornhill.

That everything would magically come right in the end. That life could be simple. That Mina might fall in love with Thornhill House on sight . . . fall in love with him, despite his numbness, his coldness.

Stupid, persistent little green blade of hope, poking up through his mind, seeking sunlight and water.

He scrubbed until his chest was streaked with red.

A knock sounded at the door. Corbyn with his heated towels and a hot jug of sugared brandy.

"Enter," he called.

Not Corbyn. *Mina.*

Marching around the screen as bold as you please with her arms crossed over her chest, eyes blazing.

He covered his genitals with a hand.

"Oh, please," she said tartly. "It's not as if I've never seen it before."

"What are you doing here, Mina?"

"You said we needed to talk." Her hair was freshly washed and still damp, spilling over her shoulders. The skin of her neck and bosom was flushed, as if warm from her bath.

The thought of all that warm, soft flesh began to do things to his cock. He added his other hand as covering for good measure.

"I'm happy to have a conversation but I'd like to do it with clothing on. Corbyn will be here any second with my towel."

"No he won't. I told him to take a walk. Well, I said it more politely than that, but he understood the message." She stepped closer to the bathing tub.

"I'd say I'm at a decided disadvantage in this interaction, wouldn't you, Miss Penny? Can you hand me a towel?"

"Oh. I thought maybe you were asking me to remove my clothing and join you in the tub."

"No," he replied hastily.

"During our dalliance you never once lost control. You never allowed yourself to feel anything, not really. You kept your distance even as your hands and lips tempted me to abandon all restraint."

She stalked closer.

What she said was only halfway true. Ever since he'd met her she'd been hammering at the walls he'd built around his heart.

He'd built those walls as a protection and a refuge.

Without those walls he'd be lost in the darkness, the ground swaying beneath him.

"You said that we needed to talk." Her expression was fierce, her words spoken with a touch of bitterness. "In my experience, those words are always followed by restrictions. When my uncle told me that it invariably ended with him telling me that I couldn't access certain areas of the estate, I mustn't converse with strange gentlemen, I was never to venture past the woods. You had that same look in your eyes, Drew. The one that said you were about to restrict my freedoms. So, Your Grace, what freedoms are you about to restrict?"

"I think you know."

She crossed her arms. "Say it."

"Very well. We can't keep doing . . . this." He would have waved his hand but he was currently covering his genitals.

"This?"

"You want a list? We can't keep kissing, staring into each other's eyes, making plans for the future, touching each other, watching each other undress."

"You forgot staring at each other's naked bodies."

"Especially that."

"Why not?"

"You know why not."

"Say it."

"Well, I met you at a ball where you were presumably displaying your eligibility to make a marriage match. Therefore, if I'm not to become your husband, then I'm not the one who gets to kiss you."

"You're too honorable to honor a girl's sincere request for a small adventure? Not a huge one, not *the one*. Just a little exploratory expedition."

"Mina," he groaned. "This isn't the direction I wanted this talk to take."

"I'm so tired of being told that I can't have what I want. I can't have adventures or freedom. We both know you'll stop. You have this iron control that you will never breach. So let's explore just a little bit, shall we? I'd like to test some boundaries, and there's no one better to do that with than you."

She knelt down beside the tub, her gaze traveling the length of his body. "I want to explore."

"I thought you wanted to talk."

"Later. Right now I want to explore."

She dipped her hands into the water, testing the temperature. "Still warm. Good."

"Mina, I—"

"Lean your head back," she said, her voice soft and seductive. "And lift your arms to the sides of the tub."

Her hair fell across his chest in damp strands. She licked her lips and that plump lower lip glistened invitingly. He wanted to gently suck it between his teeth. Then he wanted to suck on her nipples.

Then he'd suck on her . . .

Be strong, Drew.

"Lift your arms to the sides of the tub," she repeated.

That's when he stopped fighting. Barriers be damned. He was extremely talented at building walls. He'd build new ones.

He lifted his arms and spread them along the edges of the copper tub.

The head of his cock popped out of the water, aiming straight for her.

"Very good," she whispered.

She plunged her hand into the water and grasped his cock.

"He's so hard," she said wonderingly. "He's all mine, isn't he?" She stroked up and down, the water easing the glide of her movements.

"All. Yours." Teeth gritted. Stomach clenching. Mina's small hand wrapped around his cock was the most arousing thing he'd ever seen.

He watched her face as she stared down, concentrating on her task, just as she'd focused on the bookshelves when she knew there was a secret room to find.

It wouldn't take her nearly as long to unlock him.

He gripped the sides of the copper tub, his hips jerking.

"I saw you touch yourself," she said. "You like it strong and fast."

Her pace increased and he groaned. "Mina. That's so good." He lifted his head and found her lips, craving the feeling of being inside her with his tongue.

His stomach tensed and dots danced in front of his eyelids. His orgasm crept up his thighs, and down from his belly, gathering in his bollocks.

He'd have to let go soon.

He lifted his hips and thrust into her hand, using the copper tub to support his weight.

"I want to be inside you, Mina," he growled.

"I want that too," she whispered. "I'm thinking about it right now."

He came hard, shooting his seed over her fingers, into the bathwater. Ribbons of pleasure tied in silken knots and then unfurled inside him, filling his senses and rushing his heart with warmth.

"So that's what the finishing looks like," she said.

He opened his eyes.

She was still holding him, lightly stroking, and staring down in fascination.

"I was wondering what it looked like. You moved away from the window before I could see."

He sighed, pleasure still coursing through his veins. "I really need that towel now."

Drew was drying himself by the fire. He hadn't put his shirt on yet. He stood there in thin undergarments and bare chest, looking so delectable that Mina wanted to lick him dry with her tongue.

Damn his moonlit eyes, he was handsome.

All that long, lean male. She'd had him in her

grip. The power of it had gone to her head. Made her feel drunk—languid and languorous—but with a greedy desire for more power. More pleasure.

His . . . and hers.

She knew this was a dangerous game, but she wanted more. She wanted to dance right on the edge of disaster, so she sat on the edge of his bed. There were chairs available but she was sleepy and dreamy and a bed seemed like the right choice.

The sharp edges of life had been filed away, softened, and now really what was there to do but find a way to kiss Drew again?

"Corbyn also gave me that jug of brandy on the table," she pointed out.

"That was to take the edge of tension away from all that traveling. I'm feeling much more relaxed now."

"Less tense?"

"Minx. You know what you did."

"I'm feeling a little tense myself." She lay back on the pillows.

"Here, have some brandy." He held out a glass.

When she didn't move, he scooped his arm under her neck and brought her to a seated position. "Brandy, Mina. Not beds."

"Beds are much nicer than brandy, wouldn't you agree? So many wonderful things happen in beds."

"Chair." He pointed at a chair. "Now."

She slid off the bed. He pulled a white shirt over his head, leaving it open at the neck. She wanted to pull it right back off.

"We need to talk," he said.

"Oh Lord, here we go again." She took a seat. "What are the new rules?"

"I'm going to answer a question you asked me when we were in Rafe's red room."

She sat up straighter. "About the kidnapping."

"You asked me how I rescued myself." He sank to his heels and lifted the poker. He stirred the embers until they caught the edge of a piece of wood, licking into flames. "I told stories."

"What do you mean?"

"At first I was too scared to talk. The man who kidnapped me was desperate. I could see it in his eyes when he chained me to the wall. He thought of me as a symbol, not a person. A symbol of the extreme inequality of the wealth distribution in our country."

"He was your father's tenant?"

"Former tenant. He'd lost everything. He had children to feed. He demanded that my father pay a ransom—it wasn't even an extravagant amount of money—for my return. Every day my captor became angrier, more irrational. He said that my father refused to pay because if he paid one kidnapper, ten more would take his place."

"How cruel."

"The days stretched on. It was the uncertainty that was the worst. I was held in a ship's hold. At any second the ship could set sail and I might never see England or my family again."

"Why would a farmer hold you in a ship?"

"He struck a bargain with an unscrupulous privateer to split the proceeds of the ransom money for the use of his ship."

"I can't imagine, Drew. I can't imagine how scared you must have been."

"I was terrified. He only fed me a thin gruel and it wasn't nearly enough for a growing boy. I began to grow weak. My kidnapper left for several days and a boy about my own age came to feed me. I realized that this was my one chance for escape. He'd been instructed not to speak to me, but I talked until he started listening. I talked about anything that came into my mind. Anything to make him see me as a human being, and not a symbol, or an animal."

"That must have been the best thing you could have done."

"It was. The boy and I became . . . friends, of sorts. His name was Silas. He was the kidnapper's middle son. He told me all about his life. I told him about mine. We forged a bond and I was finally able to convince him to unlock my chains. I was too weak to run very far, but a constable found me and returned me to my father."

"You rescued yourself."

"No one else was going to. When I arrived home, my father immediately wanted me to lead him to the kidnapper but I pretended to be too weak to talk. I wanted . . . I know this is going to sound strange, but I wanted to give the man and his son time to escape. I didn't want Silas to be arrested, to be tried and hung for something that wasn't his fault. I don't understand it to this day, how I could have forged a bond like that with someone who was keeping me captive."

"You sympathized with their plight. That's why you've devoted yourself to improving conditions for the tenants on your estate."

"It's almost some strange penance I must do. To expiate the sins of my father. Who will create change if not those at the top? The tenants will riot if we don't find a better system."

He finished his heated brandy. "I've never told anyone about all of this, Mina. You're the only person in the world who knows about Silas and how I escaped. I never told a soul about him. Eventually his father was caught, tried, and sent to Australia. They would have hung him if I hadn't pleaded his case in court."

"What happened to Silas?"

"I don't know. He disappeared. I've never heard anything from him or about him."

"Quite possibly, you saved his life by never disclosing his role in your imprisonment."

"He saved mine. My father was ashamed of the whole ordeal. He told me never to speak of it."

"You had to be so strong. After it happened, you had to hide your emotions and pretend everything was normal. You don't have to pretend with me, Drew. Trust me. I'm strong enough to share your pain."

"I've been remote and withdrawn from my family, my friends. I've been avoiding passion of any kind, avoiding warmth and affection. You make me crave everything I've been missing, but I don't want you to be hurt. I've alienated every-

one in my life who once cared about me. I didn't
even attend my own father's funeral. I didn't feel
anything when he died. I should have been sad
or angry. All I felt was this enormous void, this
ocean of nothingness, and that's when I understood that I wasn't like other people, and I never
would be."

"It's not your fault. It's because of the kidnapping."

He laid his hand over hers on the table. "Knowing the cause of my affliction doesn't stop it from
spreading."

The instant sweet relief of his touch. Momen-
tary relief because then she wanted more.

She lifted his hand and interlaced her fingers
with his. "You can't tell me that you don't feel
this . . . this energy between us. Our bodies . . . our
minds. If you connected with your emotions, you'd
feel it too."

"If I allow myself to feel too much, I have attacks. Moments of panic and disorientation.
Mostly when I'm in London. Or in crowds, or
in small, unfamiliar dark spaces like the room
behind the bookshelf. Small things set off the attacks. At the ball, when you found me hiding in
the garden shed, it was because a drop of wax fell
on my cheek and it reminded me of something
that happened to me during my captivity."

She nodded. "I'm beginning to understand
you. You're a puzzle and I'm putting together the
pieces."

"I'm not a puzzle, I'm a dead-end street. Don't
feel sorry for me. I don't want your pity. That's

why I don't want people to know about my kidnapping. I hate the thought of people pitying me."

"I can feel you closing up," she said.

"I shouldn't have told you, I shouldn't have talked about it."

"I do pity you, Drew, you're right. But not the man in front of me, the boy you were. The one attending a celebration with his friends, happy and carefree, and then taken and locked away."

HER HAND CLASPED in his, the strength in her eyes. The tug of his heart wanting to connect with hers.

He'd confessed everything, his weakness, his mixed-up emotions, his fears and she still wanted him. It did feel good to talk about it, more than good.

The relief was instant, sweet and clear as a drink of spring water on a hot summer's day. The sweetness filled his mind, spilled over into his body.

"I don't want to burden you with my darkness," he said.

"My shoulders are strong. I want you," she whispered.

He groaned. "Mina, all I want to do is drag you into my arms. Hold you there, hold you so tightly."

"I want that too."

"I want it so badly it's tearing me apart. I want you in my arms. My bed. I want to be inside you, know you, taste you."

"Our acquaintance began with a waltz that felt more like a war," she said. "It progressed to pistols and you holding me against a wall, and from there it's devolved into passionate kissing and . . . other activities. We can never have a conventional relationship. Stop trying to shape it into something that can be classified."

"It would only be a temporary closeness and in the morning we'd still have this quest we're on. Everything would still be complicated," he said, clinging to reason.

"We're both lonely people, Drew. There is emptiness inside me too. I wanted so badly for my parents and my uncle to love me, to need me, to give me praise. This brief time with you has been the most meaningful and fulfilling adventure of my life."

"It's been unforgettable," he agreed.

"It doesn't have to end. Don't wall yourself away. Stay here with me. Give yourself to me."

Chapter 27

GIVE YOURSELF TO ME.

Was he willing to take that risk? Was she willing, knowing everything that she knew about how damaged he was?

"I crave you, Mina, I'm drawn to you, but I've lived for so long in this self-imposed prison. There are so many lines I never cross."

She was everything he'd been denying himself. Not just sex, unbridled laughter, small intimate moments, new insights, feeling drunk and not touching a drop of alcohol, feeling giddy, uncontrolled.

Mina rose to her feet and he followed. She held out her hands to him, palms upward. "It's all well and good to have high ideals, to be a provider, pay your brother's debts, give your family a good life. It's all wonderful and admirable. But what's left for you? You've been living on crumbs because you feel like that's all you deserve."

She was right.

He'd been starved. Starving for her.

"Consume me, Drew. I'm yours."

And that's when his heart leapt off the cliff. He could build new walls tomorrow. Higher, stronger, thicker.

Tonight he was going to be free.

She knew him better than anyone in the world. He almost felt like she knew him better than he knew himself. And she wanted him.

It was a miracle, because she'd seen the worst of him, she'd seen his weakness and his fears.

The lusty look in her eyes thrilled him to his core.

"I want to rip off your shirt, Drew," she said. "I need to feel your hardness against me, in my hand, in my mouth, between my thighs."

Oh, God, she was going to kill him.

"I'm so hard for you." He opened the buttons of his smallclothes with a few practiced movements and freed his cock. "This is what you do to me. Every time I think about you, every time you look at me like that, every time we kiss, this is what happens."

"That's all mine?"

"All yours. Only yours."

"To play with?"

"To do whatever you want with. Except no biting."

She giggled. "Not even a little love nip?"

"Maybe just a light one."

She walked backward to the bed and fell across it. Spread her thighs. The slit in her drawers revealed everything, the curved, pink heart of her.

He'd never seen anything so beautiful.

"This is what you do to me." She dipped a finger inside her sex. She brought it out, glistening with wetness.

She licked the tip of her finger and he almost came then and there. "Christ. Mina. Where did you come from?"

"I want to be wicked with you, Drew."

She wore a serviceable gray traveling gown that was easy to remove. She kicked off her own slippers.

Lifting her into his arms was easy. She was so light in his arms, a small bundle of curves and silky skin. He sought her lips.

She curled her arms around his neck, deepening the kiss. The soft approving noise she made in the back of her throat drove him to the edge of madness.

He placed her in the center of the bed and peeled her white cotton shift up her body and over her arms, throwing it to the floor. He untied the string of her drawers and tugged them down her body.

Her stockings came next.

He wanted her completely naked. He was going to feast so well tonight.

She was so luscious. Full breasts with erect pink nipples. The sight tied his stomach in knots and hardened his cock.

The swooping curves of her, the shadows, the secret places he couldn't see yet.

The curling light brown hair over her sex.

"You're so beautiful," he said.

"Show me that taut body of yours. Preen for me like you did in the window," she commanded.

His shirt was over his head and his smalls around his ankles quicker than lightning.

"You want a show, do you?" He flexed his arms, making the muscles bulge and pop.

"You're hired," she said breathily.

He knelt over her on the bed and kissed her breasts, exploring, teasing, worshipping.

Sliding his tongue down the center of her body, he stopped to greet her navel, her hip-bones, the curve of her belly. He slipped a finger inside her.

He slid another finger inside her, stretching the silken walls. She was so wet.

She sighed and squirmed beneath him, spreading her thighs wider. "Please," she said. "More."

He was dying to take her, to be inside her, in her wetness and heat, in the embrace of her body. But first she had to come for him, moan his name.

He angled his fingers into a curved shape inside her, fluttering them gently. He kept his fingers inside her as he bent forward and licked her clitoris.

She gasped. "Drew. That's . . . oh Lord. My new favorite thing."

He would have smiled but he was too busy licking, flicking, and sucking.

THE FIRM, GENTLE lapping of his tongue drove her wild. And his fingers kept finding new places inside her, coaxing new sensations.

She closed her eyes, forgetting everything except what he was doing to her.

She wanted his tongue to move faster now, harder, more pressure. If he moved slightly to the right and sucked in with his lips . . . but she couldn't tell him that because it would ruin the moment, ruin her concentration.

Perhaps if she nudged a little bit with her hips.

He listened, shifting the angle of his mouth and sliding his tongue faster. Then he found exactly the right place.

She held her breath, pleading silently for him to stay there. Just a little bit longer, please. A little longer . . .

She came apart, bearing down on his fingers, bucking against his tongue.

The wave of pleasure crested and continued to roll through her, carrying her mind into a night sky with bursts of gold, purple, and red.

He slid back up her body. When he kissed her, she tasted herself on his tongue.

The crown of his cock nudged between her thighs.

"Are you sure you want this, Mina?"

"All my life I've tried to please other people and I've never acted solely for myself. I want something for me. For my pleasure. I want you."

He pushed into her body. It stretched her, raw and real, and so much larger than his fingers.

"Do you want me to stop?" he asked, his gaze intent on her face.

"I need you inside me," she said breathlessly. "Now."

Slowly, with one long controlled movement, he entered her to the hilt.

His huge body made her feel small, but not helpless. She knew that she was fully in control.

His arms circled her body, lifting her hips to meet his gentle thrusts. She was surrounded, enveloped. She loved surrendering to the rhythm he set.

He moved forward, pushing into the center of her, kissing her deeply. Sweetly.

"Wrap your legs around me. Find the angle that feels the best," he said.

That low, commanding voice of his melted her into a puddle.

She lifted one leg and then the other, hooking them over his firm buttocks. He began to move again and this time it felt better, smoother.

One of his hands moved behind her and cradled her skull in his large palm, his fingers spanning her neck.

He made her feel so cherished. The way he looked at her as if she were the loveliest thing he'd ever seen.

That look in his eyes, the one that told her she was enough, with all her flaws, her fears, and her rough edges.

She was *enough*.

He didn't want anyone else. He didn't want her to be anything else.

All her life she'd been attempting to fit someone else's mold. And for what? Because she craved this—approval, acceptance. Understanding.

Communion. Togetherness.

Their bodies moving together, linked into a whole.

She was enough. More than enough.

She basked in the knowledge, kissing his lips,

tasting the brandy on his tongue and feeling replete . . . complete.

"Mine, you're mine. All mine," she said fiercely, spreading her thighs wide, clasping his buttocks to her with her heels possessively. "Give yourself to me, Drew. Not just your body. Give me your emotions. Tell me what you're feeling."

"It feels so good," he gasped. "It's like your body is clasping me, hugging me, and I want to drive home. All the way home."

They moved together faster now. Less controlled. He pounded into her and she could take it—all of it—and beg for more.

Sweat sheen, hands slippery on his back, shoulders so thick and huge above her.

Short, fast strokes that bounced her breasts against his chest.

Then long, luscious slow thrusts so deep inside her it made her want to scream. She bit his shoulder, hard, and he growled, capturing her hands and lifting them over her head.

That's what she wanted. She wanted to feel his complete ownership.

She was his and it was a sweet, hot surrender.

Skin-to-skin contact, feeding her soul.

"I want to breathe through your mouth. See through your eyes," she said.

"I see you, Mina. Only you. You're so. Damned. Perfect."

More deep thrusts, nearly lifting her off the bed. Her nipples sensitive from brushing against his chest. Arms stretched over her head.

Raw emotion on his face. His lips in a grimace, head thrown back, neck thick and muscles straining.

"Come for me, Drew," she said.

And he did.

Buried deep inside her until the very last second when he pulled out of her and spent over her belly, a guttural groan escaping his lips.

He loosened his grip on her wrists and collapsed on top of her. She ran her fingers down the ridges of his back, soothing him.

He rolled off of her and reached down beside the bed. He used his shirt to wipe her belly clean. She curled up against him, suddenly more exhausted than she'd ever been before.

He pulled a blanket over them.

"Mina, that was extraordinary."

"Wasn't it?"

She kissed his cheek. Emotion welled up in her chest. This strong, formidable man had trusted her enough to be vulnerable, to let her see his pain.

MINA WAS FALLING asleep, her body loosening in his arms, breath lengthening.

He watched her face as she slept by the light of the candles on the table near the bed. Her eyelashes fluttered against her cheeks.

What would she dream about tonight? He hoped that she would dream about him, because he'd been dreaming of her every night.

Maybe he'd wandered one too many windswept moors. Maybe he'd spent too many nights alone in his enormous bed with the crimson velvet curtains closed against the chill and the eerie sounds old houses made at night.

Maybe telling her all of his secrets had permanently changed him, and he'd never be able to bottle all of his emotions back up.

Whatever it was, he found himself stroking her hair, listening to the sound of her breath, and making plans for their future.

Could they have a future? In these sleepy golden moments, as the fire died and the candle sputtered, he almost believed that they could. If they found Rafe, and helped him capture this villainous Le Triton person, then Mina would have avenged the death of her parents. And then, maybe . . .

Mina at Thornhill House. He thought about uncorking a bottle of his groundskeeper's elderberry mead, redolent of summer sunshine even in the iciest of winters.

She would like elderberry mead. He would like kissing her after she drank it.

She liked to walk with him in the evenings. She loved orange sunsets the best.

She smelled like the honey of clover buds, but she wasn't above rolling up her sleeves and pitching in when there was work to be done on the estate. And then she smelled like good, honest sweat.

Sweat and clover and woman.

She turned that sharp mind of hers to solving agricultural problems.

Modifying and improving his hunting rifles

was a passion of hers. So was languid morning sex, when her hair was tangled and they were still half asleep.

They found new routines, new rhythms. They knew each other's bodies so very well, and yet each day there was a new discovery.

He kissed her forehead, allowing himself to dream in time with the cadence of her breathing.

Tomorrow they faced untold dangers. Choices would have to be made.

Tonight, with Mina curled inside the circle of his arms, everything was a beautiful dream.

A dream with no tomorrow.

A KNOCKING ON THE door woke Drew from a deep slumber.

Morning sun filtering through the curtains.

"Wake up, Mina," he whispered. "We overslept. There's someone at the door."

Mina dove under the covers.

"One moment," he called.

He leapt out of bed, casting about for clean clothing. He stubbed his toe as he hopped across the room on one leg, attempting to don his undergarments.

He unlocked the door and opened it a crack. Beatrice stood outside, already dressed in her bonnet and pelisse. "I thought you said you wanted to leave early."

"I must have overslept. Give me a moment."

"I can't find Mina. I think she must have taken a walk. She's ready to leave, I'm sure."

"I'll be out in a moment. Put together a plate for

me with a huge pile of sausages and mash, will you?"

He was ravenous.

"All right." She gave him a curious glance. "Drew. What's wrong?"

"Nothing."

"You look . . . happy."

"No I don't."

"You're grinning like a fool."

"Am I?" His lips refused to relinquish the smile. She attempted to peek around his shoulder but he stepped outside the door.

"Breakfast plate," he said firmly.

"I'll fetch two plates," his sister replied with a saucy grin.

Chapter 28

> ❧

"**I**T'S PARADISE ON earth, isn't it?" Beatrice twirled around the enormous library of Thornhill House with her arms spread wide, skirts a swirl of blue.

Thornhill was every bit as brooding and forbidding as Mina had pictured, perched on a hill overlooking the ocean like a glowering gargoyle with a crown of thorny spires.

Drew was waiting outside with their mounts. They were riding on horseback to the inn at Falmouth where the Inspector and his men were waiting. Mina didn't relish the idea of riding a horse, since she was quite sore from the previous night's activities.

She blushed, thinking about it.

The things she'd said. It all seemed like a fever dream now. She wanted time to think it over, but they were on an urgent quest.

Galloping into danger.

"Just look at all of these books." Only one side of Beatrice's face was able to smile but Mina would call her expression a full body smile. She flung her arms wide, happier and more open than Mina had ever seen her.

"It must have more volumes than Hatchards.

Only see the ladders on wheels. I'll buzz around from book to book like a bee in a clover field. Isn't it glorious?"

"I'm glad it makes you so happy." It wasn't Mina's idea of paradise, but to each her own. "Thorndon is going to take me for a tour of Falmouth," she said casually.

"What, this afternoon? We only just arrived."

"He was insistent."

"So that's why you're wearing that ruffled red silk gown. I thought it was a bit much for the countryside."

Mina shook a wrinkle out of her shiny scarlet skirts. "This is a London gown, but Falmouth will have to do."

"Go have your tour, I'm sure it's just like any other town. There's a cathedral and a harbor." Beatrice rolled up her sleeves. "I want to delve into these shelves."

"Then I'll leave you to it."

"Mina," called Beatrice.

"Yes?"

"Please be careful."

"Is Falmouth so dangerous?" asked Mina with a laugh.

"You know what I mean. I'm not dense. I know there's a reason you and Drew came here and it has something to do with Rafe and his troubles. I don't need to know the extent of it. You have your reasons for keeping me in the dark, but what can I do to help?"

Of course she'd guessed the true reason for coming here. "We'll bring Lord Rafe home safely."

"See that you do. I rather like him, even though he's a giant pain in the arse most of the time."

They'd bring him home unharmed. They'd all arrive safe and sound.

Mina wasn't going to imagine any other possibility.

SEVERAL HOURS LATER, they gathered around a table in a private dining room at Pierce's Royal Hotel in Falmouth. Mina's palms were sweating and her pulse raced. It was finally happening.

The man she'd hated her entire life, the monster who had stolen her parents from her, was here. She was going to meet him.

She was going to mete out justice.

Drew introduced Inspector Langley, a handsome young man with luxuriant whiskers, wearing a blue coat and a tall black hat.

"We have to move swiftly, Your Grace," Inspector Langley said. "Le Triton's ship dropped anchor three hours ago in this sheltered cove." He pointed at the map.

"A popular location for smugglers," Drew said.

"They won't unload the cargo until nightfall but we don't want your man to get away. I've stationed my officers to watch and see if he tries to escape. One thing—your brother, Lord Rafe."

"Yes? What is it?" asked Drew.

"He's on board the ship."

"They captured him?" Mina asked. This was bad.

"Not exactly. My men tell me that he came riding out to meet the ship with a lady by his side. They walked on board and haven't been seen since."

Mina and Drew exchanged a look. "Olivia Lachance," they said in unison.

"Rafe is pretending to be on Le Triton's side," Drew explained. "It's risky—one man taking on a whole ship filled with smugglers."

"He'll have a plan," Mina insisted. "He may have hired men in town who will meet him under cover of night. Or he'll ambush Le Triton while he's sleeping, drag him away by himself and hold him hostage."

"I hope he has a better plan than that," Drew replied grimly.

"Le Triton has only three fingers on one hand," Mina said. "That's how you'll know him, Inspector Langley. You'll be able to bring him to London to stand trial for the theft of the Wish Diamond, among other crimes. The Duke of Ravenwood will testify against him."

"Is there anything else we should know about him?" asked Langley.

"He carries knives on his person. At least five concealed blades and razors—his weapons of choice. He has deadly aim."

Knives that had killed her parents, she'd learned from reading Sir Malcolm's secret files. The blades marked with a golden trident.

One of the Inspector's men burst into the room. "Inspector Langley, Your Grace," he huffed, out of breath.

"What is it, Rummage?" said the Inspector.

"The gentleman, Lord Rafe, he's been captured."

Drew groaned. "I thought you said they welcomed him on board."

"They did, Your Grace, but then we saw him fighting on the deck with one of the smugglers. He fought bravely but they overwhelmed him. They trussed him up and took him down below."

"As I said, not much of a plan," grumbled Drew.

"We'll have to rescue him," Mina said, her heart sinking.

"Le Triton has a hostage now. This isn't good," said Inspector Langley.

Mina's mind sprang to action. Rafe was a hostage. They needed a bargaining chip. They needed . . . her.

"Gentlemen, here's the situation," she said. Everyone turned toward her. "I know Le Triton. I know the way his mind works. There's something you don't know. My uncle and Le Triton have a long history of enmity, my uncle being the president of the Society of Antiquaries and Le Triton being an antiquities thief. Le Triton knows about me, and he knows that my capture would wound my uncle. I could be your bargaining chip."

"You said we would help Rafe capture Le Triton," said Drew. "Nothing was said about you sacrificing yourself as bait. I'll be the one to draw his attention."

"It can't be you, Your Grace," she said evenly. "If he knows that you're here, he'll know the value of his hostage, your brother."

"Very true, Miss Penny," said Langley. "You'll have to stay in hiding, Your Grace."

"I'm not going to stay in hiding," Drew burst out.

"You won't be hiding," Mina assured him. "I have a plan. As I was saying, I have more value to Le Triton as a hostage than Lord Rafe does because of Le Triton's enmity with my uncle. Here's my proposal. Inspector Langley and I engage with Le Triton and his men from the shore. We say we know that he's holding Lord Rafe. We distract him with my presence. I know him. I know what he'll do. Quite possibly he'll offer to make a bargain, a trade."

"You'll never offer yourself as a hostage," said Drew with ice in his voice. "I won't let you."

"I didn't say I'd offer myself. I said *he* would offer for *me*. Inspector Langley, you'll play this as if all you're doing is defending England's shores from smugglers. You'll pretend to be bribable. You won't know who he is and what a prize his capture would be. You'll pretend to waiver, to be swayed by the offer he'll make you. He thinks all men and women can be bought."

"I think I'm beginning to understand," said Drew. "While you're distracting him, I'll sneak on board the ship with some of your men, Inspector, and rescue Rafe."

"And then I'll capture Le Triton," said Langley with satisfaction. "It's a good plan."

"It's our only plan," said Mina. "And we must hurry."

Chapter 29

THE RED-GOLD SUN slid behind jagged black cliffs. Mina, Drew, and Inspector Langley crouched behind an outcropping of rocks, watching the smugglers unloading crates down a ramp and into a wagon. The rowboat Drew would take to rescue Lord Rafe bobbed in the water nearby.

"I don't think this is what Sir Malcolm meant when he entrusted you to my care and I swore to protect you," Drew whispered in her ear.

"I can do this. I might look small and defenseless but you know that I'm not."

"You're not." He grabbed her hand and squeezed it tightly. "If your parents could see you right now, I know they would be so very proud."

A lump rose in her throat. "You don't have to go to the ship, Drew. There's no shame in staying here."

His jaw clenched. "Of course I'm going to the ship. I'm not letting you face this alone."

"I know it won't be easy for you to board the ship because of the kidnapping."

"Rafe's being held on that ship. He could be chained in the hold, scared and helpless. He might think he's going to die. Of course I have to do this. You know I do."

She nodded and gave his hand an answering squeeze.

"It's time, Your Grace," said Inspector Langley, interrupting them.

"Be careful." She wanted to kiss him. She had to let him go.

He crept toward the rowboat with Corbyn and one of Langley's officers, keeping to the cover of rocks. He climbed into the rowboat, one of the men untied the rope, and they glided away into the darkness.

Mina and Inspector Langley waited in the dark, watching the men unload the cargo.

"Don't worry, Miss Penny. They won't be watching the back of the ship—all of their focus is on unloading the cargo swiftly."

"That's Le Triton on the deck," whispered Mina. "The one in the gray cloak."

"It's almost time to set the plan in motion." Langley signed something to his men and they fanned out on either side of them. They would keep to the shadows while she and Langley spoke with Le Triton.

"Le Triton," shouted Langley, standing up from behind the cover of the rock. "You're surrounded. Surrender now and it will go easier on you."

The men on the ramp and in the boats all jumped to attention, drawing knives and pistols.

"Who's there?" asked Le Triton in French-accented English.

"Inspector Langley of the London Metropolitan Police!"

"You're a long way from London, Inspector."

"I'm the Inspector for the Mayfair District. I believe you're holding one of my constituents. Lord Rafe Bentley."

"We know you have Lord Rafe," Mina said, rising partially above the rock. She'd drawn her pistol when everyone else had drawn theirs.

"And who might you be, mademoiselle?" called Le Triton.

"I'm Lord Rafe's betrothed."

"Very interesting. I have another lady on board who claims to be betrothed to him."

A lovely lady with black hair and flashing green eyes appeared on deck. "*Exactement.* Lord Rafe, he is promised to me."

"Well he can't marry both of you, ladies," said Le Triton with a nasty laugh. "At least not in jolly old England. Shall we have a fight to the death?"

The smugglers laughed roughly, shouting encouragement.

"I'd win that fight," said Mina.

"Pah," spat Miss Lachance. "I think not."

"Well, well. All of this fuss over one wicked lord," said Le Triton. "Go back below deck, Olivia, and wait for me there. Perhaps I'll bring you the lady to play with later."

Miss Lachance disappeared.

"Mademoiselle, you haven't yet told me your name," called Le Triton.

"I'm Miss Wilhelmina Penny. I believe that you know my uncle, Sir Malcolm Penny."

That nasty laugh again. "Ah. This does change everything. I've been waiting a very long time to meet you, Miss Penny."

"And I've been waiting to meet you. Now let my fiancé go."

"It won't be that easy, and you know it," he replied. "Inspector Langley, shall we have a conversation man-to-man? Leave the ladies out of it. Come aboard and you have my word that you'll be unharmed."

"Don't listen to him," Mina said, turning to Langley. "He's a thief and a smuggler."

"Ah, my reputation precedes me to England," said Le Triton.

"We know you have smuggled cargo," called Langley. "And I'm not boarding your ship for all the assurances in the world. My men have you covered. Surrender or face cold, hard British steel."

"I have a better idea," said Le Triton, his voice carrying clearly on the breeze.

I'll wager you do, she thought. This was all going according to plan.

"I'll exchange Lord Rafe for Miss Penny, Inspector. And half of my cargo. You will be the hero who defended the coast of Britain and saved a duke's brother. I go back to France never to return."

Even though Mina had known that Le Triton would make the suggestion, it still chilled her to the bone. What would he do to her if he captured her?

That wasn't going to happen. They had a good plan. Drew must be on board by now. Once he rescued Rafe, Langley would move in and take the ship.

"You must be mad," said Langley. "I'll never give you Miss Penny."

"Don't be a fool, Inspector. She's only a chit of a girl. Let me see you more clearly, Miss Penny."

Langley shook his head violently but Mina decided to risk everything. She rose higher above the rock until she was standing. She flung off her cloak to reveal her scarlet gown. "I'm not afraid of you, Le Triton."

"You don't have to be. Let's go on an adventure together, no? Come with me back to France. I have uses for a young girl of your beauty and obvious intelligence."

"Stop right there," said Langley.

"I'll wager that I have more men than you do, Inspector Langley. And I'd wager they're more desperate. And they fight dirty, don't you boys?"

Shouts from the ragged and rough-looking smugglers.

"No one has to know about the girl, Inspector," said Le Triton. "Who's to even tell that she was here? Miss Penny for half my cargo and the chance to be a hero. She'll be unharmed, I give you my word."

Inspector Langley pretended to waver, to be swayed by the idea of riches and glory. "What's in your cargo?"

"Rare artworks and antiquities. One of the paintings in this hold would be more than your life pension. And I have an even greater prize. The Wish Diamond." He pulled the diamond out from his collar, holding it up by a silver chain. "I'm sure you've heard of it. It's worth a king's ransom. It's certainly worth more than one little girl."

"How dare you, sir," Mina sputtered. "Don't listen to him, Inspector. He's trying to trick you."

"How much did you say that diamond is worth?" asked Langley.

"How can you ask him that, Inspector?"

Le Triton's laughter made her shudder. "I'm afraid we all have our price, Miss Penny."

𝓕OLLOW MINA'S PLAN. Don't deviate from it.

Don't think about her bravely facing all of those evil men carrying pistols and knives.

She's no damsel in distress. She doesn't require rescuing. Rafe does.

It wasn't the belly of the ship that Drew was afraid of—it was his own mind. His mind held him captive, trapped in the past. And he could break that hold right here, right now.

Drew scaled the hull of the ship, working silently and swiftly. Hand over hand. Grip the rope, muscles knotting, heart pounding.

Don't think about anything except rescuing Rafe. Everything else was in the past.

This wasn't the same ship where he'd been held. His palm slipped against the rope and he nearly fell. Darkness danced at the edges of his eyes. His chest tightened.

Steady now. Remember to breathe.

I am not my thoughts. I am not my memories.

Mina was relying on him to be strong. To conquer his demons.

No sentries watching the stairs down to the

hold—everyone watching what was happening on the deck, riveted by Mina and the Inspector.

He heard her voice ring out, so bold and brave.

"I'm Miss Wilhelmina Penny," she shouted.

That's right, Le Triton. You've met your doom.

Darkness behind him. Small space. Panic seeping in at the edges of his mind, spilling through the cracks, ready to flood his mind until he drowned.

He steadied his breathing as he inched along the narrow corridor. "Rafe," he called in a low voice. "Rafe, are you there?"

"Thorny?" came a thin voice. "Is that you?"

He followed the sound, feeling his way along the wall, fighting panic with every step. The feel of the ship rocking beneath him. The smell of salt water and unwashed male.

He stopped to retch.

Rafe needed him. Mina was relying on him.

No one guarding Rafe. They'd stuffed him in a small cell under the stairs, hardly big enough to contain him. Drew rattled the door. It was locked.

"Rafe," he said through the rusted iron bars covering the small square hole in the door. "I'm here to rescue you."

"Thorny." Rafe's voice was weak. "You came."

"Of course I came, you big idiot. Now who has the keys to this door?"

"Hanging . . . on the hook."

Drew's eyes finally adjusted to the darkness. The keys were hanging on a hook on the wall facing the door, a cruel location meant to humiliate the prisoner who could see the keys but never reach them.

His hands trembled as he opened the door. Corbyn was watching the entrance to the stairs. "Hurry," he hissed. "Something's happening up here!"

Drew fit the key into the lock and turned. The door creaked inward. Rafe was lying on the floor, his leg twisted at a bad angle.

"How did you know where to find me?" Rafe asked.

"Mina and I translated your diary."

"Who's Mina?"

"Never mind, we have to hurry. Mina and Inspector Langley of the London Metropolitan Police Service are out there right now risking their lives, distracting Le Triton so that I can rescue your undeserving arse."

"But—"

"There'll be time for all of these questions once you're safely in a bed at Thornhill House with a physician attending you." Drew hauled Rafe upright. "Can you walk?"

"They broke my leg. I can hobble."

Rafe's face was white and his leg dragged along behind him. It made Drew sick to look at it. He tore the cork off his flask and handed it to Rafe.

"Drink this."

Rafe downed the whisky in several gulps. "I'm ready."

Drew propped him up against his chest and helped him hobble out of the cell. The stairs were difficult. Drew and Corbyn pushed and pulled Rafe up the stairs and toward the railing.

Drew was about to lower Rafe over the railing

into the waiting arms of Langley's man in the rowboat when he saw a slash of scarlet on shore and heard a shot fired. *Mina*.

He turned back, desperate to know that she was safe.

"Bring up the hostage," a voice shouted.

"I'm right here, Le Triton," Rafe shouted.

"Rafe, what are you doing? Go over the railing. Get out of here." The fool would get them all killed.

Men rushed at them. Drew stood his ground, thrusting Rafe behind him. He cracked the first one on the jaw and the man crashed to the deck.

Another shot exploded. Another man went down by Drew's fists.

His blood ran cold and hot at the same time. All he saw was scarlet. All he could think of was protecting Mina.

THIS WASN'T SUPPOSED to happen. Drew was supposed to quietly spirit Rafe off of the ship but instead a fistfight had broken out on the deck.

Mina had thought that they would be gone by now but they were still on board.

Drew plowed through men, fists huge and face a grim mask. Mina trained her pistol on Le Triton. She didn't have a clear shot. Inspector Langley's men were engaging the smugglers with fists and pistols.

One of the smugglers saw her and raised his pistol. Fear shot her full of holes as she watched him aim and fire. She unfroze just in time to move out of the way.

The bullet whistled past her, missing her by only a fraction of an inch.

Had she warned Drew about Le Triton's knives? Some of them were tipped with poison.

One scratch from a knife and Drew could die.

A bullet whizzed past her left ear. She dropped to the ground instinctively, seeking cover.

Another bullet sprayed sand in her face.

In that moment she discovered three very important things: (1) she didn't like being shot at, because she preferred to be alive; (2) she didn't want to shoot anyone else, because she didn't want blood on her hands; and (3) she loved Drew.

Of course she loved Drew.

Blindly. Explosively.

Like a bullet lodged in her chest in such a way that it would have to stay there forever because the extracting of it would kill her.

Perhaps that wasn't the best metaphor, given their current perilous situation.

She loved Drew, and she wasn't about to let him die at the hands of the same monster who had killed her parents.

"Cover me," she shouted to Langley, rising fully, balling her skirts up into one fist, and exploding into a run.

Chapter 30

❦

$\mathcal{M}$INA RACED ONTO the deck of the ship. Everything was a blur. Men grunted in pain and the deck groaned beneath her feet. Inspector Langley fought bravely, knocking people over the head with the butt of his pistol and clearing a path for Mina.

"Mina, get back," Drew shouted. He had blood dripping down his face. He was moving toward Le Triton, who was fighting with one of Langley's men.

"Drew, I love you," she shouted. "You can't die."

He startled. A knife whizzed past his ear.

"Keep fighting," she shouted. "But be careful. His blades are dipped in poison!"

Le Triton's laughter echoed into the night. "You know so much about me, Miss Penny," he shouted, parrying a blow from the Inspector's man. "Why don't you come a little closer?"

In that moment, Mina stared into the face of the man who had murdered her parents. Was this the last image her mother had seen before she died? The flat planes of his face, rust-colored hair, pale blue eyes. Had her mother asked for mercy and found none?

Le Triton threw another knife, narrowly missing Drew, who ducked just in time.

The two men circled each other. Mina trained her pistol on Le Triton's heart, but the man wouldn't stand still—he danced and leapt, always moving.

She'd have to move closer, distract him somehow.

Her uncle's voice echoed in her mind, the words he'd used when he trained agents and she'd spied on the training.

Keep your target talking. Identify weakness, hesitation, and use it to your advantage.

"Le Triton," Mina shouted. "How is Claudette? How old is she now, nineteen?" She'd read the name of his daughter in one of her uncle's secret reports.

Her enemy faltered for a second and Drew darted toward him and landed a blow on his jaw.

Le Triton staggered for a moment but regained his balance swiftly. The knife in his hand glittered wickedly in the moonlight. He slashed at Drew, who was forced to retreat.

Where was Langley? Mina caught a glimpse of him out of the corner of her eye. He was engaging more of the smugglers, keeping them from rushing to their leader's aid.

"Claudette is the same age as you, Miss Penny," said Le Triton. "She's twenty."

"The same age Sir Malcolm's daughter Rebecca would have been if you hadn't killed her."

Le Triton paused, panting for breath, his poisoned knife extended like a shield in front of his chest. "I don't kill girls. She wasn't supposed to drink that poison. It was meant for Malcolm."

"You killed his wife and his daughter."

"By accident."

"What does Claudette like to eat for breakfast? Does she have a beau?" She kept talking about his daughter, she could see it was enraging him. Drew moved closer.

Mina advanced in step with him.

If they could move close enough, Drew could kick the knife out of Le Triton's hand and Mina could shoot him.

Without warning, a knife flew through the air, but it was aimed at Le Triton. It struck home, the long, sharp blade piercing his shoulder and flinging his arm back. Le Triton's knife clattered to the deck.

"I told you I've been practicing with a knife, Thorny," Lord Rafe shouted from his slouched position on the deck.

It was the opening she and Drew had been waiting for. Drew lunged for the hilt of Le Triton's knife and flung it off the ship. In the next movement, he slammed his foot into Le Triton's kneecap.

Attacked from all sides, Le Triton fell to his knees.

Mina was on him in seconds. She pressed her pistol to his forehead. "You murdered my parents, you bastard."

Le Triton laughed, spitting blood on the deck. "Your mother was quite a woman. It was a shame to have to kill such a beauty."

Mina's hand trembled. She could take his life.

His life for the lives of her parents.

"Mina," said Drew in a low, steady voice. "He's not worth it. Let the Inspector arrest him. This isn't who you are."

A cold-blooded killer. A spy with no heart to lose.

He was right. It wasn't her. She'd already lost her heart to him.

She lacked the detachment, the coldness necessary to complete the deed.

Her finger hesitated on the trigger.

"What are you waiting for, Miss Penny? Avenge your parents," Le Triton taunted.

"Don't shoot him, Mina," said Drew. "You'll regret it the rest of your life."

A sob choked her throat. She wasn't ruthless.

She was no spy.

She flung her pistol into the ocean.

Drew grabbed both of Le Triton's wrists and Inspector Langley arrived out of nowhere with a length of stout rope.

Mina raised her eyes. All around them men lay on the deck moaning or silent. The wood was slick with blood.

She tasted blood inside her mouth where she'd bit her cheek.

Drew stepped between her and the gory scene until all she saw was the wide ocean on one side and an enormous duke on the other side.

"YOU'RE UNHARMED, MINA?" Drew asked her, cupping her face with his hands.

She loves me. She said she loves me, his heart sang.

Her voice shook and her face was drained of

color. "Some blood and bruises here or there. And you?"

"Better than I've ever been." He was stronger and more powerful with Mina inside his walls.

He'd realized while they were fighting side by side that he didn't even need the walls anymore. Inspector Langley's men rounded up the smugglers. With their leader captured, it was easy to bring them in line.

Rafe was leaning against the railing. He hadn't gotten very far with that mangled leg, but it was his well-timed knife attack that had brought down Le Triton.

One of Inspector Langley's men came up from below with a struggling Miss Lachance.

"Unhand me, you imbecile," she cried.

"We'll be questioning you, mademoiselle," said the policeman.

"Look at all of that cargo," said Inspector Langley, motioning toward the piles of linen-wrapped parcels on the shore. "Is it really priceless antiquities?"

"You will be astounded," said Mina. "My uncle will help identify everything and return the items to their proper owners, or donate them to museums. You will be hailed as a hero, I have no doubt."

Inspector Langley shrugged his shoulders. "It was a group effort. His Grace with his fists, you with your pistol. You're a very good woman to have around in a crisis, Miss Penny."

"And don't forget my knife," called Rafe. His voice was weak from pain and fatigue.

"We need to convey my brother to a physician," said Drew.

"Some of my men, and my new prisoners, require attention as well," said the Inspector.

"You brought your strumpet with you, Thorny?" Rafe asked. "The one who wants to marry me?"

"She's Miss Wilhelmina Penny," said Drew proudly. "And I'm the one who's going to marry her."

He swept her off the deck and into his arms and kissed her possessively, impulsively, with complete abandon.

He didn't think, or reason, or deny . . . he knew what he wanted. For once in his life, losing control was the clear choice.

Because surrendering his control to Mina, to the woman he trusted and loved, was the only future he cared to see.

He knew what he wanted. He wanted her.

Bold, brave, Mina.

He kissed her and his heart cracked wide open.

Chapter 31

THE KISS WAS passionate, but far too brief, in Drew's opinion. It was interrupted by pressing matters such as men bleeding from bullet wounds and Rafe crying out from the pain of his leg.

There had been no time to talk, no more kisses. They'd helped bring Langley's injured men back to the hotel, where a physician was attending them.

The physician in Falmouth had given Rafe something for the pain and Rafe had insisted on going back with them to Thornhill House, saying it was only a broken leg.

He'd even sat a horse, gritting his teeth the whole way and complaining, but they'd made it.

Mina had ridden behind Drew and remained uncharacteristically silent almost the entire ride, which Drew attributed to exhaustion. It had been one hell of a day.

Now Rafe was ensconced in a bedroom at Thornhill with the village doctor attending him. The doctor had said he'd keep the leg, but he'd probably walk with a pronounced limp the rest of his life.

Mina had gone upstairs to wash and she hadn't come back down.

Drew sat by Rafe's bedside, offering whisky

as the doctor set his leg and wrapped it in clean bandages.

"Are you comfortable, Lord Rafe?" asked the doctor.

"A little more whisky and I'll feel no pain," he replied.

"I can give you something stronger."

Rafe gritted his teeth. "I don't deserve to deaden my pain. I put everyone to so much trouble." He met Drew's gaze. "Someone could have died." His blue eyes clouded over. "I did have a plan, you know," he said. "I laid a clever trap but it all went wrong."

"I'm sure you had a plan," said Drew, though he wasn't sure of it at all.

He walked the doctor out, accepting a bottle of laudanum in case Rafe changed his mind. Drew longed to go to Mina, but he also needed to talk to Rafe. There were many things left unsaid between the brothers.

"I wasn't going to vanquish Le Triton by myself," Rafe explained. "I was going to pretend to help Le Triton set up his front—the gin palace—and then, when the moment was opportune, I'd reveal everything to Sir Malcolm and deliver Le Triton into his hands."

"You were infiltrating his inner circle. I know all about it. I know that you're a spy."

"Lower your voice."

"I still can't believe it, though," said Drew.

"Miss Penny told you."

"Do you truly not remember her?"

"Of course I remember her. I was only pretending not to—I didn't want to drag her into danger."

"It was a good thing we followed you."

"Everything went according to plan until Le Triton turned on me. He possesses a list of Sir Malcolm's former and present agents. Even the disgraced ones like me. Someone in Sir Malcolm's ranks is a traitor."

"Mina will want to know all of this. I should go and find her and bring her here."

"You love her, don't you?" asked Rafe. "I never thought it would happen to you."

"Neither did I." Drew knew he was grinning foolishly again. It was all so new and so unbelievable. Could she truly love him? He wanted to hear her say the words again.

"That was quite a kiss," said Rafe with a chuckle.

"I thought you had lost consciousness by then."

"Saw enough of it to know that you've been utterly bewitched."

"She wants to be . . . what you are, Rafe. That's why she proposed to you. It made me so angry and jealous. But that's all in the past. She said she loves me."

"I've never seen you so happy. It's rather disconcerting."

"I know. Isn't it? I'm completely off-balance and I don't ever want to regain my footing."

MINA SAT ON the edge of the bed in a guest chamber. Her entire body ached from the bruises and battle scars, but her heart ached even more.

She'd scrubbed the blood away, and the dirt, but the agonizing questions remained.

Drew was downstairs by Rafe's bedside.

So much had happened in the last twenty-four hours and the only thing that she knew for certain was that she had no idea who she was.

It wasn't about not being good enough, or not having the skills, it was something fundamental missing inside of her. The ability to distance herself, to see human beings as pawns, as expendable, to use any means necessary to achieve her goals.

The best agents had to be ruthless.

If she wasn't a spy, then who was she?

She loved Drew; there was no doubt in her mind about that. But was it enough? He couldn't be her reason for living. Marriage and living in the countryside had never been the plan.

He hadn't proposed to her, he'd informed everyone on that ship that he was going to marry her. It had been such an utterly arrogant and dukelike thing to do.

Oh, it had all become so tangled.

She wished she had a mother to talk to, someone wiser than she. Maybe she should go back to Grizzy's house. She needed time to think everything through. She couldn't think clearly when Drew was near.

She wiped her eyes with the back of her sleeve.

She had to leave. She needed space and time and she needed to decide who she wanted to become.

"WHAT DID YOU do to Mina?" Beatrice burst into the room, where Drew and Rafe were talking, her face blotched with red and her eyes fierce. She rounded on Drew. "She's crying."

"Ah." Drew scratched his head. "I didn't do anything."

"You must have done something. She was crying and now she's changing into her traveling dress. She's leaving."

"He kissed her," said Rafe.

"And she kissed me back," said Drew.

"When did you kiss her?" asked Beatrice.

"After we vanquished the villain. And before we returned home."

"Where was this?"

"On the deck of the ship. I swept her into my arms. You would have approved, it was a grand romantic gesture."

"Did you say anything?" Beatrice asked.

"He told me that he was going to marry her," Rafe said.

"On the deck of a ship, with everyone watching?" Beatrice hit Drew's arm with a small fist.

"Ow. What was that for?" Drew asked.

"I never thought I'd say this, but you're an impulsive idiot and you should have shown some restraint and control. That was the absolute worst thing you could do, can't you see that? It wasn't a proposal, it was a command."

"I thought that I was being romantic and impulsive. Mina's the one who told me I needed to lose control every now and then."

"There's a difference between being romantically impulsive and taking away a woman's choice. For a woman like Mina, that's tantamount to a declaration of war. You kissed her in front of everyone. Said you were going to marry her. You took away her freedom to choose."

He began to see why it had been so very wrong. "Oh my God. I'm an idiot. I have to go to her. I have to explain."

Beatrice moved to the window. "You'd better hurry. She's talking to Inspector Langley. He's leaving soon—he said he wanted to leave at first light."

Drew didn't wait to hear more. He was out the door and racing down the stairs.

"And don't come back until you've patched things between you," Beatrice's instructions trailed after him. "And don't forget to get down on your knees and grovel."

"Mina," Drew shouted as he ran. "Wait!"

Mina paused outside the door of Langley's coach. Everyone else was already inside.

"You're leaving?" he asked when he reached her side.

"Inspector Langley will see me safely home. Don't come any closer, Drew." Her voice was sharp and cold as the sea air. "I can't think when you touch me."

"Mina, let's go inside and talk."

"No more talking. No more kissing. I have to leave."

"What's wrong, Mina?"

"I need some time to think."

"But you love me," he said. Wrong thing to say. It was all coming out wrong. He was cocking it all up again.

He'd driven her away, and the worst of it was that he couldn't plead with her now. They were outside of a carriage filled with people. Any attempt he made at explaining himself would have an audience and she would see it as yet another infringement on her freedom.

He had to allow her to leave, to be free. She'd taught him that.

"I can change, Mina."

She turned away. "Drew," she whispered, her voice catching. "Maybe it's not enough. You can't be my reason for living. I need . . . I need to know who I am, what I want, if I'm not going to become . . . if I'm not like my mother."

He longed to sweep her into his arms again, kiss away all of these doubts and fears, but Beatrice had been right. He had to let her go. If they were meant to be together, they would find a way . . . but it would take time. Patience.

Sacrifice.

Everything in him wanted to beg, to plead with her to stay.

Fall on his knees before her and grovel.

"I understand," he said, his heart going cold as ice. "You want to make your mark on the world."

"Drew . . ." Anguish in her voice. "It's not that. I just . . ."

"I understand," he said again. "I don't want to take away the first glimpse of freedom you've ever had. Your life has been a cage, Mina, your wings clipped. You have the restless power to soar so high and I can never be the anchor weighing you down."

She laid her hand over his heart. "I just need some time to think. Can you give me that?"

He would give her anything. His heart. His soul.

He bowed his head and stepped away.

Warmth from her hand fading. The carriage beginning to move, taking her away.

It nearly killed him. His heart shattered into shards of glass. He saw it so clearly now. There could be no joy without pain. No reward without risk.

Love was a blind leap into the unknown. Mina might never come back to him.

But he had to give her the time she needed to make her own decision.

Chapter 32

Two weeks later

*L*IFE AT GREAT-AUNT Griselda's house had settled into a rhythm. They went out most mornings to see the sights of London. Grizzy was feeling better every day. They'd visited every museum, attended two operas, and even watched a public debate at the London Tavern.

Everywhere they went, people whispered about Mina. No one knew precisely what had happened between her and the Duke of Thorndon, but everyone had a theory. They didn't know whether to treat her as a future duchess or a social outcast.

Drew's mother had already left for Thornhill House when Mina arrived back in London. The duchess must be there now with all three of her children. She'd be helping Rafe recover and attempting to uncover a husband for Beatrice among the small selection of noblemen near Thornhill.

And here Mina was in London, where she'd always wanted to live, soaking in the pleasures of the city, and it all felt empty and wrong without Drew.

She missed him every second of every day. The longing to see him again was very strong. Every morning she had to wage a battle with herself not to return to Cornwall. She'd said she needed time to think, and she did.

She loved him. She would always love him. But was it enough? Would they be able to find a way to compromise enough to be together?

"You're being stubborn, Wilhelmina," said Grizzy, as they worked together on her latest taxidermy diorama, a recreation of da Vinci's *The Last Supper* featuring brightly colored goldfinches in the roles of the twelve apostles.

"I told Thorndon that I needed time to think."

"Stubborn and foolish. What's there to think about?"

"Marriage is a very serious choice." Becoming a duchess had never been the plan. Without her future in espionage she was adrift.

Le Triton was behind bars, awaiting trial for numerous international crimes. His fall had brought down a host of other criminals. Inspector Langley had visited her to tell her all of the details.

"When will Sir Malcolm arrive?" asked Grizzy. "I thought he would be back by now. Maybe he can talk some sense into that stubborn head of yours."

Mina wondered when her uncle would return. Surely the news had reached him that Le Triton had been captured. She wondered if he'd heard anything about the part she'd played.

A loud knocking at the front door interrupted her thoughts. She dropped the wire she'd been cutting and ran to the window. "It's Sir Malcolm. He's here."

She ran downstairs.

He greeted her with a nod as a servant accepted his hat and coat. "Wilhelmina, you're looking well. Where's Griselda?"

"Upstairs, working on one of her dioramas."

"I just came from Thornhill House," said her uncle.

"Thornhill?" She hadn't expected him to go there before coming to London.

"I was tracing Le Triton's path. I landed at Falmouth but I was days late. He'd already been apprehended by Inspector Langley, with help from the Duke of Thorndon, his brother, and, much to my surprise, my niece."

Mina swallowed. "About that."

"I'm not angry, Mina, I'm just so very glad that you're unharmed."

He wasn't angry that she'd defied his wishes? Mina led him into the parlor where he'd given her the Duke Dossier. He sat on the same lumpy sofa.

Grizzy's misshapen furniture and stuffed hedgehogs no longer seemed like a penance to Mina. She'd grown closer to her great-aunt in the past weeks. She was surprised to realize that she loved her dearly.

Her heart had been surprising her lately.

"Shall I ring for some tea?" Mina asked.

"No. Let's have a thimbleful of brandy. I hear from Thorndon that it's your drink of choice."

Mina blushed. What else had Thorndon told her uncle?

Sir Malcolm rose and walked to the sideboard. He poured them each a tumbler of brandy and returned.

The burn of the brandy in her throat reminded Mina of Drew. So many things reminded her of him. Everything, really. It was as though she'd been born anew the day she met him. Every memory started there.

Every hope.

Her uncle set down his glass. "I should never have kept you hidden away. I should have let you make mistakes and face dangers. Ravenwood told me that I was protecting you too closely because . . . because I lost Rebecca." He finished on a whisper, his face averted from hers.

Mina had never heard him speak of the subject.

He laid a hand on her shoulder.

She froze. She didn't know what to do or how to react. She'd always wanted tenderness from him—approval—but he'd always kept his distance.

"You did your best," she said carefully. "You gave me a safe upbringing."

"But not a happy one. But Mina, it's never too late for happiness. I hope you will find it with Thorndon. I heard the entire story from Lord Rafe, and from Thorndon. How brave you were, how you could have . . . ended Le Triton, and you made the right choice. What I don't understand is why you're here talking to me and not with Thorndon?"

Mina sighed. "I'm lost, Uncle. I'm adrift. I found I don't have the stomach for your work. I'll never become . . . what I wanted to become. Without my heritage, without following in my parents' footsteps, who am I?"

"This is what I was trying to protect you from all of these years. I was guarding you from my enemies and from this life. It's a difficult life and it's filled with danger and I wanted better for you, Mina."

He'd called her by her nickname. He'd reached out to her. What was wrong with him?

"I don't understand," she said. "I thought you would be angry with me for involving myself in the capture of Le Triton."

"I'm not. I'm proud of you, Mina. So very proud."

A lump formed in her throat. She'd wanted to hear those words for so long, and now it was too late.

"I don't have that one essential skill," she said. "I can't detach myself from my emotions."

"And I never want you to learn that skill. I want you to live to a ripe old age. With Thorndon by your side."

"I can't just give up everything I've dreamed of and become his wife."

"Who said anything about giving up your dreams? I know your strengths, Mina. I should have allowed you to use them openly. I shouldn't have forced you to hide, to be so secretive."

"You knew that I was watching you?"

"Of course I knew. Did you think you could spy on the spymaster?" That last sentence was whispered.

That's precisely what she'd thought.

"You can continue your studies," he said. "You don't have to do fieldwork. We will focus on your strengths."

Mina couldn't believe what her uncle was saying. "Do you mean that you'll allow me to join your force?"

"I have no doubt that you'll become my best code breaker."

"I also want to develop weapons that only stun or temporarily immobilize a target," she said eagerly. "Since I found that I have no taste for bloodletting, I'd like to make that my specialty."

"An excellent idea," agreed Sir Malcolm.

Mina's heart lifted. Maybe she could achieve her dreams after all. She wouldn't be a glamorous, sophisticated agent like her mother had been. She'd be behind the scenes. But she'd be useful.

Maybe she could honor her mother's legacy, while finding a way to be with Thorndon. That was, if he still wanted her. Doubt seized her mind. She'd hurt him by leaving. She'd seen the pain and confusion in his eyes as she'd left.

"He loves you, Mina," said her uncle, as if he could read her mind. "It's obvious what you're thinking about," he added.

"Did he tell you that?"

"Not in so many words, but he did give me this and ask me to see that you received it." Sir Malcolm handed her a small leather-bound notebook.

Mina read the title. *The Dueling Debutante Dossier.*

"I gather that it's a detailed analysis of the reasons that you two were meant to be together," said her uncle.

"Thank you," Mina said. "For everything."

"Well, are you going to read it?"

"I think I'll go for a walk."

Her uncle smiled. "You'll need a coach to reach Cornwall, you know."

Mina slipped the notebook in the pocket of her cloak and walked the short distance to the Thorndon town houses. The brandy still heated her belly.

The promise of reading Drew's words set her heart ablaze.

Crankshaw answered her knock. "Why, Miss Penny. What are you doing here? His Grace is still in Cornwall. I thought you'd be there with him."

"I was wondering if I might sit in your gardens for a moment."

Crankshaw paused. "Is everything all right?"

"I believe so. More than right. I think everything's going to be beautiful."

"I'm very glad to hear it. The house and gardens are yours, Miss Penny." He led her inside. "Please let me know if you need anything. Anything at all."

Mina walked the garden path. She passed the swing where she'd sat with Lady Beatrice. It seemed so long ago. The last of the summer roses clung to the bushes, petals curled and ready to fall.

She opened the door of the garden shed and stepped inside, closing it behind her. Light filtered in through the small windows, enough to read by.

Was it her imagination, or was there a lingering scent of spiced almonds in this shed? Her memory supplied Drew. Rising from the shadows.

Kneeling before her as she tied his cravat.

She opened the notebook with trembling fingers.

It was two pages long and penned in a strong, steady hand as commanding as the man who wrote it. There were moments of lighthearted silliness, and moments that made her weep.

She read it over and over, as if in the reading she could conjure him to her side.

She longed to hear him read the words to her.

Damn you, Drew, she whispered. Why are you so far away?

Because she'd pushed him away. She'd fled when she should have stayed and talked things through with him.

She hadn't given him a chance to explain, to apologize. She'd run away, not because of what he'd done, but because she'd been afraid of how much she loved him.

Afraid that loving him meant losing herself.

A knock sounded on the door of the shed. It would be Crankshaw bringing her a beverage, or telling her it was time for supper. The light was fading. She'd stayed too long.

She dried her eyes. "Enter."

"Is this shed occupied?"

Deep voice. Dark hair and glowing eyes. Broad shoulders ducking to enter the shed.

Holy Hell, he was handsome.

Mine. All mine. "Drew, what are you doing here? I thought you would be supervising the harvest."

"I couldn't stay away any longer, Mina. I tried, but I couldn't last one more day. I had to see you."

"Then you can make yourself useful and read this to me." She handed him the notebook.

His gaze met hers. He began to recite from the notebook without glancing at the writing, drawing nearer with every word, every step. "I love you, Mina Penny, because you hide scarlet dresses in garden sheds and because you have a wicked little pistol hidden in your reticule."

He was close enough to touch now, filling the shed with his oversized presence and his rich voice. Filling her with longing.

"I love you because if there's a hidden chamber, you'll find it," he continued. "And if there's a lock, you'll pick it. I admire how you stay calm while pinioned upon impolite chairs. I'm in awe of the way you decipher codes and brave hailstorms of bullets. You're kind to Beatrice. You make me laugh. And when I look at London through your eyes, I see that there is magic here, after all."

She dashed a tear away from her cheek. She knew what came next but she couldn't wait to hear it. She'd never tire of hearing it.

"I love you, Mina Penny, because you unlocked me and discovered a hidden chamber in my heart. I can never go back to the darkness. And I will never stop loving you."

"Drew," she said. "I think I'm going to kiss you now."

And she did.

AFTER DREAMING OF this moment for weeks, Mina was finally in Drew's arms. He meant to savor every second slowly, memorize it for the future, but when her soft lips touched his, all rational thought flew away.

He kissed her with the pent-up longing of a man who'd had a brief taste of paradise, and would sell his very soul for more.

She still loved him. They would find a way to be together.

He wound his arms around her and molded their bodies together. Her curves melting into his angles. Her hands twined in his hair, pressing him closer. She was small in stature, but she kissed fiercely.

When they paused for air, because they couldn't live on kisses alone, she beamed at him, her smile bright enough to replace the fading sun. "There's magic in Cornwall, as well," she said. "I felt it. It's majestic and powerful. Just like you."

He wanted to show her just how powerful he was. Lift her into his arms, carry her into the house, over the threshold, and to the nearest bed, but they needed to continue this conversation with words first.

Beds later.

"I would never ask you to give up your dreams," he said.

"Sometimes dreams require a bit of modification, just like timepieces. There's more than one kind of spy. Uncle Malcolm visited me and he agreed to train me. I'll be happy behind the scenes, cracking codes and inventing more ethical weaponry. I have no taste for bloodletting."

"I love that about you. Your heart's too tender. You'll never become jaded."

"I don't want to become one of my uncle's agents," she said. "They have to become almost inhuman. They classify people as targets, as assets or liabilities. I don't want to become hardened and brutal."

"Will you be content? You said that you didn't want to be on the sidelines of life, you wanted to be in the center, in the heart of it all."

"And I do, I do want to be in the beating heart of life. And for me, that's you."

Drew stroked strands of her hair away so that he could see her eyes. He inhaled the sweet scent of her. His heart filled with so much love he thought it might burst.

"I thought that I needed to change, to become my mother, become something I'm not," she said. "You stood by me patiently until I realized that I can just be me. Wild, messy, glorious me."

"You're perfect just the way you are."

"Do you think that we could live in Cornwall half the year, and London the other half?," she asked.

"I think that could be arranged." He couldn't stop grinning. This conversation had taken the most wonderful turn. But she still had to hear everything before she made a decision.

"You can give plants rich soil, plenty of water, and access to sun, but they still need time to grow," he began, attempting to find the words to make her understand. "That's me, Mina. You've given my heart what it needs to grow—a path to connecting with my emotions. I can feel myself changing. I want to change. But I can't make it go any faster. I'll need time."

"I know that, Drew." She kissed his cheek.

"You don't have to suddenly produce all of the emotions you've been holding back for years. I don't expect that or want it. It's enough that you're growing, changing. But there's something you should know, too. I don't want to have children yet. Maybe for several more years."

"I want an heir. But I can wait until you're ready."

"Truly?" she asked.

"Truly. I'm hoping to have many adventures with you."

"We've had quite a few already," she said with laughter in her voice. "We uncovered an extortion plot, rescued your brother, and brought an evil criminal to justice. And then you proposed marriage to me on the deck of a ship with blood-spattered hands, a bruised face, and groaning men lying all around us."

"About that proposal. I know I cocked it up. I should have fallen to my knees. Framed it as a question."

"Well?" She glanced at the floor.

He had his orders.

He sank to his knees on the rough wooden floor and clasped her hands in his.

"I love you, Mina. You captured my heart during our waltz, when you were boldly undressing me with your eyes, clearly picturing me lying in bed completely naked."

"Ha," she said. "You were the one picturing me churning your butter."

"Being with you is like sun dancing through leaves. The smell of soil after it rains. The first brave, vivid-green shoots appearing. I vow to revel in your freedom, to foster everything wild and creative in your soul. I'll always have a bottle of brandy at the ready. And I will always love you completely. Will you share your life with me?"

"Drew," she said, her voice cracking. "I told you that your heart was soft and squishy."

"It is. But that's all right, because other parts of me are hard as granite."

"Show me," she said.

"What, right here? In the garden shed?"

"There's no time like the present."

"Mina." He tightened his arms around her. "Is that a yes?"

"Yes," she whispered.

And his heart spilled over with joy.

Epilogue

T HE NEWLY, AND hastily, wed Duke and Duchess of Thorndon arrived at Thornhill House on a day when the changing seasons agreed to strike a compromise: the air would stay crisp and cool, but the sun shone brightly and the sky was a brilliant turquoise blue.

"Finally, you're here," called Beatrice, rushing to greet them as they exited the carriage.

"We're here," Drew said.

"We're home," Mina said. "I never did receive a tour on my previous visit. I hear you have a nice bed. Crimson curtains. Beeswax candles to light your way in the dark."

"You were too busy vanquishing foes."

"And running away."

Beatrice danced around them, her spectacles threatening to fly off her face. "I have so much to show you. The renovations are going well, although the most annoyingly smug carpenter has arrived to replace his father, who took a tumble off a ladder. He thinks he's God's gift to young ladies."

Mina laughed. "I'm sure you set him straight on that count."

"He makes so much noise hammering away

at walls that I can't concentrate on my writing," Beatrice said.

She chattered on and Mina and Drew followed her to the front stairs, where the servants were lined up, waiting to meet their new duchess.

Mina walked down the row, greeting each servant by name and inquiring after children and ailments. Drew had briefed her on the long carriage ride. In between other amusements.

I'm a duchess, she thought, with a sense of bemusement. She'd never thought in a million years that this would happen to her.

"It's all your fault," she said to Drew as they entered the house.

"What is, my love?"

"The fact that I'm a duchess. I never wanted to be anything so grand."

"Yes, but you're a duchess who carries a flintlock pistol in her purse and never allows anyone to tell her what to do."

"And you're a duke who grows turnips, and has dirt under his nails. I could listen to you talk about turnips for days, you know," Mina said. And she meant it.

She listened happily as he explained all of his agricultural innovations and showed her his plant conservatory and laboratory.

Testing soil temperatures, proper irrigation, defending against blight—none of these things should be interesting to her, and yet when he explained them, she pictured him poring over his research, staying up late at night, dark smudges under his eyes, hair in disarray.

Shirtsleeves rolled up and ink stains on his hands. The single-minded focus he brought to every aspect of his life.

And it filled her heart with pride.

"Maybe you'd like to put that nimble mind of yours to the task of puzzling out solutions for some of my agricultural problems," he said.

"I would be honored." Her heart jumped and skipped as they walked.

She had this overwhelming sense of rightness. She helped him. He helped her.

He was the logical one, the cool-headed one, and she led with her emotions, but together they could solve any puzzle, any code.

They'd solved the greatest puzzle of all, hadn't they?

They'd found a way to be together.

"Drew, is that a field of daisies in the distance? I can't believe they're still blooming."

"Why, yes it is."

"And aren't those sheep grazing nearby?"

"More sheep than people around here, I'm afraid."

"Then don't we have a dream to reenact?"

"You read my mind." He caught her hand and they broke into a run, the wind catching her laughter as they raced to the field.

He guided her down into the flowers. She pulled off his coat and he helped her by lifting his arms.

She opened the buttons of his shirt and pushed it over his head, nearly tearing it in her haste to see the smooth expanse of his chest above her.

He picked a daisy, pulling off the petals one by one. "She loves me, she loves me not. She loves me, she—"

"She loves you." Mina wrapped her arms around his neck. "With all her heart."

He tucked a flower into her hair. "Goddamn, Mina. You're so beautiful." He slid her sky-colored gown down her shoulders.

"What if someone sees us?"

"The sheep won't tell anyone."

"You know what I mean."

"I'm the duke. If anyone happens upon us, they'll do what's best for them and back away slowly," he growled.

"I love it when you use that rumbly voice. It makes me shiver."

"Does it now? What else makes you shiver?" His hand dipped into her bodice and covered her breast.

"That," she whispered.

"And what about this?" He kissed her possessively, nudging her lips open and delving inside her mouth with commanding strokes of his tongue.

Bees buzzed nearby. The fresh summer scent of grass and sun-warmed flowers surrounded them. The petals of a daisy brushed her cheek.

Drew stripped her down to her stockings with the practiced movements of a former wicked rake.

Former rakes were the very best kind, she'd discovered.

All of the rake and none of the risk.

She trusted him with her body and with her heart.

He made her feel reckless and free.

When he entered her with slow, languid strokes, she lifted her hips and met him halfway. Her heart expanded as wide as the sky above them as they moved together, finding the rhythm that was still so new, and still filled her with awe.

Maybe there were a few twigs poking into her back. Maybe a bee flew a little bit too close to her ear for comfort.

She was probably going to be picking burs out of her blue gown.

Life wasn't a dream. She'd always known that there was sadness and pain. Loneliness and longing.

But there was also this.

His skin against her skin. Sun on her face. Love overflowing her heart.

Life wasn't a dream.

But it came pretty damned close when she was in his arms.

Acknowledgments

MY EVERLASTING GRATITUDE to the multitude of people who helped bring this book into existence during a period in my life that included two cross-continental moves. Special thanks go to my amazing agent, Alexandra Machinist, and my erudite editor, Carrie Feron. To the fantastic team at Avon Books, especially Pam Jaffee, Asanté Simons, and Jes Lyons: you can expect abundant New Zealand treats this holiday season. Neile—you are simply the best beta reader on the planet. Plus, I get to skype with you in Switzerland and listen to your sexy French accent. *Bisous!* I'm extremely thankful for my loyal readers, especially the members of the Lenora's Bookish Belles Facebook group. Much love to all of the bloggers, librarians, reviewers, and booksellers for spreading the news about good and diverse romance reads. One of these days I'm going to visit The Ripped Bodice in person!

USA TODAY BESTSELLING AUTHOR

LENORA BELL

WHAT A DIFFERENCE A DUKE MAKES

Edgar Rochester, Duke of Banksford, is one of the wealthiest, most powerful men in England, but when it comes to raising twins alone, he knows he needs help. The only problem is the children have chased away half the governesses in London. Until the clever, bold, and far-too-enticing Miss Mari Perkins arrives.

FOR THE DUKE'S EYES ONLY

If adventure has a name, it must be Lady India Rochester. The intrepid archaeologist possesses a sharp wit and an even sharper knack for uncovering history's forgotten women. Unfortunately, she has one annoying weakness: the dangerously handsome Duke of Ravenwood. Former best friend. Current enemy. And the man who dared break her heart.

And don't miss The Disgraceful Dukes . . .

pıatkus